Alone and tired, Angela took off her eighteen-karat-gold Piaget watch—a gift from director Jon Vasta—and put it on the bedside table. She kicked off her black high heels and stripped off her jeans and sweatshirt. She reached back to unsnap her bra and noticed, for the first time, a manila envelope on the bed. She grabbed it and fell back onto the bed before prying open the little prongs and sliding out what was inside.

She sat up with a start.

It was a publicity still from *Slasher III: The Final Chapter,* a photo of her as "Jamie," standing with hand to mouth in terror of an unseen man with a knife. Written across it in bright red letters was the warning:

Forget about Tony's death, or you'll have to worry about your own.

She clutched the photo to her chest and began to shake, fighting back tears and wishing she could put the horror of Tony's death behind her.

Other books in the Veronica Slate Mystery *series:*

A VERONICA SLATE
MYSTERY

EXTREME CLOSE-UP

LARY CREWS

LYNX BOOKS
New York

VERONICA SLATE: EXTREME CLOSE-UP

ISBN: 1-55802-144-2

First Printing/March 1989

This is a work of fiction. Names, characters, places, and incidents are either the product of the author's imagination or are used fictitiously. Any resemblance to actual events, locales, or persons, living or dead, is entirely coincidental.

This book is published by Lynx Books, a division of Lynx Communications, Inc., 41 Madison Avenue, New York, New York, 10010. The name "Lynx" and the logo consisting of a stylized head of a lynx are trademarks of Lynx Communications, Inc.

Printed in the United States of America

0 9 8 7 6 5 4 3 2 1

Acknowledgments

Thanks to Robert Altman, for giving me the chance to work on a major motion picture, and to Robert Eggenweiler, Scott Bushnell, and Tommy Thompson for making it pleasant.

Thanks also to Carol Burnett, Dick Cavett, Paul Dooley, and Glenda Jackson for treating me so kindly. And, a salute to the staff of *Premiere* magazine for their "inside stuff" about the movie industry.

As always, my work is dedicated with love to my wife, Linda, who persists in loving me, and to God, who keeps on giving me "one more day" of life.

A *Veronica Slate*
MYSTERY

Extreme Close-Up

CHAPTER ONE

ON FRIDAY, APRIL 11, 1986, GARY KINES DROVE HIS NEW silver Porsche west on the Santa Monica Freeway through the deepening L.A. twilight. Angela Mastry sat quietly in the seat beside him reading the deposition by the map light. It was five legal-sized pages long. He had rounded the cloverleaf and nosed onto the San Diego Freeway heading south toward L.A.X. before she finally finished it.

"Yeah. That's everything, near as I can tell," Angela said. "I just hope this works."

Clean-shaven Gary Kines, brown hair neatly trimmed and black shoes newly shined, was dressed in what for him was casual attire, Calvin Klein jeans with creases and a white dress shirt open at the collar. Not his working uniform, certainly. But driving Angela to the airport wasn't work.

"Don't worry about a thing," he said, as he headed down Century Boulevard toward the airport. "When you get through with the shoot in Florida and you're back in town, we'll get those bastards once and for all."

He smiled at her, thinking how fragile she seemed in person. The screen didn't do justice to her oval face. Its perfection was altered only slightly by secretive eyes and a Roman nose. In person, she reminded him of a cheerleader he had craved during his Hollywood High days. Even in a U.C.L.A. sweat shirt and designer jeans, with her cornsilk hair pulled back in a hasty ponytail, Angela was beautiful.

"You're doing the right thing," he said, looking out at the humid L.A. twilight and relishing his air-conditioned car. "You're the only one who can do this. Without your testimony, we have no case." He glanced at her to underscore his words. "Without you, they win."

"Thanks," she said sarcastically. She looked at him with pale blue eyes that were nearly transparent. "Think you can scare me more than I already am?"

"Don't be scared," Gary said, adjusting the rearview mirror. "Be angry. This is the right move. You're doing what has to be done."

"I hope so," Angela said. She regarded him for a moment, then turned her head to look out the window. "I'm glad you're helping me. I don't know how I'll ever live through this."

The bright lights of Los Angeles International Airport created an orange-yellow blue in the mist that seemed to hover about twenty feet up, like the mother ship in *Close Encounters of the Third Kind*. He parked in front of the American Airlines section of the terminal. After her baggage was taken care of, he walked in with her through the security check to Gate 46.

"Okay, lady, have a good flight." He gave her a kiss. "When are you getting into Tampa? Do you know?"

"Around midnight their time." She started to hand him the folded deposition, but he waved it away.

"No. That's your copy. I've got the original. And the tape's in the safe back at the office."

Worry creased her alabaster face as she looked into his eyes. "How many of these are there?"

He smiled at her. "Just the original and two copies. You've got one and I've got one." He smiled. "Relax. It's going to be okay. And when you get back, we're going to nail Mira Loma Productions.''

"I hope so," Angela said wistfully.

An hour later Gary pulled up at his office on the northern one of the two Santa Monica Boulevards. Only in California could there be two parallel streets with the same name a block away from each other.

Like a yuppie version of the old man who lived over his pawnshop, Gary lived in an apartment on the second floor of the house he had converted to offices for himself, one other attorney, and a private investigator who worked for both of them. That house, left to him by his mother, was practically all he owned. It sometimes troubled him that his life was defined by a flashy new car, a dress-for-success wardrobe, a two-story house, and lots of debts. The Mira Loma case would change all that.

The whole way home, Angela's fear and insecurity had stuck to him like gum to a shoe. He went into the bedroom, glanced at Susan, and said hello. He took off his loafers and put them side by side on the lowest shelf of the closet. He emptied his pockets onto the dresser.

Susan looked up from the book she was reading. "You get Angie off okay?" She stuffed a bookmark in it and offered her cheek for a kiss.

"Yeah. No problem." He drank in a whiff of vanilla from Susan's clean auburn hair.

She was wearing a *Beverly Hills Cop* T-shirt, panties, and a smile, her shoulder-length hair loosely framing her face: high cheekbones and a sensuous mouth that often crippled him with desire. He kissed her.

After their lips parted, Gary walked back to the closet door and pulled off his jeans and shirt. He hung up the jeans and threw the shirt in the laundry basket. Mechanical action. Unconnected to his troubled thoughts about the power of the people he opposed in the Mira Loma case.

Finally, Susan asked, "Are you going to tell me what's wrong, or do I have to drag it out of you?" She drew her long bare legs up to her chest.

"Nothing's wrong." Clad only in his bikini briefs, he came over and sat on the bed beside her.

"Yeah, sure." She wrapped her arms around her knees and stared at him.

He read the skepticism in her brown eyes. "Okay. Yeah. I'm worried about the Mira Loma case."

"Why?"

"Winning it could mean getting out of debt. It could mean more and better clients. . . ."

"It could mean you'll finally marry me." She tilted her head to the side and smiled like the Cheshire cat.

"That, too." He sat back against the headboard and stared into the darkness beyond the window. "See, if I can prove that Tony Victor's death last fall was no accident, I'll be doing more than just winning a case. I'll be setting a precedent that could affect the *Twilight Zone* case and a couple dozen other stunt-related actions. It could have a major impact in this town."

"So what's the problem?"

"Angela. She's my only witness. She's the only one who saw what really happened. And she's a drunk."

"Not anymore, is she? I thought she'd straightened up."

He shrugged. "I don't know. Maybe. But the defense is going to have a field day with her past."

"Well, I'm not worried about you, honey." She brought her soft hand across his chest. "I know you can win. Besides—"

"Wait!" He tilted his head toward the open bedroom door.

"What?"

"What's that?" He sat up, rigid and still.

"What's what?"

"Shh!" He got to his feet and slipped open the drawer of the bedside table. "Someone's downstairs." He grabbed his short-barreled Titan Tiger .38-caliber revolver and padded to the bedroom door, naked but for his briefs. "Be right back."

Susan's face tightened as she saw the gun. "What are you doing with that?"

He put his finger to his lips and started out into the hall and down the stairs.

Alone on the bed, Susan didn't know what to do. Should she follow him? How could she help? She prayed the noise had been only a figment of his imagination, and yet she feared it wasn't. She sat perfectly still, her arms clenched around her knees, straining to hear. After a few moments, she heard voices. Unintelligible from such a distance, but definitely Gary and another man. As quickly as it had begun, the muted conversation ended.

Silence.

Suddenly, the quiet was split by the sound of gunfire. But in a rapid burst, not one at a time. As little as she knew about weapons, she knew that sound had not come from Gary's gun.

"Gary!" she screamed. "Gary! What happened?"

As the echo of her voice faded, she heard rapid steps coming up the stairs. Someone wearing shoes. Not Gary. In a panic, she jumped off the bed and reached for her jeans on the chair by the window. She had one leg in and one leg out when he appeared in the doorway. A tall man. Muscular. Grim.

Needle-sharp splinters lanced her face as bullets tattooed across the wall toward her head in a deafening burst of gunfire. She saw the blue-white blaze of the automatic weapon before little pinpoints of fire raced across her chest and pain greater than she'd ever known seared her body.

Seconds later, the pain ended, permanently.

Veronica Slate half listened as the network newsman wrapped up his midnight newscast. "Repeating our top story: Two F.B.I. agents and two robbery suspects were killed and five other agents were wounded this morning in a shootout in suburban Miami. Joseph V. Corless, head of the Miami office, called it 'a devastating day for the F.B.I. in Miami.' I'm Tom Hayes, CBS News."

As the news ended, in the glass-walled WAQT TalkStudio on Tampa's Harbour Island, Max Wilkinson pointed a finger at Veronica Slate, the signal to open her mike and begin the third hour of her late-night radio talk show.

WAQT's TalkStudio, on the second floor of The Market, a

trendy shopping center inside the Harbour Island complex, consisted of four small rooms. The studio and the producer's booth were surrounded on three sides by glass. The small lounge, with adjoining rest room, had a picture window looking out on the bay.

Across the bay, in downtown Tampa, was the rest of the station: administrative and sales offices, news department, the transmitter and satellite gear, and a tall tower dotted with flashing lights.

Superimposed on the wide plate-glass window between Veronica and Max, like a ghostly double exposure, was her own square-jawed face—green eyes, full lips, and what David called "a perfect nose"—surrounded by dark brown hair to her shoulders.

"Welcome back to the 'Slate Show.' I'm Veronica Slate, and we've got two more hours to take your calls, Tampa Bay." She smiled at the stick-figure woman with short spiky red hair sitting in the chair across the desk from her and said, "My guest is Carla Jahns, production manager of the film *Perfect Casting,* which director Jon Vasta starts filming next week at the Don CeSar Resort Hotel on St. Pete Beach." She pushed the Sennhauser mike on its heavy desk stand closer to her guest. "Thanks for being here, Carla."

"Glad to do it." A smile rippled across Carla's thin lips, making her narrow, pointy face less harsh.

"For those who have just joined us, give us a little rundown on the movie—what it's about and who's in it." She rolled down the sleeves of her soft silver-blue sweater against the air conditioning, which always seemed to reach freezing level after midnight. That was why she wore jeans most nights. She wore three-inch navy pumps because she liked wearing high heels. Besides, she could kick them off after her guest left.

Carla Jahns shifted in her chair. "*Perfect Casting* is about an elderly film director vacationing at a resort hotel with his protégée, a beautiful young girl whom he sees as his chance for a comeback. A young doctor, also on vacation, falls in love with the girl and tries to save her."

"Shades of Svengali?"

"More like *My Fair Lady* meets *Deathtrap*." This time, her whole face smiled. "It stars Raynor Fitzhugh as the director, Paul Haden as the doctor, and Angela Mastry as the girl."

Carla Jahns went on to talk about the plot of the movie, but Veronica had snagged on the mention of Angela Mastry's name. She'd known for months—since the story first hit the St. Petersburg *Times*—that Angela would be coming into Tampa Bay to be in *Perfect Casting*. Knowing it five months ago was one thing. Being reminded that she'd be arriving any day now was another.

Carla stopped talking and took a sip of coffee. Veronica fired off a question to sidestep the fact that she hadn't been listening. "Tell me about Paul Haden."

"He's the same hunk in person as on the screen." Carla put down her Styrofoam cup, bearing a red lipstick stain. The combination of the red-stained white cup and Carla's shiny black jumpsuit somehow reminded Veronica of an ad for a vampire movie.

"Do you find it difficult to breathe when he's around?" asked Veronica, as she spotted the hand signal Max had flashed her, a forefinger pointed at the light brown palm of his hand. She had to break for a spot.

Carla laughed. "Well, it's a tough job, but somebody's—"

"Got to do it, I know." Veronica finished the cliché. "Well, we've got to take this break. Then we'll come back and take some of your calls. This is the 'Slate Show' on WAQT."

As Veronica killed her mike, and a commercial for General Telephone came through the studio speaker, Max's voice, still bearing a trace of his Bahamian heritage, crackled through the tiny intercom. "It's just a thirty, Vee."

"Okay, thanks." Veronica smiled at Carla Jahns. "I'm sorry to keep you up so late."

"Hey, no problem. I'm used to it. I don't have much to do till noon tomorrow, anyhow." She sucked the last drop from her coffee cup and tossed it toward the can in the corner. "Which reminds me, when's your appointment with Jon?"

"Monday morning at ten."

"You know, don't you, that the job's not glamorous? I mean, we're talking more or less a highly paid gofer."

Veronica nodded. "I don't care. I just want to be involved." She was trying to listen for the end of the spot and talk at the same time. "I missed his *FutureBase* shoot when I left Houston. I wasn't about to miss him again."

"Well, he was impressed with your letter." She tucked one leg under the other. "The fact that you studied film in college and promised not to slobber on the stars seemed to win him over."

"I may make an exception in the case of Paul Haden." On the speaker, the General Telephone spot ended. Veronica flipped on her mike and said, "This is the 'Slate Show' on WAQT, TalkRadio TenTwenty. I'm Veronica Slate. My guest is Carla Jahns, with the movie *Perfect Casting* and—" She glanced at the Apple Macintosh screen that listed the four callers holding, and pressed a lighted button on her phone. "Ginger in Clearwater, you're on the QT."

Tampa International Airport seemed much larger than Angela remembered. She was wearing Girbaud jeans and a U.C.L.A. sweat shirt in an effort to avoid being recognized, although that wasn't really a big problem yet. With leading roles in three horror pictures, one of which hadn't yet been released, Angela was usually recognized only by teen-agers. The infrequent recognition from adult men had to do with being blond, blue-eyed, and built.

She glanced at her watch and realized she was still on California time. She walked rapidly through the huge T.I.A. terminal, littered with people even at that ungodly hour. A ride down the escalator and she reached the baggage-claim area.

"Angela!" A pretty girl, who resembled Angela except for longer hair, a smaller chest, and a good tan, waved at her. "Over here, I've got your bags." She wore denim shorts and a *Perfect Casting* T-shirt, her blond hair loose and flowing.

Angela was glad to see a friendly face. Tracy Morgan had been her friend for several years and her stunt double on all

three *Slasher* films. "Hi, Trace. Thanks for picking me up."
They kissed and hugged.

"No problem. You're gonna love it here. I got in two weeks
ago, and get a load of this tan." She made a quick circle and
struck a model's pose. "Is that great, or what?"

They exited the air-conditioned baggage area through large
automatic glass doors, and the humidity enveloped Angela
like a shroud. With a porter bringing her bags, they arrived
at a white Ford Econoline van with a magnetic sign attached
that read: PERFECT CASTING STAFF. The porter loaded the
suitcases. Tracy tipped him, then climbed behind the wheel.

As they drove around the circular road that eventually led
to the exit, Angela gazed out the window at the millions of
lights surrounding the terminal building.

"I missed you on Carson the other night," Tracy said
pleasantly. "What were you pushing?"

"*Slasher Two* was released on cassette last week. I talked
about it and about *Slasher Three*."

"Oh, that reminds me. Jon just told me. Mira Loma's set
the release date for June 6."

"Nice of him to let me know," Angela said. "I could have
mentioned that on Carson."

"It's gonna be a real change of pace for you getting third
billing in this one."

"I don't know," she said. "I don't mind. It's a better
script and it'll be less work. Besides, I do get killed this time.
That's a change." Just saying the word *killed* reminded her
of Tony.

She was surprised Tracy hadn't brought up the death of
Tony Victor. She knew that was the primary reason Mira
Loma had held up the release of *Slasher III*. Its executives
didn't want the box-office backlash that had hurt *Twilight
Zone: The Movie* after Vic Morrow and two child actors had
died during that shoot.

Tracy paid the attendant at the booth on the outskirts of
the airport and asked for a receipt.

Angela looked back at the huge terminal. "You know, the
last time I was at this airport, I was going the other way."

"When was that?"

"Seven years ago. When I moved to L.A."

"When you left David?"

"Yeah." Those awful days were etched in her mind. She had been at the end of her rope. A drunk. A pothead. A fool. She had turned her back on the man who loved her. Then, soon after she arrived in Hollywood, her sudden good fortune had almost killed her. What was it Robin Williams used to say? "Cocaine is God's way of telling you you're making too damned much money." She stared, unseeing, out the window. "I know getting away was the only thing to do, Trace, but, Jesus, sometimes I wish I had never left him."

"You gonna see him?"

"I don't know." Wanting to was one thing. Having the courage to do it was another.

Tracy paused a beat, then smiled. "Well, good news. Carla says you don't have anything to do until noon tomorrow. Jon's planning a read-through with most of the cast."

Angela wasn't listening. She was thinking about whether she should try to see David. She hadn't heard from him since the first *Slasher* film was released in 1984. He had written a short note, sent it through the studio, said she looked beautiful and was a good actress, and said he was glad she had pulled her life together. She had cried. But she hadn't written him. He probably wanted her to remain a ghost from his past. But somehow, now, almost two years later, she wanted to see him.

It was nearly three in the morning when Angela finally got into her one-hundred-fifty-dollar-a-night room on the quiet third floor of the beautiful Don CeSar Resort Hotel. The bellman left her luggage, turned down the bed, and smiled for a tip when he reached the door.

Alone and tired, Angela took off her eighteen-karat-gold Piaget watch—a gift from director Jon Vasta—and put it on the bedside table. She kicked off her black high heels and stripped off her jeans and sweatshirt. She reached back to unsnap her bra and noticed, for the first time, a manila envelope on the bed. She grabbed it and fell back onto the bed before prying open the little prongs and sliding out what was inside.

She sat up with a start.

It was a publicity still from *Slasher III: The Final Chapter*, a photo of her as "Jamie," standing with hand to mouth in terror of an unseen man with a knife. Written across it in bright red letters was the warning:

Forget about Tony's death, or you'll have to worry about your own.

She clutched the photo to her chest and began to shake, fighting back tears and wishing she could put the horror of Tony's death behind her.

Chapter Two

It was a humid, misty three in the morning when Veronica reached the door of her small, castlelike house on Coffee Pot Boulevard in St. Petersburg, across the bay from Tampa. The concrete lion by the steps watched over her as she turned the key. David's old brown Pontiac Sunbird was in the driveway. Good. The promise of wrapping herself around him had kept her going for the last couple of hours.

She unlocked the heavy oak door. "Hello. I'm home."

"Hi. I'm in the bedroom!" yelled a familiar male voice.

"I gotta feed the babies first." She dropped her purse on the couch and greeted her two long-haired feline roommates. "How's Mommy's babies?" she asked, crossing to the kitchen and snapping on the light. "Are you hungry?" Rum Tum Tugger, a grayish Maine Coon, answered by jumping up on the counter near the can opener and looking expectant. The more sedate Jennyanydots, a female tabby, waited by the food dish and mewed.

"This mommy's baby is hungry, too," David said from the bedroom. "Hungry for love."

She laughed. "You'll have to wait your turn," she called to him. "In this house, cats come first."

She slipped a can of Nine Lives into the can opener and pressed the lever. As the can opened, Rum Tum Tugger stuck his nose as close as he could to the scent of beef and liver.

She heard the padding of bare feet only a second before David wrapped his arms around her waist and buried his face in her neck. She scooped the cat food into their two little dishes.

He kissed her. "I missed you."

"I missed you, too," she said, twisting out of his grasp to set the dishes on the floor. She almost dropped them when she saw him for the first time. "Do you always walk around naked, Detective Parrish?"

"Only in your house." He spread his arms and turned around once. His dark brown eyes gleamed as a smile erupted beneath his bushy moustache. "What do you think? Wanna go to bed with me?"

She glanced down and then looked up at him with a grin. "I guess it's either that or a fast game of ring toss."

Veronica awoke with a start. She had been a prisoner in a nightmare that had plagued her most of her life. She was helpless, floating through a long dark void. There was nothing ahead or behind, just a stretch of infinity like a south Texas highway. She forced her eyes open and looked at David, asleep by her side in the rumpled queen-sized bed, grateful that he was there. Reassurance. He was alive. She was alive. All was almost right with the world.

She sat up enough to see the red digits of the clock. It was nearly six in the morning. She wanted to sleep for another five or six hours, but she was afraid to close her eyes for fear the nightmare would pick up where it had left off.

She put her long legs over the edge of the bed and sat up and stared at the tentative slits of light that had begun to slice through the darkened sky beyond Coffee Pot Bayou. Far away, she heard a police siren. Closer, a dog barked.

Sitting quietly in the darkness, her arms crossed, she recalled those nights as a child when she'd been frightened awake by fears of death. "Where do you go when you die?" she had asked her mother, never dreaming her mother would go there so long before she would, and so violently. "Is there a heaven? When I die, will it all be just blackness and nothingness?"

She finally faced the fact that—whatever the answers might be—the only way she could survive was to believe there was going to be something after death. But throughout her life, there were times when her faith—a fragile, tentative thing at best—would vanish in the middle of the night and she'd have to turn on a light and read or watch TV or do something—anything—to keep from thinking about the dark, somber questions for which she still had no answers.

This morning, now that she was awake, what she was trying not to think about was not nearly as earthshaking as life and death. David's ex-wife was coming back to town.

"Hey! Are you all right?" David's voice was mushy with sleep. "What's the matter?"

She turned and fell back on the bed beside him. "I just couldn't sleep."

"I didn't wear you out?" He smiled, then brushed a few strands of hair from her face. "What's the matter?"

She rolled onto her side and studied his face in the glow of the arriving dawn. "Do you really love me?" It was a childish question, but she felt as vulnerable as a child at the moment.

He stroked her cheek. "What's wrong, Vee?"

"Oh, I don't know."

He said nothing, a trick he used to get her to talk.

As usual, it worked.

"I'm worried about Angela coming back to town," she said.

"Why? What in the world would you have to worry about?"

"She's young, blond, and beautiful—all the things I'm not."

"You're beautiful—"

"Don't patronize me." She stopped him with a slender hand to his lips. "You know what I mean. She's glamorous. I'm not. Besides, I'm feeling a little frightened that she's going to take you back, and feeling a little stupid for feeling frightened and . . ." She looked at him, hoping he'd understand.

"Okay, let's clear this all up right now. Come here." He raised his arm and offered his shoulder. She gratefully rested her head on his strong chest, catching a subtle scent of the Royall Lyme cologne she'd given him for Christmas. "Tell me exactly what you're worried about, and I promise to tell you the truth," he said. "Is that fair enough?"

"Yeah. Okay." She ran a plum-tipped fingernail in concentric circles on his hairy chest. "Do you want to go back to her?"

"First of all, *she* left *me*. No. I don't want her back. Next question."

"But she's famous and probably rich and definitely beautiful. She could give you much more than I can."

"Bullshit! Angie's too selfish to give anything to anyone."

"Then why did you marry her?"

"Oh, c'mon, Vee! I don't really think it matters."

She pushed away far enough to look him directly in the eye. "I'm serious. You've never told me."

"Did you ever think maybe I had a reason?"

"Like what?"

"Like I don't want to talk about it."

"I want to know."

"We don't always get what we want." He closed his eyes and then opened them, staring at the ceiling.

The silence lengthened like thread unwinding from a spool. Little shafts of pinkish light played over their legs. A faint hum of distant traffic played counterpoint to early birdsong.

"Okay," he said finally. "I was lonely. It's that simple. I was lonely and she came along."

"Were you a detective then?"

"Yeah. But not like now. I was with the St. Pete police then. And I was in Narcotics, not Homicide. Only been there six months. I was alone and Angela was—like you said—

young, blond, and beautiful.'' He paused and scratched his ear.

"C'mon. Now you've started. Tell me the whole story."

"I got a call from a friend who was the director of a play at the St. Pete Little Theatre. He wanted to borrow my gun to use as a prop. They were doing a play called *Heaven Can Wait*."

"I loved that movie," Veronica said.

"Yeah. Well, the play's different. Guy's a boxer, not a football player."

"Sorry I interrupted."

"I told him I wouldn't allow the gun out of my sight. He says, 'No problem. You can play the detective.' "

Veronica laughed. "My David an actor?"

"Yeah. It was the first time I'd been onstage since Michigan State, and that was just to build the set. Anyhow, Angela was the female lead. And we just sorta got together."

Actually, he remembered as he told Veronica the story that he had been drawn to Angela Mastry because she was dramatic—her gestures, makeup, voice. She had made him feel desired almost from the first words out of her mouth. She'd faked a Mae West voice: "You carryin' a gun, or are you just glad to see me?" He hadn't laughed. "You must be the off-duty cop. Whaddaya doing after rehearsal? Wanna get a glass of wine at Denny's?"

They did. She sat across from him in the booth, locking him in her limpid gaze, and telling him things he'd needed to hear for a long time. How handsome he was and how understanding and sensitive he seemed. Not a bad analysis for a stranger after only an hour's conversation.

By the time she'd had four glasses of wine and he'd had two beers, she was nuzzling against him in the parking lot and saying she wanted to take him home to bed, only she had a roommate. He offered his own little apartment and she said yes immediately.

It was the best night he'd spent in bed with a woman in years. Almost as good as that night at the University Motel during his senior year at Michigan State. Angela was a small uncaged animal. He was surprised when she got up after their tryst and got dressed. "Where you going?" he asked.

"Home. I don't like to stay all night with a man I hardly know," she said matter-of-factly. "It's just a thing I got. Don't worry, it was hot, lover. Real hot."

For the next three weeks, their routine was the same. He'd pick her up after she got off work at the jewelry store where she was a clerk. They'd go grab dinner at the Sand Dollar or the Oyster Bar. Angela would have a couple of drinks with dinner. Then came rehearsal, where she practically ignored him. After rehearsal they'd go to his place for a couple of drinks and more sex. Then she'd go home.

After the opening-night performance, Angela and David and the other cast members went out to the Sand Dollar on South Thirty-fourth Street to drink. He was beginning to notice that drinking was something Angela did well.

By two in the morning she was very drunk, and by the time they arrived at her apartment in the Crab Key complex on the south side of St. Pete, she had passed out in the front seat of his brand-new 1979 Pontiac Sunbird.

David had to dig her keys out of her purse, carry her inside, and put her into bed. "The next day," he told Veronica, "she was impressed that I hadn't stayed the night with her."

"I thought you said she had a roommate."

"She had been lying about that. Apparently it was just an excuse for not letting me sleep over."

"She seemed to have a double standard. 'Sleep with me at your place, but stay out of my bed.' "

"Yeah. I suppose. Her friends told me she needed me to pull her life together. That was bullshit. It was a big mistake from the start, Vee." He looked sadly at her. "She was really a drunk. I couldn't stop her. Couldn't help her. Last few weeks of the marriage she was putting away half a bottle of bourbon a day. She left me three months after the wedding and took off for Hollywood. We got divorced a month later. By mail. All very civilized. A couple of expensive attorneys and lots of registered letters."

Veronica drew David's face to hers and kissed him. "Sorry I made you tell the story."

"Me, too." He gave her a tight-lipped smile. "Hey, it's okay. I'm over it now. But 1979 was about the worst year of my life." He counted off the events on the fingers of his hand. "Divorced in March. Kicked off the St. Pete police force in June."

"Kicked off? Why?"

"For killing a drug dealer." He frowned. "I don't want to talk about that right now." He dropped his head back on the pillow. "But I've never really forgiven her for taking off just when I needed her the most. I was rock bottom. And y'know what was really bad? I couldn't help her. That really pissed me off. I always think I can fix everything, take care of everyone. I couldn't do a damned thing to help her. For a couple of years I beat myself to death for failing. Failing to change her. Failing to solve her drinking problem. Failing to make the marriage work."

"Yeah," Veronica said. "See, that's what's worrying me—that you feel so bad about your so-called failure that you'll want to try again now."

David paused a little longer than she liked. "No. Angela wouldn't want me now any more than she did then. We're light-years apart." His eyes warmed as he reached out and brushed the hair back off Veronica's face. "Besides, this isn't really about Angie anyhow. It's about you and me. And you are the best thing that ever happened to me. Sure. You're beautiful and great in bed, but you know what's even better? You're a good friend. You can't imagine what it's like to sleep with a woman—"

"No, I really can't." She grinned.

He frowned. "To sleep with a woman you like *and* respect."

"Will you still respect me in the morning?" Now she was being silly and she knew it.

"It is morning, and I do respect you." He kissed her hand. "I'm really serious, Vee. My going back to Angie would be just as insane as your going back to Sam."

"I hope so." She wanted to believe him.

CHAPTER THREE

"IT'S GOING TO BE OPEN IN ABOUT A YEAR." VERONICA pointed to the new, nearly completed Sunshine Skyway Bridge to her left as she drove her blue Honda Accord across the one remaining span of the old Skyway bridge. It was a bright beautiful Florida spring day with high fluffy white clouds against a light blue canvas.

They had crawled out of bed just after ten. David had dressed in clean jeans and a blue polo shirt. Veronica wore a pale blue summery dress with a row of fake buttons down the front, and wide straps. Something about being with David brought out the femininity in her. She preferred wearing dresses when she was out with him. She even put on panty hose and a pair of white slingback heels. *Now that's true love,* she'd thought, smiling.

They had swallowed some coffee and some Entenmann's Danish, packed a change of clothes, and started out for a weekend with Veronica's father at his place on Anna Maria Island, just west of Bradenton on the Gulf of Mexico. They had to steer clear of downtown St. Petersburg, where thousands of people were lining the streets watching the annual Festival of States parade.

As they reached the peak of the old Skyway, David said, "Rick refuses to drive across this bridge for any reason."

"Rick?"

"My partner, Rick Melendez. C'mon, Vee, you remember. You met him New Year's Eve."

"Oh, yeah." She retrieved a vague image of a compact, handsome Latin type with a thin moustache. She made it over the hump of the damaged bridge and relaxed her grip on the wheel.

"Ever since the disaster he's really freaked. Says it can happen again."

"They call it Skyway Phobia," Veronica said.

No one had dreamed the old Skyway, connecting St. Petersburg to the north and Sarasota-Bradenton to the south, could topple. But a freighter called the *Summit Venture* had rammed one span of it in 1980, and thirty-five people had driven off to their death. Now, most locals were nervous about crossing the remaining span, especially if there were tourists ahead of them slowing down at the top of the bridge to look at the jagged edges of the other span.

"I'm not so sure about the new one either," David said.

"Just relax. We're safe." She smiled at him and teased, "Just keep an eye out for freighters."

Ahead of them, the thin ribbon of I-275 stretched across the shimmering pale blue bay into the dark green landmass of upper Manatee County.

Angela Mastry sat in a metal folding chair at a large portable conference table in the Del Prado meeting room on the fifth floor of the Don CeSar Resort Hotel in St. Pete Beach. She wore jeans, dance shoes, and a lavender pullover cotton blouse, no bra. Gathered in the chair around her were the primary cast members of *Perfect Casting,* and a couple of production assistants.

Angela looked across the table at her costars.

Paul Haden. Hazel eyes and sandy blond hair and a face

that launched a thousand hearts. He was Joe Casual in brown shorts and a matching T-shirt today. He was pushing forty, but was still one of the most popular leading men since Robert Redford had hit the scene.

Raynor Fitzhugh. His snow-white hair and beard reminded her of the man who played Santa Claus in *Miracle on 34th Street*. He wore a long-sleeved white shirt and blue slacks held up by suspenders. Fitzhugh was a longtime Broadway character actor who'd decided, at the age most men retired, to try his luck in the movies. He'd told her he had eight major pictures listed on his résumé.

Angela's attention was drawn to the double doors as Jon Vasta, the diminutive director of the film, entered. Right behind him were slim, angular Carla Jahns, the production manager, in khaki shirt and slacks, and Adrian Bell, the stunt coordinator, wearing jeans and a blue cotton shirt open halfway down his hairy chest.

"Sorry I'm late," Jon Vasta said with a thin smile. "I'm glad you're all here." He sat in a chair against a column by the window, looking cool in a white linen shirt and shorts. Angela had to squint to see him against the backlighting of the Florida sunshine. "Today is for problem-solving," Vasta announced. "We're just going to read through the script and discuss minor changes. We'll also discuss some of the second-unit and stunt work," Vasta said, "which is why Chuck and Adrian are here."

Vasta gestured to Chuck Hollenbeck, a tall bearded man, with black hair over the collar of his green plaid shirt. He wore jeans, and was sitting with the other production assistants. Adrian Bell sat down next to him. He was a muscular man with longish brown hair and a moustache.

Vasta smiled. "With any kind of luck we should be done in time for the golf fans in the group to see part of the Master's Tournament." With that, Vasta opened his copy of the script and began. The other voices reading the scenes became a distant hum in Angela's ears. She had tuned out and was worrying about the threat she'd found last night in her room.

How'd it go again? *Forget about Tony Victor's death, or start worrying about your own.* She had memorized the words through a mostly sleepless night. She knew whoever was threatening her was talking about the violent death on the set of *Slasher III*. If it really had been murder, as she believed, and someone knew that she had come to that conclusion, he'd have reason to threaten her in an effort to cover it up. But who? She decided she would call Gary Kines, her attorney in L.A., as soon as the meeting was over.

Veronica and David rounded the curve alongside the Manatee County Public Beach and headed north on Anna Maria Island. She remembered with a sudden chill the night last fall when she had met a disc jockey in cowboy boots on that beach to discuss the murder of one of her best friends. Some memories refused to go away even after the people did.

"So, who's this new 'lady friend' Archie wants us to meet?" David asked as Veronica drove through the small business district of Holmes Beach and headed north on Palm Drive toward her father's house in the tiny town of Anna Maria. "What's her name?"

"Barbara Robinson. She's a widow. Her husband had been president of Sunshine National Bank. She sells real estate for some company on Longboat Key." She cast a glance in David's direction. "Although I imagine it's more of a hobby than a means of survival." She turned her attention back to the street. "She's involved in that new theme park outside Sarasota, too."

"What new theme park?"

"CircusLand." She looked at him and her jaw dropped. "You haven't heard about it?"

"I've heard of Circus World. Out by Lakeland."

"That's closed. This one is different. It's supposed to open in May. They say it's going to be a real shot in the arm for Sarasota's economy."

"I didn't know Sarasota's economy needed a shot in the arm."

"You can't go on forever with two dozen theaters, an opera company, a performing arts hall, hundreds of artists, writers, and performers, a hundred banks and three Mercedes dealers. These days, almost any new business that doesn't have a smokestack is welcome in Sarasota."

"I hear you." He rolled down his window another inch, letting in more fishy smells and gull songs. "So, this Barbara. You've met her?"

"Not yet."

"Think your dad will get married again?"

Veronica almost drove off the road. "Jesus! Don't scare me like that. He just met her," she said. She straightened the wheel and checked her rearview mirror. "I'm glad to see Daddy's dating. After all, Mom's been dead more than seven years." She thought for a moment. "But I don't know about getting married. I'm not so sure that's a good idea."

"Just because you hate marriage doesn't mean he does." He added, "You worry about him too much."

"I don't hate marriage," she said grimly, as she made the turn around the Island Players theater onto Pine Avenue. "And I've been worrying about Daddy ever since he retired from the Bureau," she said. After leaving the F.B.I., except for four years as Manatee County sheriff, her father had done little but fish. As she slowed at the corner where Fast Eddie's restaurant was located, she added, "I don't want him to be alone."

Archie was waiting for them, sitting on the deck of his rustic pine-and-driftwood house on Bay Boulevard just beyond Fast Eddie's Place, one of the most popular restaurants south of the Skyway. His short-cropped white hair seemed to glow against the tan of his face. He was dressed casually in tan cotton slacks and a dark brown knit shirt. "Hi, Ronnie." He stood and hugged his daughter, then shook David's hand. "How's the cop?"

"Doing okay. You hear about the shootout in Miami yesterday? Big piece on the front page of the St. Pete *Times* this morning."

Archie's smile faded. "Good Lord, yes. I talked to Joe Corless this morning. He's head of the office there. Jesus! It was awful. I knew Ben Grogan personally. He'd been with the Bureau twenty-five years."

"Was he one of the agents who was killed?" Veronica
asked, as she fiddled with one of her gold-and-blue earrings.

"Yeah," Archie said. "Just a year away from retirement.
Good guy. A marathon runner. He was a legend in the Miami
office." He looked grimly at David. "The son-of-a-bitch
nailed Ben with a Ruger Mini-Fourteen. Killed him instantly."

"Who were the perps?" David asked.

"Couple of hotshot bank robbers. They both bought it,
too, thank God." Archie led the way into the living room.
"It just makes me sick to hear about it."

Inside, as Veronica sat beside David on the long couch,
Archie walked to the walnut bar that separated the living
room from the cheery white-and-tan kitchen.

"Well, enough gloom and doom. Can I get you guys anything to drink?"

Veronica asked for a Dr Pepper, David requested iced tea,
and Archie grabbed three glasses from behind an old brass
ice bucket and went into the kitchen. Reflected in the pat-
terned mirrors on the wall around the bar, a dozen antique
enamel-on-steel advertising signs filled the walls by the front
door.

David looked around the room. "You know, I've always
been meaning to tell you, I really like this place," he called
to Archie. "Like what you did to it."

From the kitchen, Archie said, "Yeah, it's like me.
Weather-beaten and old." He came back into the room and
handed them their drinks. "Ronnie and I did it ourselves,
you know. It used to be an old boathouse."

How well Veronica remembered those six months in early
1980, a year after her mother was killed. Remodeling the
house was their way of marking time, trying to start their
lives again.

"Actually, I'm talking about the living room," David said.
"The way it looks."

Archie sat in his bamboo chair with the green padded seat.
"Okay. That's something I can take credit for. The living
room was the one room Ronnie let me decorate by myself."
He looked around. "I guess I didn't mess it up too much."

"No, Daddy," she said, "you did a great job." He'd chosen a mixture of bamboo, driftwood, and dark walnut, with two bamboo chairs and a seven-foot couch dominating the room, and a heavy walnut coffee table for magazines or feet.

Archie glanced at the Regulator clock on the wall. "Barbara will be here soon. What do you think of spending the afternoon at the Ringling Museum, then dinner at Fast Eddie's?"

"Sounds good," David said.

"Yeah," Veronica added, "but let's go to Old Hickory for dinner. It's just a few blocks from the museum. We go to Fast Eddie's all the time."

"Well, Barbara wanted to go to Fast Eddie's. She's never been there. You don't mind, do you?"

Veronica shrugged. "I guess not."

"Good. It's settled." Archie took a long sip of his iced tea and smiled at his daughter. "So what's this I hear about you trying to break into the movies?"

"That's not exactly it, Daddy. I'm just interviewing Monday with Jon Vasta, the director. He may hire me as a P.A. That's movie shorthand for a production assistant."

"Jon Vasta. Should I know him? Is he famous?"

"You could say that." She wrinkled her nose. "I keep forgetting you're not a movie fan, Daddy."

Archie grinned. "I just don't like sitting in tiny matchbox theaters with a bunch of teen-agers and three-dollar popcorn."

"Well, he won the Academy Award for directing *Jeremy Starr* almost twenty years ago. It was also the film that launched Paul Haden's career."

"Was he in the TV show?" Archie asked. "I saw the TV show."

"No. Steve Ellis played Jeremy Starr in the series," she explained patiently. "Paul Haden's in the movie they're making at the Don. That's one of the reasons I want to work on the film." She poked David in the ribs. "To meet Paul Haden."

David seemed to miss the jibe. "Paul Haden was in a sci-fi movie that long ago? He must be older than he looks."

She folded her arms across her chest. "Good grief, David, he was twenty-one when he won Best Actor in '69. The movie won Best Picture. Where were you, for God's sake?"

"In Nam," he said evenly.

"Oh, yeah. Sorry."

Veronica was saved from further embarrassment as a car pulled up outside. Archie stood expectantly and said, "That's Barbara."

Barbara Robinson was a petite woman who appeared to be in her late forties, but Veronica guessed she had probably passed fifty. Her short-cropped blond hair and large blue eyes gave her a youthful aura. Even in an expensive-looking aqua pantsuit and sensible white low-heeled shoes, she reminded Veronica of an older Angela Mastry. *I've got Angela on the brain,* she thought, as Barbara entered and they shook hands. It struck Veronica that Barbara seemed the exact opposite of her mother. Elizabeth Leigh Slate had been a tall, dark-haired beauty with uncommon intelligence.

Angela Mastry stuck her head in the door of the production office and told Liz, the brunette secretary, "Meeting's over. I'm going to change and lie on the beach for a while."

"Is everything okay so far?" asked Liz.

"Listen, after shooting the *Slasher* pictures in Canada, this is heaven." Also, she thought, but didn't say, this was her first chance—since her sudden rise to semi-fame as the only person left alive in three horror movies—to play someone older and more glamorous than "Jamie" in *Slasher, Slasher II,* and *Slasher III: The Final Chapter.*

Angela unlocked the door to her room and went directly to the closet, where she pulled off her dance shoes and jeans and began to take off the cotton blouse. She had it up over her face when someone kicked her in the back. The wind knocked out of her, she fell face first on the carpeted floor.

"Please do not move or I will most assuredly kill you." It was a low, even man's voice with an accent she couldn't immediately place. He straddled her back and hit her outstretched wrists with something metallic. Handcuffs. He snapped them shut, got off her back, and dragged her by her arms across the carpet. The blouse still covered her face, and her breasts burned against the carpet. He put his foot in the center of her back and pressed down. "Now, listen to me."

"I can't breathe," she mumbled into the blouse. She couldn't see, either.

"Don't breathe. Just listen. You should not have talked to that attorney before you left L.A. That was a mistake."

Angela's heart fell. She had counted on Gary Kines to protect her if it came to that, and now it had come to that.

"If you go to the police, or anyone else, you can be absolutely certain that you will die."

She was beginning to feel light-headed. "Okay, I won't talk." Her arms ached, her breasts burned, and her back hurt where he had his foot. But she had finally figured out the accent. Irish.

"Do you promise?" he asked sarcastically.

"I promise." Her mouth was cottony from the fabric. "Now let me up, you bastard."

"In a moment." He took his foot off her back and she gulped in a breath of air. He asked, "Have you ever heard this before?"

There was a click and Angela's horror mounted as she heard the tape of her own deposition given to Gary Kines in L.A.

After a few moments, he shut off the tape and said, in a soft, emotionless voice, "You should not have done that, Angela. We were not sure how much you knew until we heard the tape. You should not have done that." He put something cold and metallic on her bare back.

She flinched.

"Time for you to give a performance, Angela. Remember when you were cornered in *Slasher*? You were up against the wall and Kevin was coming at you with the knife. Remember what you said?"

Her mind raced, trying to recall that film, made two years before, but they all blended together. If there was anything unimportant in the *Slasher* pictures it was the script. "I don't remember."

"You said, 'Oh, please don't kill me! Please . . .' "

She waited, trying to reason it out. If he had meant to kill her, surely he would have done it already. He was just trying to scare her.

He removed the cold metal object from her back. "I don't like to use knives. Too messy. Guns are more efficient."

She heard the hammer click as he drew it back.

"It's your line, Angela."

At first, Angela was so terrified she didn't know what he wanted. Then she caught on. The line from her movie. "Oh, please, don't kill me!" She wasn't acting. "Oh, please, don't kill me!" She twisted wildly, fighting against the handcuffs, as she imagined the bullet coming down the barrel into her back. "Oh, please, don't kill me!" She was whimpering like a baby.

Nothing happened for a moment.

Then: "Good-bye, Angela." He squeezed the trigger, and the last sound she heard was a loud metallic click.

CHAPTER FOUR

"I'M REALLY EXCITED BECAUSE IT LOOKS LIKE HARCOURT, Brace, Jovanovich is going to buy Circus World," Barbara said from the front seat of Archie's 1980 Buick. David and Veronica sat close together in the backseat.

"Aren't they in the book-publishing business?" David asked.

"Well, yes, dear." Barbara turned to face him. "But they also own theme parks and other things."

"I don't understand the connection with what you're doing," Veronica said. "How does this help you?"

"Well, if they do buy Circus World, they're probably going to close it down and reopen as some other kind of theme park someday. That means we may be able to buy much of their equipment and even some of their animals for CircusLand."

"That's the theme park Barbara is working on for Sarasota," Archie explained, as he turned south from Cortez Boulevard onto the Tamiami Trail.

"It's opening in late May or early June," she said to Veronica. "I hope you can come see it."

"Sure."

"Enough about me," Barbara said, smiling at David. "Archie tells me you're with the Tampa police. What do you do?"

"I'm a homicide detective."

"My! That must be dangerous, exciting work."

"Sometimes it is, usually it isn't. It's not like on TV."

"Or in Miami," Archie added darkly.

Barbara turned her attention to Veronica. "And you have a talk show, dear? How sweet. Can I hear you in Longboat Key?"

Veronica forced a smile. "I'm sure you can. Our signal covers from Clearwater to Venice."

"Where do I find it on the dial?"

"It's ten-twenty on the A.M. dial. But I'm on pretty late at night," Veronica said. "Ten to two."

"Two in the morning?"

Veronica nodded. Her cheeks hurt from smiling.

"That must make it difficult for you to have any kind of a social life."

Veronica cast a conspiratorial smile at David. "I manage."

"I don't know what I'd do if I had to work at night," Barbara said, squeezing Archie's arm and smiling at him. "Archie and I are getting to be such late-night people."

Veronica was surprised to feel a pang of jealousy.

Where the northern limits of the city of Sarasota began, clinging to the Tamiami Trail, or what the natives called "the North Trail," there stood one of Florida's major attractions. The Ringling Museum and surrounding grounds may have been less exciting than Disney World, a couple of hours to the northeast, but the complex was well known and revered as a cultural landmark.

There was a major art museum featuring America's most important collection of baroque art; the state-supported Asolo Theatre, housed in an authentic eighteenth-century Italian theater; the magnificent mansion Ca' d'Zan—former home of John Ringling; and the more contemporary Museum of the Circus.

Veronica, David, Barbara, and Archie stood just inside the entranceway of the museum in a small mixed group of men, women, and children, listening to the tastefully dressed guide. "The John and Mable Ringling Museum of Art, opened to the public in 1930, was styled after a fifteenth-century Italian villa and built with columns, doorways, sculptures, and marble that circus magnate John Ringling had bought in Venice, Rome, Genoa, and Naples and had shipped to America.

"As you can see," she said, pointing through large windows, "the galleries are laid out on three sides of a garden court, and connected on the fourth side by a raised bridge dominated by a bronze statue of David by Michelangelo."

She walked to the door leading to the north gallery and smiled. "When he died in 1936, John Ringling left the art museum and its collections, the surrounding sixty-eight-acre estate, his sumptuous residence, and his entire fortune to the State of Florida. The Asolo Theatre and the Ringling Museum of the Circus were added later. We hope you enjoy your visit today."

Allowing the rest of the group to go on, Veronica stopped just inside the first door, to gaze at the huge canvas of *Abraham Receiving Bread and Wine from Melchizdek*. According to the notes, it was painted around 1625 to 1628 by the great baroque artist Peter Paul Reubens. Archie joined her. David and Barbara had begun working their way farther into the gallery.

"It's wonderful, isn't it?" Archie said.

"Absolutely beautiful." She pointed to a bearded man in the lower right corner of the large painting. "Look at the detail. The shoulder muscles and the expression on his face."

"Coming here always gives me a sense of timelessness," Archie said. "Like I can live forever."

"I know what you mean, Daddy."

"So what do you think of her?" Archie asked eagerly.

"I just met her." She noticed the glimmer of disappoint-

ment in his eyes and lied, "She seems nice." She regretted
the noncommittal tone in her voice. "Attractive, too."

"Did I tell you I met her at Selby Library?"

"No. Really?"

He followed Veronica as she started edging into the next
room. "She was in the stacks looking for books on the circus
and she literally bumped into me. I picked up her books for
her."

"That's nice, Daddy." Something about the conversation
was bothering her, and she hoped he didn't notice. "Maybe
we should catch up with them."

Archie put his hand on her bare arm and stopped her. "You
don't like her, do you? Tell me the truth."

"Daddy." She smiled. "I just met her. Give me time. I'm
sure I'll like her." She was sure she was lying, too.

Archie looked at her for a moment without removing his
hand from her shoulder. "You seem a little down. Are you
okay?"

"Yeah. Mostly." She bit her lower lip and moved on to
the next painting. "I'm just a little nervous."

"About meeting that director? Getting the job?"

"That. And about Angela Mastry." Suddenly the museum
seemed cold to Veronica.

"Angela . . . ?"

"David's ex-wife." She rubbed some warmth into her
hands. "She's starring in the movie."

"Why are you nervous about meeting her?"

"Good grief, Daddy! Why do you think?" Veronica
pushed a few strands of dark hair off her face. "She used to
be married to David. I'm afraid she might want him back
now that she's a star."

"A star, huh?" He moved out of the way for an elderly
woman who was looking at paintings instead of where she
was going. "You couldn't prove it by me. I've never seen
her."

"They're not really your kind of movies, anyhow." She
walked slowly past *The Building of a Palace* by Piero di Co-
simo.

"Wait a minute, Ronnie. Let's sit." He pointed to a low

bench against the wall. "I know you hate it when I tell you that you're being immature, but that's the truth." They sat and he touched her hand. "Now, I don't know much about this young lady, but I know a little bit about David, and I know a lot about you. David chose to be with you. That should be enough." He took her hand in his and traced out to the end of a finger. "One thing is for sure, honey. You can't let your fear of someone from David's past interfere with your present, or your future. Don't you think he loves you?"

"Yes. I know he does." The air in the museum suddenly seemed still and close. She took a deep breath.

"See? He loves you. You love him. You can deal with Angela what's-her-name when it comes up. *If* it comes up. It's like, what would you do if Sam came to town? Would David be jealous of him and worried about your relationship? You two were married, but that's been over for years."

"But this is different. Angela ran away from David. I left Sam. You can't compare the two."

Archie stood and offered his hand. "Sure I can." He grinned. "I'm your father. I can compare anyone I want." He pulled her up and kissed her lightly on the cheek. "Now, cheer up, okay? Don't be a gloomy Gus."

"Okay." She squeezed his arm. "Gloomy Gus? I haven't heard that in twenty years. In fact, I haven't heard of anyone *named* Gus in twenty years." She flashed a quick smile, but it slipped as soon as he walked away.

After Angela regained consciousness she gradually realized that she had not been shot. She must have fainted. But the sensory details were different now. She was on her back, apparently in bed. She was naked and blindfolded with what felt like gaffer's tape. Her hands were still handcuffed, but now behind her back. The circulation in her hands had stopped.

"Is our little princess awake? Is she ready to listen?" It was the same male voice with a slight Irish lilt.

"What do you want with me? Why are you doing this?"

"Very simple. You saw us kill Tony. You told an attorney.

We don't want you to tell anyone else. Consider this afternoon a warning. If I had wanted to kill you, I'd have done it days ago in L.A., or at the airport in Tampa. I don't want to kill you unless I have to. You have a movie to make. All you have to do to save your life is shut your mouth.''

"Okay. I'll shut my mouth. I won't tell anyone. I promise. Just let me go. Don't hurt me. Please.''

He uttered a low, guttural laugh. "You're very good at begging, you know that? Very good. If you tell anyone what you know, I'm going to kill you slowly. So you can beg me not to.''

Angela was drifting in a cold, clammy world of fear and she mostly wanted it to be over. "Please. I swear I won't tell anyone. Please. Let me go.''

"Okay. But first I've got something nice for you.''

He grabbed one of her cuffed arms. "Let me see if I can find a vein.''

Angela knew immediately what he was about to do and she cried, "No! No! No!'' The needle jabbed into her arm.

"A little sweets for the sweet,'' her attacker said. "And here's a chaser.''

The ponderous warmth of the drug began to relax her muscles. He poured what smelled like whiskey on her lips. She clamped shut her mouth. She heard him set the bottle down.

"Good night, princess.''

It was nearly four in the afternoon by the time Veronica, David, Archie, and Barbara had seen enough of the museum and had walked back through the lush landscaping to the Ca' d'Zan, Venetian for "House of John.'' The sun was dipping toward the Gulf of Mexico ahead of them as they entered the ornate mansion.

John Ringling reportedly had said he'd be satisfied with just a little place back in the early twenties, but Mable Ringling had hired an architect to fashion a one-and-a-half-million-dollar Venetian gothic palazzo combining elements from two of her favorite buildings, the facade of the Doge's Palace in Venice and the tower of the old Madison Square Garden. Quite the unique combination.

They all stood in the foyer on the first floor of the Ca' d'Zan. According to the sign Veronica was reading aloud: "The house is two hundred feet long and the tower extends sixty-one feet above ground level. On the Sarasota Bay side, an eight-thousand-square-foot terrace of variegated marble enclosed by terra-cotta balustrades creates a piazzetta between the house and the dock."

"Are you going to read that whole thing?" David asked.

"I'm just impressed that she can pronounce 'balustrades' and 'piazzetta,' " Archie said with a chuckle.

Veronica continued. "Just one more thing. 'There are thirty rooms around a two-and-a-half-story roofed court.' "

"Great," David said. "Let's see some of those rooms."

"You just have no patience for culture." Veronica pushed him. "Go ahead. I'll catch up with you."

David and Archie headed into the State Dining Room as Barbara and Veronica stood reading the rest of the sign.

"He seems like a nice young man," Barbara said after they'd finished. "Have you known him long?"

"Since September."

"I know Archie thinks very highly of him." Barbara smiled up at Veronica.

It bothered Veronica that her father was confiding in Barbara. "Daddy likes him because he's a cop. It's a fraternal thing. Shared experiences and so on, I guess."

"I'm sure there's more to it than that. There's more to Archie than that."

Veronica looked at her for a between-the-lines reading, saw none, and smiled. "Yeah, Daddy's really great."

David and Archie were on the second floor looking in at the ornate carved wooden bed in Mable Ringling's bedroom.

"Ronnie tells me your ex is coming to town," Archie said without preface. "You going to see her?"

David's startled look gave way to a thin smile. "I don't think so, Archie. I don't have any reason to see her."

Archie ran his hand over the thick velvet rope barring entrance to the room. "She's worried, you know."

"Vee?"

"Yeah." He peered at David. "I told her not to worry."

"That's what I told her last night. She's just overly impressed because Angela's famous. But that doesn't make her a better person."

"True." Archie walked toward John Ringling's bedroom.

"I just want you to know something," David said as he followed Archie into the room. "I wouldn't knowingly do anything to hurt Veronica. I really care about her."

Archie smiled and patted David on the shoulder. "I know you do, son. I'm glad. She's a good girl. Deserves a good man."

The women caught up to the men in John Ringling's large red-carpeted bedroom. David pointed to the oval painted ceiling decoration overhead and said, "See? At night, old Johnny would slide that painting back and there was a mirror there, and he'd invite one of his circus ladies in for some fun and games." David made a move, as if opening a bathrobe. "Heeeere's Johnnny!"

"Hi-ho!" Archie chimed in.

"You two are incorrigible," Barbara said. "You're ignoring the lovely French Empire furniture. Isn't it marvelous?"

"Could you sell a home like this?" Archie asked.

"Who would want it?" Barbara said. "It's probably cold and drafty and impossible to keep clean. It's better that the state take care of it and show it to tourists. I have enough trouble selling three-bedroom homes on Bird Key."

"Why did you quit the F.B.I., Archie?" Barbara was sitting across from him at a table in the noisy but pleasant main room of Fast Eddie's Place, famous all over the Southeast for "Warm Beer and Lousy Food." By six o'clock it had begun to rain, and the weary four had skipped the Museum of the Circus and driven to the restaurant for dinner. Veronica and David were still in the lobby talking to the genial owner, Eddie Porter.

"I didn't exactly quit. I retired."

"Did your wife ask you to?"

Archie's hand shook slightly as he picked up his glass of

water. "No. Elizabeth had already been dead a year when I retired."

"Oh, dear, I am sorry. Was she ill long?"

Archie was uncomfortable but candid. "She was killed in a car-bomb explosion. It was meant for me. She—"

"How dreadful." Barbara put her small, pale hand over his. "I'm so sorry, Archie. I didn't mean to pry."

"That's all right. It's about damned time I get over it."

"But good memories die hard," she said. "I understand. Frank died of cancer. Not nearly so violent a death as your Elizabeth suffered. But I still think of him a lot."

"At least you probably had a chance to say good-bye and tell him you loved him. I never had that chance." Archie took his napkin and wiped away an imaginary drop of perspiration so he could sneak it up to his eyes and soak up an errant tear as David and Veronica returned.

"Guess what. Eddie says he's opening another restaurant in Tarpon Springs before long," Veronica said.

"Great," Archie said wryly. "Then I can drive for three hours instead of walking for one minute."

"C'mon, Daddy. I was just telling you the news."

Barbara looked up from the menu at Veronica. "What do you suggest? Is there anything especially good?"

"I like the shrimp," David said.

"That's all he likes," Veronica said, tweaking his ear. "I can't believe this guy. Lives in the heart of some of the greatest seafood eating in America, and all he ever orders is shrimp. Shrimp cocktail. Shrimp scampi. Shrimp fried in beer batter. Fried in pecans. Fried in coconut." She grinned at David. "You really should try some mullet."

"Or stone crabs," Barbara said.

"Or gator," Archie added, and everyone laughed.

Carla Jahns stood by as the bellman, dressed in tan slacks and a burgundy tunic, opened the door to Angela Mastry's room. When Angela had failed to show up for the pre-dinner press conference, it was up to Carla to go and find her. After knocking on the door for several minutes, Carla had called the front desk.

The moment the door was opened Carla nearly reeled from the strong odor of whiskey. She handed the bellman a five-dollar bill and thanked him, shoving him out before he could get a good look at the scene before her.

Carla shut the door and flipped on the light. It was as she had feared. Angela was back on the booze again, or worse. She was spread out on her back sound asleep or dead drunk. She was naked. On the bedside table was a nearly empty bottle of Johnny Walker Red. In the wastebasket was a used hypo and a small vial. Carla had been around Hollywood long enough to know what that meant. She grabbed the phone and called the front desk. "We need a doctor in Miss Mastry's room. Right away."

She replaced the phone and sat on the edge of the bed.

"Oh, baby," Carla said out loud. "I'm afraid you've really blown it this time."

CHAPTER FIVE

IT WAS MONDAY MORNING, THE END OF A NICE WEEKEND with David. Although Veronica had spent an inordinate amount of time worrying about Angela Mastry and trying to warm up to Barbara Robinson, she had enjoyed being with David. Saturday night they'd made love in the guest bedroom, with raindrops beating a tattoo on the window while Archie and Barbara visited friends on Longboat Key. Then they'd put on some clothes and curled up on the couch in the living room and watched *Nashville* on Channel 13's Late Show, looking as innocent as a couple of teen-agers after a make-out party when Archie and Barbara returned.

Sunday evening, on their way back to St. Pete, David and Veronica had spent an hour at Bradenton Beach watching the sun streak into the Gulf of Mexico. Shared times with David were always good, and this weekend—knowing that Angela was in the wings—Veronica had been storing up good times.

Now she sat cross-legged on her couch, in terry shorts and a huge Denver Broncos jersey, eating Frosted Flakes and milk

39

from a Tupperware bowl, and watching the "Today" show, while David finished his shower. Rum Tum Rugger climbed onto the couch and stuck his gray fuzzy face in her cereal bowl, lapping up the leftover milk. Jennyanydots was asleep in the window.

David stepped into the living room, naked except for the big brown towel he carried in his hands. "Hey, Vee, would you—"

"Would I dry your back?" she finished for him. It was a ritual they'd developed over several months of overnighters. "Come here, where I can reach you." She pointed to a spot in front of the couch. "You know, this nakedness is becoming a habit with you."

"Sorry." He stood in front of her, turned his back, and asked, "When's your appointment with Jon Vasta?"

"Ten." She rubbed his back dry and finished with a quick squeeze of his hairy buttocks. "There, you're all dry."

"Thanks." He turned, leaned over, and kissed her.

She hit the TV remote, turning off a loud ad in which a guy was yelling into a hand mike and pounding a brand-new van, and followed David into the bedroom. "Promise you won't laugh at me if I tell you something?" She didn't wait for his response. "I'm getting nervous about having a person-to-person talk with Jon Vasta himself." She sat on the edge of the bed and watched David dress, thinking for a moment about helping him reverse the process. "It's more than just his fame. I've seen every one of his films." She leaned back against the headboard. "I can still remember when I first saw *Jeremy Starr,* his first big hit. Christmas week, 1968, after Sam and I got married. He was off flying an F-Nine Cougar. Sam, I mean. There I was, this pathetic eighteen-year-old bride, sitting in a dusty Texas navy town all alone the week before Christmas watching a movie."

"Poor baby," David said.

She watched as he shrugged into the shoulder holster bearing his Smith & Wesson .38 Police Special. Somehow, seeing the gun gave Veronica a chill. It was a reminder of what David did for a living and that he could die before she'd see him again.

Soon after they'd begun dating, in an effort to get her over her fear of his gun, and because of the danger she'd been in from a child pornographer she'd discovered, David had enrolled her in a handgun course at the Lou Rosa Pistol Range in Pinellas Park. She was very good at it. She'd qualified on a Smith & Wesson .38 like his in a matter of weeks, but didn't even try to get a license, despite her ability with the weapon. Besides, in Pinellas County, it was very difficult to get a permit even if one needed to carry a gun. And Veronica had decided she didn't need to carry one.

She shook her head, bringing her mind back to the present. "I get the nagging feeling I've told you this before."

He started toward the door. "You probably did. You know what a lousy memory I have for ex-husbands."

"How about for ex-wives?" It had slipped out, her thoughts made verbal on the spur of the moment.

"Touché." He paused at the door.

"I'm sorry, I didn't—"

"It's okay." He looked at his watch. "I gotta go. Can I have a kiss?"

She stood and walked to him. "Sure." She kissed him and held him a little tighter than usual. Was it seeing the gun, or the thoughts of Angela? "I love you," she said.

"Call me after your meeting, okay?" David headed for the front door, then turned to say, "I love you, too."

Veronica stepped out of her Honda, straightened her skirt, and looked up at the imposing pink hotel before her. The sun was warm through a blue cloudless sky, and a breeze off the Gulf of Mexico whispered through the tall palm trees. Somewhere in the distance, she could hear a steel-drum band playing a calypso version of Schubert's *Marche Militaire*.

Built at a cost of more than a million dollars in 1928, the Don CeSar Resort Hotel was a flapper's dream, with its daring flamingo-pink exteriors, opulent Moorish interiors, and peekaboo gulfside verandas. Almost sixty years old, and refurbished a couple of times, it still reminded Veronica of a giant Disneyesque wedding cake, with its multitiered design, white-frosting window moldings, and six figurine towers. She crossed the street and headed for the side entrance.

She remembered reading that the Don had played host to everyone from F. Scott Fitzgerald to Robert Altman, who shot his 1979 film, *Health,* there. She had been working at WSUN Radio in St. Pete when Altman came to town to use the Don as the backdrop for a fictional health-food convention. Despite a cast featuring such stars as Carol Burnett, Glenda Jackson, Lauren Bacall, and James Garner, the film had sunk like a stone.

Now, Hollywood had ventured into the Don CeSar again with the production of *Perfect Casting* by Jon Vasta, a director who'd had as uneven a career as Altman. Between *Health* and *Perfect Casting,* a couple of memorable scenes had been shot in the hotel for the gangster epic *Once Upon a Time in America,* but a butchered edit had sunk that film. Jon Vasta had told reporters he hoped his picture would be the first hit to be made at the Don CeSar.

Veronica checked her appearance in one of the mirrors on the dark wood-grained wall of the elevator as she traveled to the third floor of the Don CeSar. She wore a burgundy dress with puffy half sleeves, a belted waist, and a trumpet skirt. She'd kept it simple with a gold chain and a pair of gold dot earrings, and showed off her good legs with high-heeled black pumps.

The doors opened on the third floor, and the relative silence of the elevator was shattered by a computer printer and a dozen voices talking at once. She stepped out and headed for a room that sported a temporary sign reading PRODUCTION OFFICE.

Inside, a pretty brunette in a green sundress sat behind a desk talking on the phone. A long, low couch held two burly men reading papers and smoking. She recognized Raynor Fitzhugh, the elderly character actor, sitting at a small table near the windows talking loudly to a young man in Bermuda shorts.

"What did I tell you?" Fitzhugh said. "I told you Nicklaus would win the Master's. Adrian says he's 'too old.' Bullshit! Forty-six is not old. He's a mere babe. And a hell of a golfer. What did I tell you? The sixth damned time he won that sucker.''

The model-slim brunette hung up and smiled at Veronica. ''Hi. We're not casting extras till Friday. If you want to leave your résumé—''

''I'm not an actress. I'm Veronica Slate. I've got an appointment with Mr. Vasta.''

The woman shook her head as if to clear the cobwebs. ''Sorry, I've got casting on the brain. I'm Elizabeth Barney, but you can call me Liz.'' She waved a small pink piece of paper between her thumb and finger. ''I've got the note right here, honest. Jon's expecting you. He should be back any minute.''

''Okay.'' Veronica sat on a folding chair next to Liz's desk, the one remaining chair. ''Can you tell me anything about Mr. Vasta? Anything to help me not make a fool of myself?''

''First, don't call him Mr. Vasta. He hates that. Call him Jon. He's real nice, very low-key. Quiet.'' Liz leaned toward Veronica, lowering her voice. ''I almost missed getting this job because I talked too much. He hired me when he did *Denver Boot* in Colorado. He said, 'Elizabeth, I'll hire you if you shut up once in a while.' ''

''Are you from Colorado?''

''Yeah. Castle Rock. It's a speck on the map between Colorado Springs and Denver.'' She was interrupted by the ringing phone. She answered it. ''Production. This is Elizabeth.''

Elizabeth. Veronica couldn't help thinking of her mother. She still burned inside at the memories of that day in Arlington. The explosion. Ripped metal sizzling in the slush. Archie on his knees in the snow, crying. But most of all she hated the random unfairness of it all. The bomb had not been meant for her mother, a fact that had tormented her father ever since.

''Excuse me. Are you Miss Slate?'' The man who had silently appeared at her side was shorter but more distinguished-looking than she remembered. Prematurely gray hair. Blue eyes like Yoda's in the second Star Wars movie. Smooth skin. He offered his hand. ''I'm Jon Vasta.''

She stood, and regretted it as she towered over him. He

didn't seem to mind. She shook his hand. "I'm Veronica Slate."

He started out the door and said over his shoulder, "Come with me. It will be less noisy in this other room." He wore a white linen shirt and matching shorts and New Balance running shoes. She noticed his arms were tan and his legs were pale, the sign of a man who seldom wore shorts.

They arrived at the end of the hall and entered a room with large windows on two sides, the inside of one of the hotel's great turrets. Through the windows, the sun brightened the water of Boca Ciega Bay and the expensive homes surrounded by tall skinny palm trees that rimmed the water. The hum of traffic three stories below was faint but persistent.

"Let's sit," he said, clearing a stack of scripts off the couch onto the floor. "And perhaps you can clear up a profound mystery for me."

"What's that?" She sat on the other end of the couch, put her purse beside her, and smoothed her dress over her knees.

"What's a nice girl like you . . ." His deep blue eyes sparkled. "I'm sorry. What's a nice woman like you doing in a place like this? Why do you want to get into the movies?"

"Actually, I don't want to get into the movies in the sense of being an actress or something like that. It's just that I studied film and I love films and I wanted to work behind the scenes of at least one movie before I die."

"Are you going to die soon?" His eyes twinkled.

"I hope not."

"Good. We've got time to work on a picture together."

"*FutureBase* was what gave me that desire," she told him. "I left Houston just before you filmed there. When I saw the movie, it was so exciting to see the way you had turned 1977 Houston into a city of the future. I saw the film five times."

"Good Lord!" he said, bringing the back of his hand to his forehead in mock horror. "I don't think even I could stand to see it that often." He paused, looking curiously at her. "Did you ever see *Magic Morning*?"

"Yes, and I loved it."

"Someone had to." He chuckled. "Well, you must really

be a film buff to remember *Magic Morning*. I guess it was a mistake to make a gentle love story so soon after *Jeremy Starr*. Critics loved it. Audiences hated it. No laser blasts, you know? It was an artistic success that lost money."

"Hey, look, even Michael Cimino had *Heaven's Gate*."

"Ah, but that picture wasn't even an *artistic* success. Why anybody would hire him again is beyond me. But I digress."

He glanced out the window for a second, then back at her. "So, you really want to work on a movie?"

"Yes. When Ron Howard was in St. Pete shooting *Cocoon,* and later when Carl Reiner did *Summer Rental,* I tried to get a job with them doing anything, helping out, just to be involved." She smiled and spread her hands. "But they had their own people."

"Yes." He studied her. "Well, about the job. As a production assistant, you'll be running errands, keeping the bar stocked—I drink Soave Bola and piña coladas—and you may help in the casting of extras, and do some crowd control. Most of the time you will report to Carla. What hours are you available?"

"My show on WAQT is from ten P.M. to two in the morning, so basically I'm available from, say, ten in the morning to about eight each night. And, of course, I'm free on weekends."

"That's fine. I don't plan to work you as hard as most P.A.'s since you do have another job. I have several other P.A.'s, so the full burden won't fall on your shoulders." He gazed out at a swooping gull, then looked back at her.

She waited.

He studied her for another moment, then smiled. "You're very pretty. We'll see if we can't get you into the picture, too. A little walk-on, perhaps." He looked at the gold Rolex on his wrist. "Well, if you'd stop by the office right next to the production office and see the accountant on your way out, you can fill out the forms. You may start tomorrow."

It had come so suddenly, so easily, that she could scarcely believe it. "You mean, you want me?"

He stood and issued a gentle smile. "I hardly know you well enough to want you, my dear, but I certainly want to hire you." Veronica picked up her purse, and was about to rise when a blonde in jeans, dance shoes, and a slinky black silk blouse burst into the room. She had a manila envelope in one hand. It took a second for Veronica to realize it was Angela Mastry, David's ex, and a chill raced down her back.

"Goddammit, Jon! I've been trying to find you for an hour!" Angela exclaimed. "We need to talk! Right now!" She finally turned to see Veronica sitting on the couch with her knees pressed tightly together and her purse in her lap. "Sorry."

"Angela Mastry, this is Veronica Slate," Vasta said. "Veronica's going to be working on the picture with us as a P.A."

Angela's mouth smiled but her face did not. "Hi." She wheeled back to Vasta. "Can we talk?"

Veronica got the cue and stood, offering Jon Vasta her hand. "Thank you, Jon." She started to say something civil to Angela, but the diminutive actress seemed impatient for her to leave.

Outside the door, Veronica was still breathing rapidly. She had prepared herself for eventually meeting Angela, but she'd had no idea it would be so soon or so sudden. As she headed down the hall to the accountant's office, she realized that seeing Angela Mastry off the screen in ordinary clothes had been a good thing. She had clear blue eyes, short blond hair, and a compact but well-built body. But she wasn't the glamour queen Veronica had expected. Somehow the unknown was always worse than reality. Angela Mastry looked like a hundred other blue-eyed blondes, except that there was something veiled or seductive hidden in those translucent pale blue eyes.

Angela walked to the doorway and watched as the tall, attractive dark-haired woman in the burgundy dress headed down the hall. Then she shut and locked the door and returned to where Jon Vasta was sitting on the couch, her stomach tied in knots. "Jon, you've got to hire some professional protection for me," she pleaded. "Someone's out to get me."

"Now, Angela, calm down. That's hard to believe." His

face spread into a sweet smile. "Who would want to *get* you?"

"I don't know. But look at this." She thrust the envelope into his hands and sat on the edge of the couch while he slipped out the photograph and read the threat written on it in red.

"Well, this could be considered a threat, I suppose." He looked up. "But how do I know you didn't write this yourself?" He sat again and his Yodalike eyes steeled. "I think the larger problem is the fact that you have violated our agreement," he continued. "When I hired you for this picture you signed an agreement that you would not abuse drugs or alcohol. What about Saturday?"

"That's just it, Jon!" She leaped to her feet. "I didn't! Someone jumped me in my room and shot me up! I was set up! Can't you see that?"

"You expect me to believe that someone forcibly administered cocaine to you? Why? What possible motive would anyone have?"

"How about your fucking completion clause?" Angela's agent had agreed to a clause in her contract that protected Mira Loma Productions against the possibility of her hitting the bottle again and not being able to finish the film. They had the right to fire her and hire another actress at any time, with only minimal severance pay, if they could prove she was too drunk to work. She had almost refused to sign the contract until her agent explained that she might not get another chance unless she proved she was sober. "Someone's trying to stop me from making this movie," Angela insisted. "You've got to give me some protection. A guard or a cop or someone."

"Okay, Angela, that's enough!" He stood and the anger in his voice startled her. "I'm not going to hire a police officer or a guard just to keep you from drinking and imagining that people are after you. We begin tomorrow, and you had better be on the set, sober and ready to work, at nine in the morning." Vasta walked to the door and turned, playing it like a scene from one of his films. "If I have another incident like you pulled Saturday night, you can be assured that I will take you off this picture so fast . . ." He glared. "Do I make myself clear?"

Angela stood, tight-lipped, as Vasta left the room. Damn! After almost four months without touching the stuff, just a few drops of whiskey spilled through her lips had set her off again.

As Angela got on the elevator to return to her room, Tracy Morgan came down the hall. "Hey, Angie! Hold the elevator!"

Tracy's blond hair was tied in a ponytail with a piece of pink yarn. She wore a French-cut *Perfect Casting* T-shirt and Levi's cutoffs. Her pink-canvas shoes matched her shirt. "Thanks." She did a double take. "You look like you could kill someone. What's the matter?"

Angela kicked the wall of the elevator as the door closed. "That little prick Vasta won't hire someone to protect me."

"Protect you from what? Fans?"

"No. Not fans." Angela looked closely at Tracy's pretty, uncomplicated face. Could she even trust her best friend? She needed to. "Someone's threatened to kill me."

"My God!" Tracy's eyes widened. "You're kidding."

As they reached the fifth floor and walked the carpeted hall to Angela's room, she told Tracy about the photograph the first night and about the attack on Saturday night.

Inside her room, Angela sat on the edge of the bed and reached for the phone.

"So someone set it up to make it look like you were drunk and doing drugs?" Tracy asked, as she sat on a chair by the window, her hair framed by a halo of sunshine.

"Right." Angela pulled the business card from her purse and dialed Gary's number in L.A. "It had to be someone who knows that I can get thrown off the picture if I'm drunk or doing drugs."

"Lots of people know that."

"Really?" Angela was surprised. Maybe that explained the veiled looks from some of the crew. Probably everybody was waiting for Little Miss Movie Star to go under for the last time.

On the phone a voice said, "Lawyers Incorporated."

"Hello. This is Angela Mastry in Florida. I need to speak to Gary Kines right away."

There was a pause. "I'm sorry. That is quite impossible."

"Why? This is important."

"Who did you say this is?"

"Angela Mastry. I'm a client."

"Hold on, please."

"What's the matter?" Tracy asked.

Angela covered the mouthpiece in her hand. "They say it's not possible to speak to Gary."

On the phone: "Miss Mastry?"

"Yes."

"This is Howard. I was Gary's partner. What case is this in reference to?"

Angela had noticed the word *was*, and a chill washed down the back of her neck. "The Mira Loma case. About the death of Tony Victor. I had . . . What did you mean, 'was'?"

"I'm sorry. I thought you knew." There was a long pause. "Gary was killed last Friday night here in his office." Another pause. "It was in all the papers."

Angela's hand started to shake.

"Angie," Tracy said. "What's wrong?"

"Hello? Are you there?" Howard's voice from the phone startled her out of her daze.

"Yes. I'm sorry. What did you say?"

"Someone killed Gary, and Susan, his girlfriend. It was awful. I've tried to take over most of his cases. Give me some more information and I'm sure I can help you."

"No. That's all right. Thank you." Angela hung up and turned to look at Tracy, her eyes welling up with tears. "They killed my attorney. I'm next."

Tracy joined Angela on the edge of the bed and put her arm around her. "No, you're not. If Jon won't give you protection, why don't you call David? He's a cop."

Angela jerked her head around. "I can't run to David. I gave up any claim on him when I left him."

"I'm not talking about romance. I mean, call him for advice or for protection. You can keep it strictly business."

Angela smiled through her tears. "Think so, huh?" She

shook off Tracy's arm and stomped into the bathroom, closing the door behind her. As quietly as possible, she lifted the top off the toilet tank and reached into the cold water. She grabbed her bottle of Beefeaters. Brought it out and held it, dripping, over the sink as she wiped it dry with some tissue paper. She poured an inch into her bathroom glass, then put the cap back on.

It wasn't until she had drunk it down that she saw herself in the mirror.

Still blond. Still beautiful. Still a drunk.

She closed her eyes and cried.

CHAPTER SIX

VERONICA WATCHED AS A HANDSOME MAN IN A TUXEDO AP-
proached the beautiful young blonde. She sat alone at a table
just inside the double doors of the elegant King Charles restaurant on the fifth floor of the Don CeSar Resort Hotel.

He came up from behind, a gun fitted with a silencer aimed
at the blonde's back. She was unaware of his presence, but
none of the thirty-odd people standing in the hall and sitting
at the marble fountain outside the door even tried to warn
her. They were too busy being quiet while a huge Panavision
camera filmed the scene.

It was a curious juxtaposition: A few elegantly dressed
extras were seated near the actress, whom Veronica had immediately recognized as Angela Mastry, while the crew to
the side and behind the camera wore T-shirts and shorts,
cutoffs, or jeans.

The magic of movie-making, she thought, as two "foomp"
sounds erupted from the gun and a pair of "squibs" under

Angela's blond hair popped open, spilling special-effects blood on her dress. She fell forward over the table.

After a few seconds, Jon Vasta gave the command to cut. At once, two dozen people broke their silence, Angela stood and peeled off part of her neck, and the huge lights were turned off.

The man who had just killed Angela turned to Veronica as a young man took the gun from his hand. "You're new, aren't you?"

She smiled. Carla was right. Paul Haden was just as handsome in person as he appeared on screen. She wished she were wearing something nicer and sexier than the unofficial uniform of the film crew: shorts, running shoes, and a pink *Perfect Casting* T-shirt. "Yes," she said. "I'm Veronica Slate."

"I'm Paul Haden." As if she wouldn't know that. He sat in one of the upholstered restaurant chairs and loosened the bow tie he wore. He looked up at her, his hazel eyes clear and bright. "Are you an extra?"

"No. I'm one of Jon's assistants."

"Ah, yes." He smiled and brushed some lint from his tux pants. His eyes darted away to Angela, huddled in discussion with Jon Vasta. He asked Veronica, "Are you from California?"

"No. St. Petersburg." She was trying not to stare at his classic face, molded in the image of Robert Redford.

"That's near here, right?"

"A few miles due east of where you're sitting."

"Forgive me." He flashed what she was beginning to recognize as an artificial smile. "I'm new in town."

She started away. "I'm new on the job, so forgive me if I get back to work." She gave him a real smile, and added, "It was nice to meet you, Mr. Haden."

"Call me Paul," he called after her. "And let me know if you want a walk-on. I can help you."

She started away, but a young girl who looked remarkably like Angela Mastry intercepted her. "Hi. I'm Tracy Morgan. Carla said I'm supposed to show you the ropes." She offered her hand and Veronica shook it.

Tracy Morgan looked to be about five-foot-three. She had long ash-blond hair tied back in a ponytail, wideset blue eyes, and full lips. She was wearing a *Perfect Casting* T-shirt, Levi's cutoffs, and pink-canvas shoes. They sat on the flat marble wall around the fountain.

"Do people often tell you how much you look like Angela?"

"I hope so," Tracy said. "That's how I got the job."

"What?"

"I'm her stunt double. Since the first *Slasher* film."

"You're a stuntwoman?"

"And an actress," Tracy said quickly. "I've got my SAG card. I've done a few supporting roles in other pictures."

"So you know Angela?"

"I guess you could say that. When she's in a good mood we're buddies. When she's playing 'star' she ignores me. It's that kind of relationship. I've worked three shoots with her before this and watched her act—so to speak." She giggled. "Don't repeat that, please."

"I won't." Veronica glanced at Angela, who was now arguing with Jon Vasta in front of the elevator, waving her arms and pacing in front of him. "Maybe you could explain something to me."

"I'll try."

"Why is Paul Haden's character killing Angela's character? I thought they were supposed to fall in love and walk off into the sunset."

Tracy smiled. "This was a dream sequence. See, the old director, played by Raynor Fitzhugh, warns Angela to stay away from Paul because he's dangerous. She worries about that and falls asleep and dreams that he kills her. It's just a dream."

"Guess it would help if I'd read the script," Veronica said.

"Good luck. Carla is protecting the script with her life." Tracy stood and yanked on her shorts. "Well, it's nice to meet you, Veronica."

"You can call me Vee. My friends do."

"Vee?"

"It's a horrible in-joke," Veronica said. "Several years

ago there was this science-fiction TV series called *V,* and a friend of mine at the TV station where I was working then started calling me Vee. It caught on.''

''TV? You were on TV?''

''Not a big deal,'' Veronica said, as she stood and hitched her jeans. ''I did weather for about a year on a little station down in Sarasota. Never again, please.''

''Veronica,'' Carla Jahns said, as she came out of the restaurant through a door with an etched C in the glass. ''I've got a job for you.'' She looked over at Angela, and asked Tracy, ''Is Little Mary Sunshine causing trouble?''

''Looks that way.'' Tracy stood. ''Nice meeting you.'' She offered a small, soft hand to Veronica, who shook it. ''See you later, Vee.'' As she walked away she mumbled, ''Vee. I like that. That sounds good. Vee.'' At the door she turned and smiled at Veronica. ''Maybe I can get people to call me Tee.'' Her musical laugh faded as she walked into the restaurant.

''What's this V stuff?'' Carla asked.

''Nothing important. Just a nickname.'' She glanced at Angela, still arguing with Jon Vasta, and turned back to Carla. ''What's wrong with Angela?''

''I don't know.'' Carla leaned closer and lowered her voice. ''She didn't show up at a press conference Saturday. When she didn't answer my knock, I had the bellboy open her door and I went in, and she was stretched out on her bed, naked and dead to the world.''

''Was she drunk?''

''Yeah. But Angie doesn't limit herself to booze. She had done some coke.''

''I'm sorry. This is really none of my business.'' Veronica felt uneasy discussing Angela. ''Well, what can I do for you? You said you had a job for me.''

Carla pulled out a cigarette almost as long and slim as she was, and lit it. ''Okay. Here's the skinny: Jon's moving across the hall to the east penthouse, room eight-oh-one, because he's decided to shoot a few scenes in eight-oh-two, the west penthouse. He needs a couple of suitcases and some clothes bags moved across the hall. Okay? They're in the bedroom on the second level."

Veronica was up and moving for the elevator. "Okay."

As she rode up in the service elevator, the only one that went to the penthouse level, Veronica mused about Angela. Despite David's reassurance, she was worried about her. True, she wasn't as beautiful in real life as she seemed on screen. But there was something strong, something seething beneath the surface that concerned Veronica. She could see it in Angela's eyes.

The elevator opened to a tiny foyer that contained the surprisingly small doors to the two penthouse apartments, a padlocked door to the roof, and a door to the stairway. Both penthouse doors were wide open. She stepped into the west penthouse and found her Adidas sinking into lush, off-white carpeting leading into a living room. Straight ahead a narrow spiral staircase wound up to the second floor of the penthouse. To her right, centered amid the expensive furniture, was a large backgammon table made of some sort of inlaid wood.

The glass doors to the balcony stood open. She couldn't resist going out into the cool late-morning air and gazing off into the distance. The day had dawned gray and windless, as if the sky intended to hold its breath until it turned blue.

A sailboat with its sails unfurled was moving lazily, and closer to the beach a few jet skis buzzed along the gray-green surface of the water.

The balcony stretched the full width of the penthouse, and the floor was covered with Astroturf, of all things. She walked over to the waist-high concrete wall, touched the piece of statuary on the corner, and looked south toward Pass-A-Grille. The narrow, tree-covered peninsula stretched off into infinity, where Tampa Bay met the Gulf of Mexico and the sky, almost like an art exercise in perspective.

She moved to the center and looked down at the roof of the fifth floor. Beyond the roof, she saw the outdoor swimming pool and the tennis courts behind the hotel. What a fall that would be, she thought.

"That would be a hell of a fall, wouldn't it?"

She jumped involuntarily at the sudden voice behind her, and turned to find herself face to face with a muscular man with brown hair and a moustache.

"Yo! I'm Adrian Bell. Carla said I'd find you up here." He strode over to the concrete wall and looked down. "I did one of these last year. Working a Chuck Norris shoot. Free-fell off the side of a building and crashed through the roof into a room filled with Nazis." He looked down again, as if measuring the distance. "Little bit more than this drop, though."

Veronica belabored the obvious. "You're a stuntman?"

"Stunt coordinator on this shoot. Yeah." He stood with his feet apart, heavy boots beneath tight jeans, his gray cotton shirt open halfway down his chest. "You Jon's newest bimbo?"

She fought the flush heading for her cheeks. "No. I'm too tall," she said evenly, determined not to take the bait. "I'm just another production assistant."

Bell let loose a deep, resonant laugh. "How tall are you?"

"Five-ten."

"Yeah, you are too tall for *Jon*."

She noticed the stress he put on the word "Jon" and sensed he wanted to play her like a raw recruit, a new kid in town. She wasn't having any part of it.

Still laughing a little, he covered his brown eyes with aviator-style sunglasses, and walked back toward the doors. A breeze brought the scent of a spicy cologne back her way.

She started toward the doors, a few paces behind him. At the open door, he turned. "Oh, yeah. I almost forgot why I came up here. Carla says you can work crowd control for me when we do the jet-ski gag on the beach. I'll need you about one o'clock." He raised his glasses and peered at her. He stood, feet apart, grinning at her like Brenda's big brother in *Good-bye, Columbus*. The moment was two beats away from awkward when she spotted Tracy Morgan coming through the living room. Adrian Bell turned to follow Veronica's gaze, looked back at her with his smile gone, and said, "Okay. Nice meeting you. See you on the beach."

He strode in through the sliding-glass doors and stopped

in front of Tracy. He threw his arms around her, lifted her a few inches off the floor, and kissed her. He said something Veronica couldn't hear, then disappeared around the corner toward the elevator.

Tracy came out onto the balcony, blushing a little. "I see you met Butch the Wonder Dog. Did he make a move?"

"Not exactly."

"Well, he'd better not," Tracy said lightly. "He's mine."

"Don't worry. I'm taken."

The scent of White Shoulders drifted by as Tracy walked to the wall of the balcony and looked at the beach. Veronica could never forget that scent. Her mother had worn it all the time. A steel-drum band had begun playing somewhere behind her, probably down at the beach bar.

Tracy turned back and looked up at Veronica, shading her eyes with her hand. "Angela got in a big fight with Jon and locked herself in her room, so Carla sent me up to help you— something about moving some stuff from Jon's bedroom."

"Oh, shit! That's what I'm supposed to be doing," she said. "I'm supposed to move some stuff to the other penthouse."

"Well, c'mon," Tracy said cheerfully. "I'll help you."

The two women crossed the living room and started, single file, up the narrow spiral staircase.

In the first bedroom, Jon Vasta's clothes were on hangers but bound together in four dark brown clothing bags. She was grateful for that. Four small blue suitcases sat on the bed.

Veronica picked up two suitcases, then started for the door, narrowly missing a large Chinese vase in the corner. Tracy grabbed the other two and followed her into the hallway.

As they carefully picked their way down the wrought-iron spiral staircase, Veronica asked, "What's wrong with Angela? Do you know?"

"Jon wanted her to do the shooting scene again and she started yelling at him. She goes: 'You're a perfectionist, Vasta.' She called him 'Vasta.' He hates that. Then she goes: 'I'm not going to get shot again, you son-of-a-bitch.' Can you believe it? Then she storms off and locks herself in her room.'' As they reached the level of the living room, she added, ''But I think what's really got her upset is that her ex-husband lives around here and she's strung out about seeing him again.''

Something akin to an electric shock jolted through Veronica. Was Angela planning to see David? Did David know that? Had he already planned to see her? She chided herself. *C'mon, give the guy the benefit of the doubt.* ''When's she seeing him?'' she asked, trying to sound nonchalant.

''I don't know.'' Tracy came off the last step and they crossed the hall and went, single file, in the door of the east penthouse. They took the suitcases inside and up another staircase, the twin to the one they'd just come down. But for the view, the east penthouse was a mirror image of the one on the west. They reached the top of the stairs.

''She hasn't seen the guy in seven or eight years,'' Tracy said. ''My ex is the *last* person *I'd* want to see.'' She set down her suitcases.

''Same here.'' Veronica put her two suitcases by the closet door, and noticed there was a small green zippered suitcase already there.

Tracy laughed. ''My ex is the last person you'd want to see?''

''No. I mean, *my* ex is the last . . . Oh, you know . . .''

Tracy noticed Veronica looking at the green suitcase. ''That's Jon's stash,'' she said matter-of-factly. ''He's real generous with it.'' She started for the door. ''You do coke?''

''No. I do Dr Pepper and Coors.''

Tracy turned in the doorway and laughed. ''That's great. I don't do it either. But lots of people in the business do.''

''So I've heard.'' She followed Tracy, and they retraced their steps to the other penthouse. As they reached the top of the west penthouse staircase, Veronica said, ''I'm getting really sick of spiral staircases.''

Tracy laughed and grabbed two clothes bags from the closet. ''I hear you. Sometimes, 'life at the top' ain't all it's cracked up to be.'' Coming down the spiral stairs with two bags each was an extremely difficult task, which Tracy solved with a giggle by dropping both her bags to the floor below.

Veronica did the same. Then they both circled on down the steps and retrieved their bundles. "Smart move, Tracy."

"Just call it street smarts."

Angela was sitting on the bed in her room, waiting. She had forced the fight with Jon Vasta so she could wait in her room for David's call. And so she could take just a little sip from her bathroom gin bottle. The man she had talked to at the police station earlier, a cop named Rick, had told her David would call her back about noon. It was twelve-thirty, and Angela was wondering if he'd return her call at all.

Instead of a ring, there was a knock on the door. She didn't say anything. She didn't want to face Jon Vasta, Carla Jahns, or one of their underlings. Not until she talked to David.

"Angie? You okay? It's Tracy."

A friend she could use. She stood and opened the door just enough for Tracy to slip in. "You're not here to take me back to the set, are you?"

"No. It's cool. Chuck's shooting Paul's arrival scene out front of the hotel, and Jon is rehearsing with Raynor Fitzhugh. You're off till tomorrow morning."

"Thank God."

"But don't get the idea Jon's not angry. He is."

"Tough shit. This is more important." She gestured toward the phone and sat back down on the edge of the bed.

Tracy eased into a wing chair. "Waiting for your ex to call?"

"Yeah. I'm beginning to wonder if he will." She could visualize as clearly as the trailer for a new movie the last time she had seen David. She had been planning her escape for several weeks. It was pure chance that it came the same week he was hauled up before his bosses at the St. Pete police for killing a drug dealer. She should have been there for him. Instead, he came home early, surprising her as she was packing her suitcase. Some men would have become angry and violent. Not David. Not that wonderful, understanding son-of-a-bitch. He just said he was sorry their marriage hadn't worked out, and wished her luck.

It was his understanding and his attempts to help her beat

her problems that had turned her on him. She felt like a child or a victim or a patient when she was around him, and that was why she had to leave. She knew she couldn't keep on living with a man who only wanted to help her. She hated the pity and concern she'd seen in his face back then. Now, with the advantage of time and maturity, she wished she had stayed.

The ring she had been waiting for split open her memories and startled Tracy.

"Want me to leave?" Tracy whispered.

"No. It's okay." She spoke into the phone. "Hello?"

"Hi, Angie. It's David."

The years rushed back in a blur at the sound of that warm, masculine voice. She thought about hanging up and having another drink, but knew she couldn't with Tracy sitting right there.

"Hi," she said. "Thanks for calling."

CHAPTER SEVEN

DAVID STOOD AT A PAY PHONE ON THE WALL OF A CIRCLE K store on Hillsborough Avenue in Tampa wondering whatever happened to phone booths people could sit in. His partner, Rick, was in their unmarked Dodge Diplomat, with the motor running, reading the Tampa *Tribune* sports page.

When David got the message to call Angela, he had spent a half hour batting it around with Rick. Should he call her or not? Rick said, "If Angela Mastry called me, I'd sure as hell call her back."

David had said, "Yeah, but you weren't married to her."

"Thanks for calling me," Angela was saying over the phone.

"Sure." Noncommittal. "How you doing?" Easy question.

"Okay."

"Good." He didn't know what the hell to say. Hearing her voice had tightened his chest. His battered sport coat felt hot on his torso.

"How have you been?"

"Not bad." He wanted to say, "Better than ever since you skipped out on me." Instead, he just told her, "I'm working for Tampa P.D. now."

"I know."

How'd she know? Who'd she talked to? Had she thought about him in the last few years? He made more conversation. "So, you're making a movie in St. Pete Beach, right?"

"Yeah. It's not a *Slasher* flick this time."

"I saw the first one." He'd seen it a couple of times. Saw the second one, too. No need for her to know that. But she deserved something. "You looked great." She had.

"Thanks." There was a long silence. Then Angela said something in a small voice. He couldn't hear her for the traffic on the nearby highway.

"What did you say?"

"David . . . this is very difficult for me."

"What is?"

"I . . . that is . . ." Another pause.

He could have made it easier for her. He didn't.

"I need to see you, David. I need to talk to you. Could we have lunch or dinner or something?"

He hesitated. Her voice was beginning to sound panicked. "I'm sort of 'involved' with someone these days," he said. Sort of involved? Where the hell had he come up with that? He was deeply involved with Veronica. Maybe too deeply.

"No. That's not what I mean," Angela said hastily. "No. This has nothing to do with us. It's my problem, but I can't handle it alone."

"I don't get it." He loosened his tie.

"David, someone's trying to kill me!"

"What do you want me to do, arrest him?" He hadn't meant to sound flip, but it came out that way.

"Dammit! I'm not kidding! I need some protection and I need some advice." Her anger turned to pleading. "Couldn't you just see me for dinner and talk it over with me?" Pleading became sincerity. "I'm not trying to come back and screw up your life." Sincerity gave way to fear. "I just need help."

What an actress, David thought. But there was something

real at the core of her movie-star monologue. She did sound frightened. It wouldn't hurt to see her and talk to her. Have dinner. See if he could put her in touch with the right people.

"David. Please. I need your help."

"Okay. Look, maybe we can make it tomorrow night."

"Could you possibly make it tonight? I'm really scared."

He thought about it. Probably better to get it over with. "Okay. You at the Don?"

"Yeah."

"I'll pick you up at eight."

"Thank you, David."

David walked to the car, his mind racing with doubt and confusion. He wasn't sure he'd made a wise choice, and he wondered why he was suddenly eager to see her again. He lumped in beside Rick.

"So, she wanna come back and be your baby?" Rick asked. His dark eyes brimmed over with mirth. "What'd she say?"

"She just wants to have dinner."

"Fucking A!" Rick exclaimed, as he put the unmarked Dodge into gear. "Dinner with a movie star!"

David looked at his watch and grabbed the mike. "I'm going to call Dispatch and tell them we're taking a break for lunch." He smiled at Rick. "How'd you like to visit a movie set?"

Angela put the phone on its cradle. Her hand was shaking. It had been an okay phone call, no recriminations, no veiled barbs or nasty comments. But it had tied her stomach in knots—to talk to David after all those years and know that he was probably less than twenty miles away, apparently happy, healthy, with a good job and some sort of romance going on. It wasn't that she still loved him. It was just the knowledge that he'd known her so well during a time in her life when she was screwing up so badly. The fact that he knew more about her past than any of her present-day friends. It made her nervous and filled her with mixed emotions.

"I'm finding it hard to put this into words," Angela said, turning to look at Tracy, who had been sitting silently. "Talk-

ing to David like that was nerve-racking, and I can't explain
why. It shakes my courage. My belief in myself. Probably
'cause I still feel I fucked up our marriage.''

"Is he going to see you?"

"Yeah.''

"Great! You think he'll help you?''

"I don't know." She walked to the window and looked
out at the cloudy day, which matched her mood. It looked
like rain. "I think so. He's a really good guy. That was part
of our problem. He was too good. Always trying to save
me." She touched the window with her hand and laughed.
"Isn't that a hoot? Now, I *need* him to save me.''

"Are you going to tell him all about Tony's death and Gary
Kines and everything?''

"Of course," she said, turning to face her friend. "The
only way he can help me is if I tell him the truth. All of it.''

"Yeah. I suppose you're right." Tracy checked her watch,
the gesture looking suddenly phony and staged to Angela.
"Look, I gotta go. Your call tomorrow morning is at eight-
thirty, so don't stay up too late." She headed for the door.
"And I think it might be a good idea if you call Jon before
you leave for dinner and apologize. He really likes you, you
know. Just tell him you're sorry. It'd be a good idea.''

"Okay," Angela said, but she knew she wouldn't.

Tracy left, and Angela flipped on the TV set, then headed
for the bathroom to prepare for her dinner with David. And
to visit her English buddy in the toilet tank.

Veronica sat on the octagonal rim of the pink concrete outdoor fountain—temporarily turned off for maintenance—
which graced the second-floor main entrance of the Don
CeSar. Access to the lobby of the glamorous hotel was gained
from a fifty-foot concrete ramp that came up from the parking
lot and circled under a peaked tile roof at the front doors.

In the center of the circle was the fountain, two small trees
in wooden planters, and a couple of semicircles of orange
and yellow flowers. Sitting and standing all around the fountain were other production assistants and a couple of technicians listening to the second-unit director, a tall, muscular

man with a beard, long hair, and—she'd noticed it when he moved—a limp. Carla had told her his name was Chuck Hollenbeck and he had been a stuntman until an explosion took part of his leg. Veronica had been tempted to tell him how an explosion took part of her life.

"This is going to be basically two setups and some SteadiCam work, and it'll probably take the rest of the afternoon," Hollenbeck told the group. "Here's the gig: Paul drives up the ramp from down there and pulls in right under the roof in front of the doors. He gets out and is greeted by Raynor Fitzhugh. They doobie-doobie-do a few minutes and then go inside. That lets us do the close-ups and two-shots in the shadow of the roof," he continued. "We've got some lighting problems because the hotel faces east, but it'll only be a problem for the long shots." He allowed a thin smile to escape his lips. "Naturally, that's what we'll do first." Hollenbeck checked his clipboard and said, "Sound. As you guys can tell, the main problem you've got is the traffic on the street under this ramp." He pointed down to the surface of Pass-A-Grille Boulevard, a narrow two-lane street that was the only access to Pass-A-Grille, a small peninsula community to the south. "The only time that comes up is in the half page of dialogue at the door when Paul arrives. If we have to, we'll close one lane for a while or slow things down a little."

Veronica's mind wandered, and she gazed out at the hundreds of tall, thin palm trees that dotted the land around the high-priced homes beyond the parking lot. She wondered what it would be like to work on movies for a living, all the time. Probably boring as hell.

She jolted back to attention when the bearded second-unit director said, "P.A.'s. Your job is crowd control. The access to this ramp is the entrance down there." He pointed to where the ramp began in the parking lot. "And a set of stairs on either side of the ramp." He gestured to the gaps in the concrete railings that edged the entire ramp and the circle. "When I give you the word, you gotta close off those stairs. The entrance to the ramp can be closed after the long shot. Before that, we'll have to keep them out of range any way we can.''

Veronica was surprised to see a couple of dozen people already standing around in the parking lot, trying to look casual but obviously hoping for a glimpse of Paul Haden or Angela Mastry. For her, one glimpse of Angela today had been enough.

"Okay. Questions?" Hollenbeck looked over the small group. "No? Okay, let's get ready." He checked his clipboard. "Veronica Slate?"

She raised her hand and said, "Here."

Hollenbeck approached her and said, "I need you down at the foot of the ramp. Until we're through with the long shot, you'll have to keep people out of sight. There's some other P.A.'s down there. They'll help you."

As Veronica started down the sidewalk of the ramp, Hollenbeck was stopped by a young man in an ornate doorman's uniform with epaulets and braid. "What do you think? How do I look?"

Hollenbeck snapped, "It looks good."

Behind him, two of the real Don CeSar bellmen were laughing at the costumer's idea of a Florida hotel doorman's uniform.

''Excuse me, ma'am. Could you please move back about six feet?'' Veronica was trying to urge a middle-aged woman with enough costume jewelry to stock a K Mart out of the way for the fifth attempt at a long shot of Paul Haden's character driving up the ramp.

The first take had been scrubbed when two little boys climbed over the railing and waved at Haden's car. Takes two and three were called back for technical flaws. On the fourth try there had been noise problems. Veronica was learning that there was nothing glamorous about making a movie. It was mostly long periods of waiting punctuated by short bursts of activity.

Finally, Veronica walked over to the woman and whispered, "Paul Haden is out at the pool signing autographs. The man in the car is a stunt double." It was a lie, but good enough to spur the woman into a mad dash for the rear of the hotel.

Through the bullhorn Chuck Hollenbeck announced, "This is for real, folks. I need quiet. Stand by. Roll camera."

The cameraman said, "Rolling."

"Roll sound," Hollenbeck said.

The soundman looked up and said, "Speed."

"Mark it, Tommy." Hollenbeck nodded at a skinny kid with the clapstick. He held it in front of the lens and slammed it shut, and Hollenbeck yelled, "Action!"

At his cue, Paul Haden drove from his position in the parking lot into the camera's view and up the ramp. When he reached the top there was a moment's hush while various technicians checked something.

Then Hollenbeck's voice came through the bullhorn. "It's a keeper. Thank you, everyone. Let's set up for the close work. On the double."

Veronica was about to start up the ramp when a familiar Dodge sedan pulled up Casablanca Street and into the parking lot and David climbed out.

"Hi, Vee. How's your first day?"

"Boring. But fun." She kissed him on the cheek. "What brings you out here?" She waved at Rick, behind the wheel.

David's smile slipped from his face. "I need to talk to you. I need to ask you a question."

"Okay." She felt uneasy but curious. "What?"

"I got a call from Angela today." Discomfort showed in his face. "She wants to see me. For dinner." He quickly added, "Just to talk. She's got some trouble and needs advice."

Veronica was working hard to remain calm. She had always wondered what she'd do when David left her for another woman. She hadn't really expected he'd go back to his own ex-wife, though. "Well . . ." She killed some time trying to decide what to say. *Wait a minute, she told herself, it's just dinner we're talking about. Don't you trust him? Yeah. But do you trust her?* "What kind of trouble?" she asked finally.

"She didn't tell me over the phone. She did say someone's trying to kill her."

"And you believe her?"

"I don't know." He stared off toward the hotel. "She did sound terrified, though."

"She's an actress, David."

"Yeah." He looked back at her. "I thought about that."

"Oh, hell. We might as well face this right now," Veronica said, leaning against the concrete railing. "You know what's the matter with me. We talked about it. I'm afraid you'll take her back, and you tell me that's not possible."

"It's not possible. That's right. I meant that. I just feel like I should at least talk to her, try to help her."

"Like you tried to help her before?" She regretted the words the minute she'd said them.

"Cheap shot."

"I know. I'm sorry." She forced a half smile. "So when did you want to do this?"

"Tonight." He fidgeted. "Get it over with."

"Well, I don't know what you expected from me. A blessing or something?" She could hear her own unreasonable words but did nothing to stop. "Did you want me to drive the two of you to the restaurant?"

"Christ, Vee. At least I asked you first. That should count for something. I wouldn't have met her if you'd said no."

"Bullshit."

"C'mon, don't be mad."

She didn't say anything, trying to keep from hitting him.

After it was obvious she wasn't going to speak, David shrugged and said, "Right. See you after work."

"Don't cut short your dinner date," she said bitterly.

A glance, and then David returned to the car. Rick tossed a small farewell salute as they pulled out of the parking lot.

Veronica stood very still, waiting for her jealousy to subside. Sam's jealousy was what had caused her to divorce him. She didn't want her jealousy to screw up a great relationship with David. But she was beginning to wonder if the relationship was really that great after all.

* * *

Adrian Bell stood at the desk just off the lobby of the Don CeSar. He punched in the number on the house phone. "Hi. I have some very interesting news," Bell said. "Angela's going to see her ex for dinner tonight. She says she's going to tell him everything." He paused for effect.

"Tell Derek tonight's the night."

CHAPTER EIGHT

"WELCOME TO T. NELSON DOWNS. IN WHICH ROOM WILL you be dining tonight?" The young greeter was dressed in a tuxedo and a white ruffled shirt. Not that the T. Nelson Downs restaurant was especially high class. What it was, was magic.

T. Nelson Downs, near the Hilton on the Gulf side of Gulf Boulevard, was the newest theme restaurant on St. Pete Beach. It was immediately obvious that the theme was magic, from the white neon rabbits peering out of black top hats on either side of the entrance to the red plush and black velvet decor of the lobby, adorned with posters of famous conjurers of the past. Filling the sprawling restaurant were different dining rooms, each named after a different magician.

"What rooms do you have?" Angela asked, handing the umbrella back to the valet who had whisked them from David's Pontiac through the rain to the door.

The young man showed his well-manicured hands to be empty and reached behind Angela's head to produce a colored fan, which he spread open. He read from the fan: "In the Robert-Houdin room, you may order French cuisine, in honor of the nineteenth-century conjurer who was such an influence on Harry Houdini that Houdini adopted his name."

The young man with neatly trimmed black hair passed the fan over his empty hand, and a small Oriental parasol appeared. He handed it to Angela. "Okito's Den features both Japanese and Chinese food," he explained, "because the real Okito wasn't actually Oriental. His name was Theodore Bamberg and he operated a New York City magic shop in the early days of this century."

David looked at Angela, radiant in a shimmering blue dress with simple lines and a layer of glittery stuff across the front. She was obviously enjoying the performance. He was glad he had worn a sport coat over his tan slacks and off-white shirt. It covered his gun, safely holstered on his belt.

The young man's smile seemed genuine, as if he enjoyed this as much as they did. "Blackstone Bay is an intimate little room with fine seafood and steaks. It's dedicated to both Harry Blackstone and his son, who is still performing." He snapped the fan shut with a flourish and said, "While you wait for us to call you, we invite you to visit our new David Copperfield Lounge, which is an English-style pub, or the Thurston Terrace, which affords a wonderful view of the Gulf."

"We'd like the Blackstone Bay room," David said, without consulting Angela. "And we'll wait on the Thurston Terrace. How long a wait?"

"Perhaps twenty minutes. We'll call you."

"I have a question," Angela said. "It's probably a stupid question. Who was T. Nelson Downs?"

"In vaudeville, they called him the 'King of Koins.' He was one of the best coin manipulators in this century." At that, the young man took a half dollar from his pocket and held it in front of Angela. In an instant, it changed to a small red flower, which he handed to her as he bowed. "For the lady."

"T. Nelson Downs is one of the few theme restaurants

around here that I can stand,'' David said as they followed a young lady in a short black dress to the Thurston Terrace.

"I didn't know you liked magic," Angela said.

"Ever since I was a kid. I can still remember reading the Lou Tannen catalogue cover to cover when I was in high school, and saving my money to send away for the Temple Screen and a book about Houdini.''

David and Angela sat on the Thurston Terrace drinking and watching the flickering lights of the boats on the Gulf of Mexico through the thin sheet of rain. Some sort of soft jazz eased out of cleverly concealed speakers.

Angela was beautiful in the candlelight. She'd been only twenty when they had married. Despite the life she'd apparently led since then, her complexion was still flawless. Now there was an added edge of sophistication he'd never seen. There was something about her face he could barely describe. The lips, red tonight, the slightly large but still attractive nose, the light blue eyes that seemed filled with tears even when they were not. She had become an even more beautiful woman than before.

"Did I tell you I saw *Slasher*?'' he asked, to get the conversation started.

"Yes." She held her glass in both hands, staring at her Black Russian as if she were reading tea leaves. "I wasn't real good in that one, but it was my first major role, so it was important to me.''

"Well, you looked good. You look good tonight, too.''

She flashed a tentative smile. "Thanks." She set down her glass and looked around. "This place is great." She gestured, and her tiny gold bracelets tinkled like wind chimes. "It's so theatrical. Have you been here before?''

"Yeah. We came out the week it opened.''

He saw a shadow pass through her nearly transparent eyes as she caught the significance of the word "we." He stared at the rain beating against the wide plate-glass windows. She traced the rim of her glass with a pink fingernail. The silence lengthened. To him they seemed more like a blind date than a former husband and wife.

"Is she pretty?''

He was startled from his reverie. "Who?"

"Your girlfriend. Is she attractive?"

"We don't need to talk about this, you know."

"I know. I'm interested."

"She's beautiful. Dark brown hair. Green eyes."

"Are you in love with her?"

"Probably. Why?"

"Just curious."

"Look, it's not that I don't want to talk about my love life, but we did come here so I could help you out of a jam. I need to know more about what's going on."

"I know." She fingered the square black paper napkin under her glass, tracing the white top hat and rabbit-ears design. "It's a long story."

"We've got all night." He regretted the implication of that, but she apparently didn't catch it. "Tell me what happened."

"I might as well start at the beginning." She drained her drink and looked at him with serious blue eyes. "About a year after I hit L.A., I met Tony Victor. You probably heard of him."

"Heard about his death last fall."

"This was before he made it big in *Dealer's Wire*. We started living together and he got me into acting classes and off booze."

"How'd he do that?" David slouched in his chair and picked up the damp napkin in one hand and his drink in the other. "I wish to hell I knew his secret."

"What do you mean?"

"I tried to straighten you out once. Couldn't do it. I'm just curious." He fingered his napkin. "How'd he do it?"

"Lots of love and patience. He really loved me." She looked at him with the hardness in her eyes. "He didn't treat me like a fucking leper or a sicko."

David glanced over his shoulder at the other couples waiting on the dimly lit terrace. "You saying I did?"

"Yeah. That's why I left you. I felt like a second-class citizen. You made me feel that way."

"I wish to hell you had told me that then." He shredded the napkin into little pieces.

"Come on, David! I tried to tell you. But you were so damned busy being Mr. Goodbar and trying to save me. You wouldn't listen."

"How could I? When you were drunk—which was a hell of a lot of the time, I might add—I couldn't reason with you."

"Who the fuck said anything about reasoning? I just wanted you to understand what I was going through." She leaned forward on her chair, her bracelets jangling. "I just wanted you to accept me the way I was and help me deal with life. Why couldn't you accept me the way I was?"

"Because you were killing yourself, Angie. I loved you too much to let that happen. I was trying to save you."

"Oh, yeah? Who crowned you Jesus Christ?"

The waitress crept up to their table like a civilian in a war zone. David was thankful for the interruption because he had no answer for why he was always trying to save people. It was what drove him to be a cop, but it had also driven a number of women out of relationships with him.

"Would you like another drink?" the waitress asked.

David shook his head.

"Bring me another Black Russian," Angela told the waitress, who scurried away, apparently relieved not to be in the middle of a lovers' quarrel.

"Besides, I had my own problems then. If there had ever been a time I needed you . . ." He balled up the pieces of his napkin and dropped them in the ashtray. He stared at her. "Okay. Let's forget about us for a moment," David said.

"Okay." She crossed her legs, making him tight with desire. He was furious with himself that she could still reach him on a sexual level. "Well, Tony had done a movie when he was just a teen-ager, but it had never been released. Yet he had lots of money. Finally, I found out his money came from dealing coke."

"Did he tell you?"

"In a way. He sold me some." She ignored the frown that spread across David's face. "Anyhow, I had this job as a secretary for this sleazoid videotape production company. After Tony hit it big with *Dealer's Wire* he had some pull, and he helped me get some commercials, some showcase stuff, a guest bit on a 'Matt Houston' episode, and speaking roles in a few independent pictures. Then, in 1983, Mira Loma Productions—Jon Vasta's company—came along with this script for a movie called *Slasher*. They wanted Tony for the lead. He said yes, but only if I got the female lead. They grumbled, but he was hot from *Dealer's Wire* and he had another picture in the can that was getting some heavy publicity.''

''So they backed down and gave you the lead?''

''Yeah. They released it in 1984, and it grossed about ten times what it cost to make it. Right away, they signed both of us to three-picture deals. A few months later we did *Slasher II*. It came out last summer and did more than thirty million dollars.'' She looked earnestly into David's eyes. ''That's what got me started doing coke. But I'm not doing it anymore. I did for a while, but I'm not anymore.''

''Does that matter?'' He didn't believe it anyhow.

She looked down. ''It does to me.''

''Why did you ever start doing it in the first place?''

''You wouldn't understand.''

''Try me.'' He sat back in his chair.

''I started because I wanted to belong. To fit in. The first time I did it was at the wrap party for *Slasher Two*. Tony says, 'Let's do some coke.' I go, 'Okay, why not?' The feeling it gave me was this incredible euphoria. This feeling like I was brave and strong. It gave me courage.''

''You needed courage?''

''Yes. I was scared. It was all happening too fast. I came out of nowhere, and suddenly I was the star of a major motion picture. Anytime anyone criticized me I felt wounded. I felt like I really wasn't good enough for all the acclaim I was getting. For me, cocaine had healing powers.''

''So why did you stop?''

''Because I finally realized it's a lie. Cocaine kills. I was obsessed with cocaine. I was so out of control, so ashamed, so humiliated. I realized the only way to get off the stuff was to move out. To leave Tony. Because he was my dealer.''

''How did you do it?''

"At first I cut down to doing it only at home off the job. Then I did it only at night, then only on weekends, then two weekends a month, then one weekend a month." She slumped in her chair and took a long drink of her Black Russian. "Finally, it just sank in that I was not having a good time, that I was killing myself, that I was spending all my money. So I quit."

"Just like that?"

"Just like that."

David wiped the sweat off his glass with one finger and didn't look up. "Look, I appreciate this movie-industry primer, and I'm sorry about what you went through with the coke and all, but what's the point to all this? What's the danger you're in?"

"Tony Victor was murdered last fall."

He looked at her. "I thought it was an accident."

"That's what they'd like everyone to believe. But it was no accident. I know that." She leaned in closer over the table and he caught a glimpse of her pale soft breasts. "They killed him. I saw it happen."

A pretty young woman in a short sequined costume and legs that went on forever came out on the terrace and announced, "Parrish, party of two? Your table is ready."

"That's us," David said, as he drank the rest of his beer in a quick gulp and stood. "We'll talk more, later."

"Could you ask the waitress to bring another Black Russian to our table?" Angela said to the girl as she followed David from the terrace.

"Don't you think you've had enough?" David asked as he held the door for her. She ignored him.

Tuesday night.

Open calling, thank God. No guest to fool with. Veronica was sick to death of all the talk about income tax and the IRS that had dominated her show in recent weeks. Talk about death and taxes being inevitable. For radio talk hosts, late March and early April each year meant accountants and IRS people as guests and a million questions from listeners. At least tonight was the filing deadline. Maybe they'd forget about it for another year. For herself, Veronica had decided years ago that it was worth it to pay an accountant to do her taxes. She'd always been better in English than in math.

She was driving through a steady downpour across the narrow Gandy Bridge linking St. Petersburg and Tampa, on her way to work at WAQT. Her car windows were rolled up against the rain, which had come with the sunset. She was listening to WUSF-FM, the college station, humming along with Brahms's *Second Symphony*.

It occurred to her that probably the best topic to get into on the show tonight was the bombing of Libya that morning by U.S. jets. It had been prompted by the West German disco bombing ten days earlier and some other acts of terrorism, and it was likely to bring out some vocal listeners both for and against.

As she got off the bridge on the Tampa side and drove through the corridor of fast-food outlets and shopping centers leading to the On ramp of the Crosstown Expressway, she thought it over again, trying to decide what better course of action she could have taken where David and Angela were concerned.

David was having dinner with his ex-wife tonight in spite of how she felt about it. That bothered her. And yet, was it really her place to tell him what to do? They'd been together only a little more than six months.

On the other hand, Angela and David's entire marriage had lasted only three months.

She wished she had asked him not to see Angela. But if she didn't trust him enough to let him have dinner with his ex-wife, she must not trust him at all.

Veronica pulled into the Fort Brooke Parking Garage and pushed the button for a ticket. The striped barrier arm jerked upward, and she drove to the third level. She locked the car, walked to the people-mover station on the same level, and waited for the people-mover car to return from Harbour Island. She stared through the hard rain at the N.C.N.B. bank building.

Tampa had changed from the first time she'd seen it nine years ago. Tall glass office towers were everywhere. On the ground were postage-stamp-sized parks and modern right-angle traffic lights that arched out over the intersections.

Veronica got a token out of her purse, dropped it in the slot, and eased through the turnstile when she saw the brightly lit people-mover car make the slight jog a couple of hundred feet down the track and pull into the station.

She had the car to herself. She grabbed one of the vertical chrome bars and planted her feet for the takeoff. She was wrestling with her feelings tonight, and at the core of her discomfort was the conclusion to which she had come, grudgingly, over the last few years. That men could be so unpredictable.

As the car passed over it, Veronica looked down at the Crosstown Expressway, where diamonds were going one way and rubies the other. She had started with David because, frankly, she hadn't been serious about a man for more than a year when they'd met. Her last real love before that had been a fellow student at U.S.F., a handsome communications major who'd turned out to be bisexual. That had hit her hard. Being dropped for another woman was one thing, but being dropped for another man was tough to take. But it was all history. Danny had been killed just five months ago, and now she was even casual friends with his lover.

Moments later, she could make out the lights of Harbour Island through the heavy rain pounding the bay. Veronica thought of the old song from *My Fair Lady.* "Why can't a woman be more like a man?" She sometimes wished men could be more like women: sensitive, understanding, faithful, and loving.

After working her way through The Market, the two-floor shopping area of Harbour Island, Veronica came in WAQT's glass door, through the lounge, and into the producer's booth, a five-by-ten glassed-in room. At the control board, Becky Hummel sat looking straight ahead through the plate-glass window at Ralph McCormick, who was just wrapping up his "Consumer Helpline" show. In front of Becky, on the desk, were an Apple Macintosh keyboard, a ten-line telephone, and a legal pad.

Becky, a young girl with extremely short black hair and a

large nose, had joined WAQT as a high-school trainee. Now she was putting herself through Hillsborough Community College as a talk-show producer thanks to Ralph McCormick. He liked her because he could boss her around and she wouldn't complain. She didn't look up as Veronica came in the room.

Veronica's producer, Max, was sitting in a folding chair at the back of the room, reading *Tampa Bay Metromagazine*. Maxwell Penrose Wilkinson was a handsome thirtyish black man from the Bahamas who had come to Tampa to attend the University of South Florida and stayed on after graduation. By day, he owned and operated VideoMax, a videotape sales-and-rental store on Kennedy Boulevard. At night, he screened calls and ran the equipment that kept the "Slate Show" on the air.

A wide smile spread under his well-trimmed moustache as he saw Veronica. "Hey, lady. What's happenin'? You look great."

She had forgotten that she'd worn a brown-striped pink sweater and a brown skirt to work. It was such a change from the jeans and sweat shirt she usually wore. Somehow, tonight, she wanted to feel pretty. Could it be insecurity?

"Thanks," she said. "Just thought I'd be different."

"You keep dressin' like that and you be married," Max said, smiling as he took an obvious look at her legs.

"Not this lady. No way."

He held up the magazine. "Hear the news? *Tampa Bay Metromagazine*'s calling it quits. May's gonna be the last issue. Something about not enough advertising."

"I figured it was too slick to last," Veronica said. She stood by Becky's chair and looked absently through the plate-glass window at Ralph.

"You okay?" Max asked. "You seem a little off."

"She's having dinner with him tonight," she said, turning and sitting on the other folding chair in the back of the booth.

"Don't tell me. Let me guess. You're not thrilled?" His smile turned to concern. "You jealous, babe?"

"Not exactly." She thought about it. "Hell, yes. I'm jealous. She hasn't seen him in years, and now she comes breezing into town and decides she needs his help. I hope to God she apologizes for leaving him.''

"That would be decent of her," he said sarcastically. "You think she wants him back?"

"Not really. David and I had a long talk about that. No." She absently flopped one heel in and out of her brown pump. "But I'm not a hundred percent sure he doesn't want her back. He can be easily dazzled."

"Apparently," Max said. "He was dazzled by you."

"Nice try, Max." She sighed. "Oh, I guess I'm just letting jealousy and envy rear their ugly little heads. It'll be okay."

"Well, I could really get off on dinner with Angela Mastry," said Max. "She's hot stuff at the box office. Her first two *Slasher* films are big sellers at the store."

"Are you turning on me, too?" She smiled, letting him know it was just a joke. Through the studio window, Veronica glanced at the rumpled-looking man sitting behind the mike. "Looks like the savior of the consumer is nearly done."

Ralph McCormick wore his usual uniform: a white dress shirt, which always looked slept in, and green slacks that had lost the struggle to remain permanently pressed. Ralph glanced at Veronica. He was talking to a caller.

"They can't take you to court, my friend. No chance. You write that letter, and then you call me next week and let me know what happened. In that letter, mention that you have been in contact with Mr. Ralph McCormick of 'Consumer Helpline.' "

Ralph was a balding, middle-aged ex-corporate attorney who'd spent five years with the Small Business Administration and then discovered the power of radio. He'd been divorced twice, and had represented himself both times.

McCormick was wrapping up his show. "My apologies to you folks who are waiting. We've got to go. Don't forget that you've got to have that income-tax return in the mailbox by midnight tonight. You've got just two hours to get it together and in the mail. I'll see you tomorrow night. CBS News is next, followed by the 'Slate Show' with WAQT's lady of the evening, Veronica Slate.''

Ralph's little dig.

With Ralph and Becky signed off the logs and out of the studio, Veronica sat in her chair behind the mike and kicked off her shoes. As she smoothed her skirt she remembered why she nearly always wore jeans to work. It was cold in the studio.

"Coming up in thirty, Vee." It was Max over the intercom. CBS News came to an end and her cart intro played: "You're on the QT," said the impossibly deep recorded voice. "WAQT Talk Radio TenTwenty. And now, the phone lines are open for Veronica Slate and the 'Slate Show.' "

She turned on her mike. "Good evening. Welcome to the 'Slate Show.' I'm Veronica Slate and it's open calling tonight. But please, let's not talk about income tax. I'm sick and tired of that. Besides, Ralph McCormick's the expert on income tax."

She picked up a piece of wire copy torn off the Associated Press printer.

"As you probably heard on the news, eighteen air force F-one-elevens and fifteen navy A-six Intruder light bombers attacked five targets in Libya late last night, our time. The President says the U.S. is striking back at terrorism. Some other countries say we're becoming terrorists ourselves. What do you think? Did we do the right thing? Give me a call."

After years in the business, radio people gained a skill most humans didn't have to such a finely honed degree. They could talk about one thing and think about another. Veronica was talking about the numbers to call, but she was thinking about David's dinner with Angela. Was she going to lose him to his ex-wife?

Tracy was worried. She had wanted her chance for quite a while. But now, with the distinct possibility that the opportunity was about to be hers, she was concerned. She knew she was a better actress than Angela Mastry. The only thing that had held her back, as Adrian was always telling her, was that Big Break, the opportunity to show what she could do. Now it was about to be hers.

Dressed in a pink silk nightgown, Tracy was in bed trying to fall asleep. She had the TV set on for company. Adrian had left right after they made love and returned to his own room. Probably to drink some wheat-germ shake or whatever the hell it was he did to maintain that body.

She was watching the local eleven o'clock news delivered by a pretty young blond anchorwoman named Kelly and a serious-looking older man named Hugh. They were talking about the U.S. attacking somebody in the Middle East, but Tracy wasn't really paying attention. She was wondering what they were planning to do this time to convince Jon Vasta that Angela was back on the bottle and doing drugs. As much as Tracy wanted her chance, she didn't really want to see Angela hurt.

She rolled over on the bed and switched off the TV, trying to convince herself that it was a tough business and one had to get one's break any way possible.

CHAPTER NINE

DAVID AND ANGELA SAT AT A TABLE FOR TWO IN THE BLACKstone Bay room at T. Nelson Downs. Angela finished her latest Black Russian, and David stared at the cards and coins embedded in the laminated tabletop as the waitress cleared their dishes. The napkins were black with tiny white stars, and the salt and pepper shakers were reversed rabbits and hats; salt was a white rabbit in a black hat, and pepper a black bunny in a white hat.

They had made small talk, mostly about movies and Hollywood, while they ate their dinner—smoked mullet for Angela, and shrimp scampi for David—and Angela had ordered another Black Russian before getting back to the subject.

"I thought you said you weren't drinking anymore," David said, gesturing at her drink. He had promised himself he wouldn't judge her or try to save her as he had when they were married, but he couldn't keep silent because her drinking really worried him.

"I still drink," she said defiantly. "It's just that now I know when to stop." Her eyes betrayed a lack of conviction.

Soft jazz music from speakers concealed in the black ceiling blurred with the conversations of the dozen or so other diners in the room. She adjusted a pearl earring and crossed her legs.

David looked away. Did she expose that extra bit of thigh for his benefit? Or was he just troubled by his renewed and pointless desire for her? The same things about Angela that had captivated and fascinated him years ago had been magnified and perfected with age.

"Okay." He forged ahead. "So you got the threat the first night and then the guy jumped you. . . . When was that?"

"I told you. It was Saturday afternoon. The day after I got here. The day after the threats."

"And then you called your attorney. . . ."

"His partner told me Gary had been killed." She leaned forward, hitting the table with her knee, spilling a little from her water glass. "Don't you see, David? Gary must have been killed by the same people who killed Tony Victor. Because Gary knew everything I did about the murder."

"Great. So now you're telling me so they can kill me."

Angela finished her drink and signaled the waitress for another one. "Y'know, you're not making this easy for me."

"Who says it should be easy?"

She said nothing, took a cigarette from her purse.

"I'd rather you didn't," David said.

She glared at him. "When did *you* stop?"

"Right after you left."

"Did *she* ask you to quit?"

He decided to leave that alone. "You said Tony Victor didn't die accidentally. What did you mean?"

"I don't know how much you remember about what the papers and TV said about it last fall, but the official story is that Tony died accidentally filming the dream sequence."

"Dream sequence?"

"Yeah. The idea behind *Slasher Three*—"

He snorted. "There's an idea behind one of those movies?"

She didn't even smile. "The idea is that Jamie, the character I play, is recovering from the deaths of her friends in the first two movies and the attack on her at the end of *Slasher Two* by staying in her uncle's mountain cabin with the young forest ranger she met in the first film and fell in love with in the second one. The forest ranger was played by Tony."

"I don't need the whole story."

"Yes, you do." Angela's eyes flashed. "Anyhow, she falls in love with him. He keeps having these recurring nightmares about being in Vietnam."

"Great," David said, with more than a trace of disgust. "I love to see what Hollywood screenwriters think Nam was like."

She ignored him and went on. "In the Vietnam dream sequence Tony's character is in a battle with a bunch of Vietcong with automatic weapons."

"Don't tell me. Let me guess. One of the guns was loaded?"

"C'mon. That's such a cliché they even make TV movies about it." She took another sip of her drink. "No. The weapons were all checked before and after the scene. None of them had live ammunition in them."

"Then how did he die?"

"That's the part I noticed that apparently no one else did. There were twelve extras playing commandos in that scene. There were a few Vietnamese actors and a couple of guys from Japan. Anyhow, they were all Oriental-looking. They surrounded him like in the opening battle in *Ninja Three: The Domination.*"

David sat back and smiled. "Does everything in Hollywood have a sequel?"

"I was hanging around the set watching Tony's scene. On the third take, I noticed one of the commandos was standing slightly behind a tree. I remember thinking how stupid that was. I mean, the guy was out of camera range, and if there's anything an extra tries to do it's get screen time. Something else weird about him was that his commando suit—"

David laughed in spite of himself.

"His costume, okay?" Angela was not amused. "His costume was different from the others. Not a lot, just cleaner, like it was brand-new, and with some gear on it that the others didn't seem to have. And he wasn't Oriental. He looked like you.''

"So what did this *extra* extra do?''

"Well, I was looking at him and Jon called, 'Action!,' and all of the commandos fired at Tony, and he fired back and then did his death scene, and it was over and everybody started getting ready for the next setup, and then the makeup girl noticed that Tony wasn't moving. We all ran over to see why.'' Angela stopped as her eyes filled with tears. "He *was* dead.''

As if the waitress had been waiting for a cue, she showed up with Angela's Black Russian. She cast an inquiring glance at David and he covered his glass with his hand.

As the waitress returned to the shadows, Angela continued. "In all the excitement, I guess the other guy got away. They immediately closed the set and checked all of the weapons and called the cops.'' She took a drink.

"So you think a mysterious stranger in a commando suit joined a bunch of extras just long enough to kill Tony Victor and then vanished? That's crazy. Wouldn't someone else have noticed? Don't they keep track of the extras?''

"Only at the start of the day and at lunchtime and at the end of the day. The rest of the time extras are almost invisible, unless they get drunk or cause trouble.''

"Do you have any proof at all?''

"No. But Vince Westfall does.''

"Who's that?''

"The senior editor on the *Slasher* pictures. He has all the leftover raw footage shot from *Slasher Three*.''

"Wait a minute. You mean to tell me they *used* Tony Victor's death scene in the movie?''

"No. They hired a replacement. Reshot Tony's scenes. But I'm sure that Vince has the film of Tony's death scene.''

"So where is it? Did your attorney get it?''

"He was going to. He was going to get a court order or whatever the Monday after I left L.A. Woulda been yesterday.''

"Why didn't you call this film-editor guy sooner, or go to the police or something?"

"I was scared, for one thing. How the hell was I supposed to know why they killed Tony? I had been living with him, for Christ's sake! They could have been after me, too."

"And now they are?"

"Yes." Angela drained half of her Black Russian and began to show some of the old signs David remembered so well. She was drunk, but still coping. She sat up rigidly, as if trying not to slump over.

"I still don't understand why you couldn't just talk to the editor and ask to see the film."

"He was in fucking Africa, David! On location for *Ivory Coast,* Paul Haden's big one for next Christmas. He was doing rough cuts of the dailies. Living in a camp where you had to ride camels or some shit to even get there. When he finally came back, I called him and he said the cops had impounded the footage. Something about a lawsuit brought by Tony's parents."

"So, who knows what you know?" Now he could see that familiar glazed look in her eyes.

"Who knows?" She sucked the last of her drink.

"C'mon, Angie, this is no time for Abbott and Costello. I need to know who could be after you."

"The only people I've told were Gary Kines, my attorney, and Tracy Morgan, my best friend. But whoever killed Gary took the tape of my deposishh . . . my depuhzis . . . the tape of what I told him. The guy who grabbed me Saturday played it for me. Trying to scare me."

"So the end result is that you were an eyewitness to a murder that everyone else thought was an accident, but the only proof is under wraps in L.A., except for your taped deposition, which someone wanted so badly they killed your attorney to get it."

"Yeah." She pulled her skirt down over her knees and stared at a spot somewhere between her and David.

"What was the motive? Why kill Tony?"

"I don't know. But I have an idea." She slowed like a tape recorder with bad batteries. "Like I said, Tony was dealing."

"Coke, right?"

"And crack."

David picked up his cloth napkin and absently folded it as he spoke. "I don't know what I can do for you. Obviously, it's mostly your word against a mysterious killer with no definite motive."

"I told you. Tony was dealing." She spoke slowly and with effort. "Wouldn't my testimony be enough to get the film out and open up the case and get whoever did this?"

"Face it, Angie, you're not going to be the most creditable witness. I mean, you were living with the guy. And you're . . . well, maybe not a totally reliable witness."

"Are you saying I'm a drunk?" Her eyes lit like frosted light bulbs.

"Not exactly. But attorneys love to use a drinking problem to discredit testimony. Unless you find some more definite evidence or another witness or something, I'm afraid—"

So quickly that her glass fell to the tiled floor with a crash, Angela stood up, unsteadily, and pointed a finger at David. "I should have known you'd cop out on me, you son-of-a-bitch. I come to you for some fucking help and you—"

"Angie, cool it." David looked around warily. "People are staring." It was a bad dream from their past, relived.

"Well, let them stare. I'm a fucking movie star." Her voice was louder now. All other conversation in the room had ceased. To David it seemed that even the music had stopped. "Hi, folks. Remember me? I'm Angela Mastry. Star of the *Slasher* movies. Anybody want an autograph?"

The manager appeared in the doorway and reached Angela just as David stood and went to her side. "I'm sorry," he told the manager. "She had too much to drink."

"I had too mush to drink," Angela repeated. "Can I have a recount? How about a fucking recount . . ."

"I'll just get her to the car." David reached in his wallet and handed the manager a fifty-dollar bill. "Keep the change for your trouble and for the waitress. I'm really sorry about this."

"You certainly are a sorry excuse for a cop, you stupid

son-of-a-bitch,'' Angela slurred, as David hustled her out the door into the rain. ''Are you going to fucking arrest me?''

The cold, dismal rain was still falling as David drove up the ramp that circled one story above the parking lot in front of the Don CeSar's main lobby. A doorman in a heavily decorated uniform came to the car.

Angela was sitting in a lump, her head against the window. David stopped, left the car running, got out, and came around to her door. The doorman joined him. David said, ''She's had too much to drink. Can you help me?''

''Sure.'' The doorman pulled open the door and smiled. ''Hi, Miss Mastry. Let me help you.'' He was tall and in his twenties. His fancy uniform jacket seemed a little too large for him.

She looked at him and mumbled, ''Hello, Todd. What are you doing here?''

''I work here, Miss Mastry.''

Together the two men got her out and up to the door. She was standing, which surprised David.

''Look, I'll seat her just inside the door,'' the doorman said. ''I need you to move your car, and then you can come back in and we'll get her to her room. You can't leave your car there.''

''But it's raining.''

''I'm sorry. I don't make the rules.''

''Okay.'' He looked at Angela, leaning against the doorman's shoulder. ''I'll be right back, Angie.''

David slipped his Pontiac into first gear and started on around the half-circle ramp. He had to pull tightly on his left to avoid a green van parked against the side railing, facing down the ramp. The exhaust showed in the downpour, indicating its motor was running. Its rear doors were open, lights were off.

Although he was pissed off about having to move his car and walk back up the ramp in the rain, David was grateful for the help from the doorman. He had almost forgotten all the times he'd had to carry Angie into their bedroom after she'd passed out in the car. It was a bitter memory that reminded him of why he didn't want to be involved with her again.

He looked forward to returning to Veronica's apartment, where she'd meet him after work. He needed to talk to her alone. He glanced in the rearview mirror and noticed something odd in the splash of light from the lobby. The doorman had his arm around Angela, walking her *away* from the door toward the van.

In an instant, David realized what was happening. He slammed on the brakes, yanked up the parking brake, and threw the shift into neutral. He jumped out of his car, and walked rapidly toward the doorman and Angela. "Is everything okay?"

Angela screamed. They were about twenty feet away, heading for the van. David saw the small handgun the doorman had wedged against Angela's chin. The tall young man had a handful of Angela's hair, pulling up. She had her hands around his, trying to ease the pain.

David pulled his .38 from under his jacket and aimed it— held in both hands—at the doorman. "Drop the weapon and let her go. I'm a police officer."

"Leave me alone, man! This is none of your business!" yelled the doorman. He was only a few feet from the rear doors of the van and still moving, with Angela's hair in a death grip. Puddles on the ramp held rippled reflections of the pair.

"You kill her, you'll be dead a moment later!" yelled David. He looked up at the pink hotel, looming like a mountain between them and the Gulf of Mexico, and wondered why people weren't leaning out their windows watching this little drama.

The doorman looked visibly shaken but he toughed it out. "Go ahead! Shoot me!"

The steady rain, nearly obscuring the distant full moon, beat down on his head. He checked the front of the van and couldn't see anyone in the driver's seat. He looked at Angela, measuring his chances of hitting the man and not her.

The doorman and the frightened actress were only a foot from the open doors at the rear of the van now. He knew he had to do something fast. "Last warning! Drop her or I shoot!"

Suddenly, someone in the van shone a bright light in David's face, temporarily blinding him. He moved to the right, and the light followed him. He heard the rear doors of the van slam shut, and the van raced by him, splashing his pants. The van skidded. It clipped David's Pontiac as it raced away. He holstered his gun, ran to his open door, and jumped in. He shifted into first and released the hand brake at the same instant.

Ahead of him, the van hydroplaned south on Casablanca. It took a tight right just beyond the parking lot. It rolled left onto Pass-A-Grille Way. That told him that they were probably from out of town. Anybody from around St. Pete Beach knew that Pass-A-Grille was basically a dead end, a peninsula. The only way out was the way he was now going in after them, a narrow-two lane street.

He memorized their taillights about two blocks ahead as they raced down Pass-A-Grille Way. They ran the red light at Twenty-first Avenue. They narrowly missed a pickup truck backing out of the parking lot of a fire station a half block beyond. David crossed Twenty-first. Now the pickup truck was across both lanes. It had stalled. A man in a dark raincoat got out and lifted the hood. David honked his horn. The man gave him the finger. David tried to get around the truck, but telephone polls, newspaper boxes, and a couple of trees made the sidewalks unreachable. David cursed his luck. He rolled down his window. "Get out of the way!" The man didn't look up. "Police emergency! I've got to get through!" He realized the man couldn't hear him. "Dammit!" David pounded the steering wheel. Just then, the man slammed the hood and moved the truck.

David took off. It had been just a few minutes, but it was enough to give the van a hell of a lead. He drove down Pass-A-Grille Way, catching glimpses of the shiny waves of the Pass-A-Grille Channel and the lights of the expensive homes on Tierra Verde, across the water. The numbers on the street signs diminished as he drove on, looking to the right at the old Florida homes mixed with an occasional modern house in a geometric arrangement of cedar.

He strained to spot the van. At the end of the street his high beams flashed on a sign attached to a weathered two-story building directly in front of him: ISLAND'S END COTTAGES. Aptly named since the street ended there.

He was forced into a right turn that went one block past the Pointe Pass-A-Grille condo complex, and into another right turn onto Gulf Way at the beach.

David slowed under a streetlight to get his bearings. On his left a concrete wall about two feet tall separated the street from the beach. Shadowy sea oats were waving in the windy rain. There were no other moving vehicles on the street. The only sound was the surf from the nearby Gulf of Mexico, the rain pelting his car, and his defroster fan running at high speed.

David inched across Second Avenue past one-story houses with large awnings, searching the driveways and avenues to his right for any sign of the van. No luck.

It wasn't down Third Avenue.

It wasn't down Fourth, where a little blue concrete-block building bore a sign that read THE HOTEL CASTLE. Because of the angle of Pass-A-Grille, David could actually see the spotlit Don CeSar ahead of him, off in the distance. A far cry in distance and status from the Hotel Castle, he thought.

A tall condo building cast a shadow on the Fifth Avenue sign. David was beginning to think he'd probably have to come back and drive up and down each avenue. They were mostly just a block or two long, connecting Gulf Way on the west with Pass-A-Grille Way on the east, but it could still take precious time. Besides, there was a chance that the van had kept going, looped around, and left the peninsula altogether.

David was so busy trying to find the street sign on what had to be Sixth Avenue that he almost didn't notice the ugly old house about a hundred yards down the street with a green van parked in the alley just beyond it.

The van.

The street sign had apparently been ripped off, but the van

engine was still running and its doors were flung open. He guessed they had come up Sixth from the other side when he was slowed by the pickup truck. Could it have been deliberate?

David turned off his lights and eased slowly down Sixth Avenue past the house and van, checking to see that no one was in the van. He went on about a half block, pulled to the curb, and turned off his engine. Checking his .38, David emerged from the Pontiac and trotted up the street to the house, trying to keep out of sight as much as possible.

As he came closer, he saw that the house had apparently been abandoned. It was a one-story affair with a peaked roof and what seemed to be an attic window with the glass broken out. In the bright glow of the condo security lights across the street, David studied the front of the house—five side-by-side jalousie windows, an open glass-paned door, surrounded by faded brown shingles. The painted doorframe was chipped away to the point of oblivion, and a small piece of wood by the door bore the ghostly image of what had once been a house number.

One-zero-something.

Two tall palm trees with trunks that were bare as far as twenty feet up cast shadows over the house.

Peering in the open front door, he saw a hallway that ended with another open doorway on the left. There wasn't a sound except the rain beating on the roof of the small porch.

Tired and miserable, his clothing soaked, David crept in the open door, gun in hand. He had just cleared the doorway when the tall young man appeared at the end of the hall. He had shed his doorman's jacket and wore only a T-shirt and slacks. In the semi-bright light, mostly from the streetlight outside, David could see that the man was pointing a gun at him.

"Where is she?" David asked, glancing cautiously to either side and taking a step forward.

"She's dead, man. And you're next." He raised his gun and fired at David.

David saw the flash and he rolled to his right, landed on one knee, and squeezed off two shots in quick succession.

David watched him fall before he stood up and started cautiously forward. The rain had increased outside and the pounding on the roof made it impossible to hear. Without warning, David felt a dull thud and a sharp pain behind his right ear.

Then he didn't feel anything at all.

CHAPTER TEN

DETECTIVE CHRISTOPHER CROSS OF THE ST. PETERSBURG Beach Police Department got out of his car, cursed the rain, and crossed the narrow street to the ugly little house in Pass-A-Grille. The officer who had answered the report of shots being fired just after midnight Tuesday had been smart enough to call it in by phone so that the media, usually listening to their police scanners, wouldn't find out.

It was almost one in the morning according to his black digital watch as Cross ducked under the yellow crime-scene ribbon. The I.D. unit was already there. Cross nodded at the uniformed officer at the door and went in. The light from the videotape camera one of the technicians was using illuminated the scene, a hallway from the front of the house to the rear.

Just inside the door was a curly-haired, middle-aged man facedown in a small pool of blood with a Smith & Wesson .38-caliber gun in his right hand. Two E.M.T.'s were working on him. An I.D. tech was taking still photos of the gun.

"Hi, Bill. What've we got?" Cross asked the technician.

"He's a cop," Bill told him. "We found his shield. Tampa P.D. Homicide."

One of the E.M.T.'s raised his head and said, "This one's unconscious, but he'll probably be okay. We'll take him to Palms."

"Was he shot?"

"No. Could be a skull fracture. He hit his head on something." He gestured toward an antique iron doorstop on the floor a few inches from David's head. "Maybe fell and hit his head on that."

Cross nodded at the other end of the hall. "What about the woman?"

"She's stone dead," said the E.M.T. "Shot a couple of times."

Cross walked to the end of the hall and found a much more horrible scene. The small blonde was crumpled like a sack of potatoes in a pool of catsup. He looked closer. She had been shot in the chest. There was a great deal of blood on the wall and the floor. The brownish-red stains clashed with the blue dress she wore. Without touching her he leaned closer. There was a gold watch on her left wrist. Several thin gold bracelets on her right. But there were also red marks around both wrists. The kind one got from being tied with ropes.

There was a commotion as the E.M.T.'s carried the man's body to the waiting ambulance outside. Cross stepped outside and asked another detective to go with them to the hospital, then came back in and walked over to the technician who was still examining the weapon with rubber-gloved hands. "Smith and Wesson?"

"Standard issue."

"Ammunition?"

Bill carefully opened the gun and dropped the four remaining bullets into his gloved hand. "Semi-jacketed hollow-point."

"How many rounds fired?"

"Two."

Cross walked back to stand behind the technician, looking over his shoulder. "Was there a round under the hammer?"

"Yeah."

"Probably trained in double action," Cross said to himself. He knew that many local police departments and sheriffs' offices taught their officers to fire without cocking the hammer.

"Yeah," Bill agreed. "In fact, the hammer is bobbed. Cut off so he's not tempted to use it."

Cross glanced at the video man, who was shooting every square inch of the wall and floor surrounding the woman's body, and went out into the windy rain, pulling his clear plastic raincoat closed. He approached the uniformed officer. "State attorney's office notified?"

"On the way."

"How about the body-removal service?"

"Speak of the devil," said the officer, pointing at the white mini-van with gold-leaf trim and no other markings, which had come to a halt at the curb.

"Do me a favor," Cross told the uniformed officer. "Call the medical examiner and see if they can do the autopsy before noon. I got to get busy doing an I.D. on the woman, and I need to check in at the hospital on the guy."

Cross went back into the hall and stepped around the woman's body. He looked at the wall. There were several holes. Not just bullet holes. More like nail holes. He remembered the rope burns on the victim's wrists and told a nearby technician, "Make sure your guys do careful measurements. And I want you to spray this wall with T.M.B. I need to know if the woman was standing when she was shot."

Cross came out the door, followed by the technician named Bill, who was carrying several plastic bags filled with evidence. The largest held the gun.

"Be real careful with the weapon," Cross said. "I want you to send it to F.B.I. Washington."

"What's wrong with F.D.L.E. Tampa?" Bill asked. "F.B.I. will take a couple months."

"I want the best ballistics on this one. The F.B.I. techs

are solid gold as expert witnesses. I don't want to take any chances in court. I think it's going to be a hot case.''

"Because a cop's involved?''

"No. Because the dead woman is a movie star.'' Detective Cross pulled his clear raincoat closed and trudged toward his car. His first stop would be the Don CeSar Hotel. He had recognized the actress immediately from the videotapes his teen-aged son had rented several times. In both movies, he recalled, Angela Mastry had been one of the few characters left alive. *But now, in real life,* he thought ironically, *she's dead*.

Veronica pulled into her driveway, disappointed but not really surprised that David's Pontiac Sunbird wasn't there. She had hoped he'd come back to her apartment after he delivered Angela to the hotel. Like a storm cloud in a blue sky, the thought crossed her mind that he'd probably decided to spend the night with Angela instead. "No,'' she told Rum Tum Tugger, just inside her door. "I've got to have more faith in him than that.''

She fed the cats quickly, then went to her office. No matter what she had told her cat, Veronica was upset. She sat at her desk and grabbed the phone. The number for the Don CeSar Hotel was still on a little yellow Post-it note stuck to her computer screen.

She felt betrayed and perverse enough to cause some trouble, to call Angela's room like a wife checking up on her errant husband.

"Hi. Could you connect me with Angela Mastry's room?''

"Not at two-thirty in the morning, ma'am. I'm sorry.''

She tried a different tack with the night clerk. "Could you help me? I'm trying to locate Detective David Parrish of the Tampa Police Department. He was supposed to be—''

"I'm sorry, ma'am. The police left hours ago. But they weren't from Tampa.''

"What?'' She sat up, confused.

"You're talking about the commotion in the parking lot, right? The police left hours ago. But you can call them. They might be able to tell you something.''

"Which police?" Irritation crept into her voice.

"What?"

"Which police? There are a dozen police departments in Pinellas County," she said harshly. "Which one?"

"Oh. St. Pete Beach Police."

She hung up and dug her phone book out from under the April issue of *Suncoast* magazine. A commotion in the parking lot? What could have happened? Was David involved? Her fingers stumbled through the pages, found the number, dialed.

A sleepy-sounding woman answered. "St. Pete Beach P.D."

"There was some trouble in front of the Don CeSar last night. Can you tell me anything about what happened?"

"No, I can't. I'm sorry." Her voice sounded bored, not sorry. "I can't give out that information."

Veronica slammed the phone down and tried to think logically. If David was involved in whatever had happened at the hotel, he still might have called her at the station, or at least called her recorder at home. Her recorder! Of course. In her haste to call the hotel, she hadn't even checked her phone recorder.

She rewound the chattering tape and listened. The first call was a hang-up. The second message was someone from the Florida Orchestra asking for a donation. The next message was David's partner. "Hi. This is Rick. I'll try you at the station. I forgot what hours you worked. It's almost two A.M. If I miss you at work, call me at Tampa P.D., Detective division. I'll be here for a couple hours. It's about David."

The tone at the end of his message went through Veronica like a knife. She called Rick.

"Detective division. Detective Melendez."

"Rick, this is Veronica. What's happened to David?"

"Look. Try to stay calm."

Jesus! she thought. *Cops never know the right thing to say.*

"David's alive, but he was injured in some sort of trouble over on Pass-A-Grille Beach last night."

"Oh, my God! Rick, where is he? I've got to see him!"

"They took him to Palms of Pasadena, but I don't know—"

"Thanks, Rick."

As she slipped her shoes back on, she berated herself for the bad thoughts she had been thinking about him all night. What in the world had happened? Had the people who were allegedly after Angela tangled with David instead?

Veronica drove westward on Twenty-second Avenue North, trying to avoid skidding on the rain-slicked street and replaying good memories of David, as if keeping the memories alive would somehow keep *him* alive. She remembered the early morning just a few weeks after she had started her job at WAQT Radio, the morning she'd met David.

Veronica and Max had stopped at the brightly lit twenty-four-hour Krispy Kreme doughnut place on Kennedy Boulevard in Tampa after work, just after two that morning. David had just finished the paperwork after a homicide that had fallen to him because he'd been stuck with what he called the "midnight detective" duty that night. They'd all gotten into a conversation about the hurricane that had grazed Tampa Bay a week earlier, and before long Veronica had made a new friend. A friend who'd soon become a lover. That had been almost seven months ago, and they'd been together ever since.

She waited impatiently for the light at Tyrone Boulevard, and jabbed at her radio buttons seeking music that wouldn't make her more rattled than she already was. She could visualize his rumpled comfortable face, deep brown eyes straddling a prominent nose above a shaggy moustache. She fought the feeling that she'd find him seriously injured or even dead and pressed on into the intersection through the pouring rain.

Palms of Pasadena was a small hospital, just across the Intracoastal Waterway from Treasure Island, a few miles north of St. Pete Beach. In daylight, the palm tree that poked up through a specially created rectangle in the overhanging roof of the emergency-room entrance probably looked romantic.

At nearly three in the morning, it looked shadowy and haunted in the light fog that the nonstop rain had brought.

Veronica pulled her Honda into a no-parking space, jumped out, and headed for the entrance. The tall windows and double doors of the emergency room were coated with a reflective sunscreen film, turning them into giant mirrors reflecting the fear in her face and the rain on the concrete walk behind her.

She hurried in to find a nearly empty, tastefully decorated waiting room filled with Danish-modern chairs and tables. A young man in jeans was talking on the pay phone to the right of a darkened TV. Subtle prints hung on the walls, and ficus trees were distributed throughout. The eighties version of modern medicine.

Two alcoves marked Cashier and Registry were to the left of a wide hallway, which probably led to the main part of the hospital. She identified herself to the first person she saw, a young girl in tan slacks and an off-white blouse sitting in the Cashier alcove reading *Glamour* magazine. The girl's bright red hair clashed with the blue cabinets behind her.

"Veronica Slate?" The young girl repeated her name. "You do that talk show on the radio?"

"Yes."

"Wow! I listen to you every night. I come on duty at eleven."

"Thanks." She looked at the girl's casual clothes and asked hesitantly, "Are you on duty here?"

"Yes." She smiled and gestured to her slacks. "We aren't required to wear uniforms on the eleven-to-seven shift."

"Okay. I need your help. A man I know was injured last night out on Pass-A-Grille. He was brought here. I need to know his condition."

"Oh." She checked a pad on the desk in front of her. "Well, a man was transported here from Pass-A-Grille just after one this morning. He's about to undergo surgery. I can't release his name."

"Did you happen to see him?"

She looked startled, as if Veronica had read her mind. "Yeah, as a matter of fact, I did."

"Can you tell me what he looked like?"

"Dark hair, a moustache, nice-looking man. Older."

"Older?"

"Older than me, I mean." She giggled, revealing laugh lines around her brown eyes. "He might have been late thirties, early forties."

"That's David. Are you sure you can't confirm the name?"

"I'm sorry." She looked as if she really was.

"Isn't there anyone I can talk to?"

"Talk to me, ma'am."

The deep voice came from a tall, craggy man in his thirties, wearing gray pants, white shirt, a tie open at the neck, and a clear plastic raincoat over it all. "I'm Detective Cross." He snapped open a small notebook and looked at her. "Chris Cross."

"Chris Cross?"

"Spare me the jokes. I've heard them all."

"No. I wasn't . . ." Veronica's earnest protest was cut short by the suspicious look on the detective's face.

"Why are you interested in this guy?" A few droplets of water clung to his brownish moustache. "Were you there?"

"Please," she begged, "just tell me his name. Can you confirm that he's David Parrish, a Tampa police detective?"

"Why?" Cross asked suspiciously. "You related to him?"

"No, I'm not. We're just good friends." She flinched at the inadvertent cliché. "I mean, I've known him for a while."

Cross pointed the way to a pair of chairs in the center of the room. His raincoat was dripping on the tasteful charcoal gray carpet. She remained standing, too tense to sit down.

Detective Cross sat. For the first time, a smile creased his lined face. "I'm sorry if I was giving you the third degree. I'm just tired. Spent an hour at the scene and another hour at the hotel finding someone to I.D. the body."

Veronica gasped. "The body? Oh, my God!"

Cross held up an outstretched palm. "Wait a minute. I'm not talking about the man. I mean the woman."

"Angela's dead?"

"Boy, you're determined to sucker me into telling you all the names, aren't you?" He chuckled and glanced at his notebook. "Okay, look. Maybe you can help me. I've been trying to locate a next of kin on the guy. Doctors said they needed the signature of a next of kin in order to operate." He looked up at her. "You know where we can find somebody?"

"Operate? You mean David's alive?" she asked hopefully.

"Now, did I say his name was David?"

"Please, if it is David, I can help you. He's divorced and his parents are dead."

He glanced at her, and apparently finally realized how concerned she was. "Yeah, the guy's Detective David Parrish," he said. "The doctors went ahead and started on him."

"Started on him? I thought you said—"

He flipped the notebook closed. "They can operate without an okay in the case of life-threatening injury."

"Life-threatening?" She collapsed into a waiting-room chair and finally cried.

After an hour of counting the segments of the suspended ceiling and trying to watch a late-night movie on Channel 44, Veronica was drowsy and exhausted. What kept her in the waiting room was the promise from the young red-haired girl that the doctor would talk to her soon. Deputy Cross had finally left to meet Carla Jahns and Adrian Bell at the medical examiner's office so they could I.D. the body. He said he'd call her if he needed more information.

"Miss Slate?" The doctor flashed the artificial smile doctors used when pretending all was well, and walked in long strides to where she was sitting.

He was very tan, a sharp contrast to his jacket, which had probably been white before the hospital laundry washed it to death. With curly black hair and a prominent nose, he reminded her of David Brenner, the comedian. But the doctor was no longer smiling. "I want you to know what I know at this point. You're the only person who seems to know Mr. Parrish." He frowned. "That wasn't quite the way I meant that, but we did try to contact a next of kin."

She stood. "I understand. How is he?" The doctor was

the same height as she. They saw literally eye to eye. His were a cool gray.

"Mr. Parrish has a skull fracture."

"Skull fracture?"

"Apparently he fell and struck his head on something. We don't know. We do know that, had it been just an inch to the left, it would have totally destroyed the hearing in his right ear. It is possible that could still happen if he is struck again on that portion of his head. Of course, partial hearing can be restored with a hearing aid. What we're concerned about is the possibility of damage to the brain itself. We've done what we can at this time. I have scheduled further tests. However, we cannot do anything until he comes out of the coma."

"Coma? He's in a coma?" A wave of despair overtook her. "You said *until*. Does that mean he *will* come out of it?"

"Yes, I think so."

"Has he been unconscious since he got here?"

"Yes. That's not at all unusual considering the type of trauma he has sustained. He may regain consciousness in a few hours or a few days."

"I hope so." She looked away, staring at the darkened, silent TV set and trying to control herself. "I really hope so."

"As I said, we'll know more after he's conscious and the tests are completed. I will keep you informed." He pulled up his sleeve and checked his watch. "Now I suggest you go home and get some sleep. The sun'll be up in a couple hours."

"When can I see him?"

"Probably this afternoon. Call first."

"Thank you, Doctor."

He managed a smile, revealing bright white teeth in his dark, tan face. "Get some sleep. He'll be all right. Don't worry."

Veronica watched the doctor stride away. She picked up her purse, threw away the damp tissues balled up on the table, and trudged to her car. To her amazement, it hadn't been towed. Nice thing about a small place like Pasadena.

CHAPTER ELEVEN

"I DON'T LIKE THIS AT ALL!" TRACY MORGAN EXCLAIMED. "You never said anything about killing her! Jesus Christ! I can't do this picture with her blood on my hands." Tracy paced in her room, stabbing a cigarette between her pink lips in between sentences. Adrian Bell, the stunt coordinator, was on his back in her bed, naked. The ornate clock on the dresser read a quarter to eight in the morning.

Adrian had come to Tracy's room after midnight and shaken off his damp clothes. He hadn't said anything about Angela. He'd drunk two glasses of Tracy's white wine, and still hadn't said anything about Angela. Finally, he'd carried Tracy to bed and they'd made unusually intense love.

The phone had rung about two in the morning and Adrian had answered. As he dressed, he'd told her, matter-of-factly, "By the way, baby, you're the female lead now. You don't have to worry about Angela anymore. She's out of the picture."

"What do you mean?" Tracy had asked.

"She's dead," he had told her, as if it were no big deal. "That was Carla. I'm going with her to the medical examiner's office to identify the body. I'll be back in about an hour."

Now, two hours later, Tracy pulled at the thin strap of her sheer pink nightgown and sat on the edge of the bed, jamming the half-smoked cigarette into the ashtray that already held a half dozen others. "I thought the plan was just to get her drunk and screw up her contract. You never said anything about killing her. You know I'd never go along with murder."

"What makes you think I killed her?" Adrian asked, putting his hands behind his head in a show of insouciance.

She glanced at him, hoping it was possible. "So maybe you had one of your trained stunt monkeys to do it. Same damned thing."

"Ever think that maybe her ex-husband did it?"

"Yeah, sure." Her eyes flashed. "That's insane. After all she's told me about him over the years . . ." She turned and stared at the early-morning pinkness outside the window. "He's just not the type to kill his wife."

"People do strange things sometimes."

Tracy turned her head like a slow-motion replay and regarded Adrian's brown eyes. "What are you talking about?"

"Believe it or not, babe, I'm telling you the truth. He really did kill her. No shit." He reached for her arm and pulled her alongside his muscular body. "When the cops check his gun they'll know it. It's a fact, Jack. He takes the fall. We're clean." He pressed against her, and his moustache tickled her lips as she resisted his kiss. He broke just enough to whisper, with his lips brushing hers, "Of course, he had a little help." He told her how they had done it, and she smiled in spite of herself.

"That's straight out of *F/X*," she said.

"Whatever works. It's foolproof. He's going to go down for the murder. Make lots of people happy."

The muscles in her neck tightened at the implied evil in his voice and she pulled away. "What do you mean by that?"

He just smiled.

She sat up again. "Look, I need to know what's going on. What if the police talk to me?"

"Why would they do that?"

"I have a motive."

"You have an alibi." He kissed her fingers. "And so do I. I was here all night, wasn't I?"

The intensity of his stare told her he needed her, if only for an alibi. "I just don't like this. Why did you do it?"

Adrian sat up beside her and grabbed Tracy by both arms, staring into her eyes. "Angela had to go for reasons bigger than you getting her part. And I'm getting well paid for what I did, helping to set it up."

"But surely someone will find out. You'll go to prison." Her eyes were misting up again. "I could go to prison."

His fingers dug into her slim, tan arms. "No one's going to prison. But I need your help. We need to keep a lid on how this whole thing happened. Some very important people are counting on me. On us."

Tracy stood, pulling out of his grasp, and lit another cigarette, her hands shaking. "What can I do?"

"You've made friends with that tall chick from the radio station, right?"

She spun around. "Veronica? Yes. But what—"

"She's been going with the cop that was married to Angela. That's why she got her job here."

"Oh, Jesus! You didn't kill him, too?"

"No. Relax. I just bopped him on the head. He'll be okay. But I don't know how much the girl knows. It's a cinch she'll find out something when he comes around. Whatever Angela told him. And she knew a lot." He smiled. "I need you to find out what his girlfriend knows. When will you see her next?"

"I don't know. Probably today."

"Good. Try to make friends with her, get her away from the hotel and pump her for information. But don't be too obvious. I don't want her to suspect you're involved in this."

At that, Tracy's tears started again. "See, I *am* involved in this. Even though I didn't know what you were doing." She ground out the cigarette, wrapped her arms around his neck, and settled onto the matted hair of his chest. "What are we going to do? What am I going to do?"

"You're going to have a conversation with this Veronica chick, and you're going to take over Angela's role, and you're going to be a star. It's real simple."

"But Angela was murdered. What if Jon doesn't give me the role? What if he hires someone else?"

He lifted her head and looked into her eyes. "I won't let that happen."

Tracy hesitated, then wiped her tears away with the back of her hand. "But I feel so guilty."

"It wasn't your fault."

Tracy closed her eyes and laid her head back on his chest. She realized she'd have to keep repeating that over and over to keep her confidence high enough to give two of the greatest performances of her career. One would be on screen. The other would be in public.

"I'm sorry, ma'am, but you'll have to leave. Doctor's orders. You can see him again tomorrow." Veronica realized the nurse had been patient, but she didn't want to leave David's bedside. He was under a white sheet and a yellow blanket in a bed circled on three sides by a pale green curtain on a suspended track. Aluminum bars were raised on both sides of the bed, like a crib for grown-ups. Being careful not to disturb the I.V. tube in his hand, Veronica leaned over and kissed him on the cheek.

The fear of losing him and the elation that he was alive had filled her to capacity. As the sun began to rise over Tampa, she had finally gone to sleep, getting a few hours in until she could return and see him at eight Wednesday morning. Carla had told her the whole shoot was on a temporary hold for the day because of Angela's death and not to worry about being late.

"Mrs. Slate? I'm sorry. You really must go."

For the past two hours, Veronica had waited by David's bed praying he'd come out of the coma. Now she was being forced to leave. She traced his bushy moustache with a plum-tipped finger and said, "I love you, David. Please, wake up."

It was sunny and warm as Veronica finally bowed to pressure from Tracy Morgan and agreed to escape the Don CeSar for lunch with her. She had been on edge for so long that a relaxing lunch seemed a good idea. Besides, Carla had insisted they take off.

Principal photography had been called off for the rest of the day. Some second-unit work was being done and the construction crew was hard at work, but the actors had the rest of the day off. When they left, Carla was on the phone trying to explain things to the executives back at Mira Loma Productions in California.

"This is really weird," Tracy said, as Veronica pulled out onto the Bayway in her '83 Honda Accord. "Angela's been a little shit sometimes, and she's locked herself in her trailer more than once, and she's been on an all-night drunk quite a few times, but why the hell would anyone want to kill her? And what was she doing down in Pass . . . down in . . ."

"Pass-A-Grille," Veronica said.

"Pass-A-Grille. Isn't that what they call that area south of the hotel?"

"Yeah. Did Carla tell you anything what happened?"

"Only that Angela went out to dinner with her ex last night. A couple of people from the crew were there having dinner."

"Where?"

"A place called T. Nelson Downs. It's a magic-theme restaurant."

"I know." *That son-of-a-bitch*, Veronica thought. *He took Angela to our favorite restaurant.*

"Anyhow," Tracy continued, "they said Angela and her ex got in a fight and left."

"Did they come back to the hotel?" She moved to the exact-change lane of the tollbooths. "Where did they find David?" She fished in her blue canvas purse for change.

Tracy gave her a quizzical look. "Angela's ex? The same place they found Angela. Some little house on Pass-A-Grille.

She was dead at one end of the hall. He was knocked out at the other.'' Tracy frowned. ''It's probably none of my business,'' she said, ''but there was something in the way you said 'David.' Do you know him?''

''Yeah.'' She paid the toll, smiled at the elderly man in the booth, and drove on. ''We've been dating for almost seven months.''

''No shit?'' Tracy turned in her seat. ''Angela said he had a girlfriend, but I don't think she knew it was you.''

''I *know* she didn't know. And I'd just as soon nobody else knows either.'' She looked at Tracy. ''Do you mind?''

''My lips are sealed.'' Tracy removed her sunglasses, rubbed her eyes, and put them back on. ''So, have you seen him? Did he tell you anything?''

''He can't. He's in a coma.''

''Bummer. What's the doctor say?''

''He says David should come out of it. Just can't say when.''

''You must be really worried.''

''You got that right.'' She braked for a red light.

''I don't mean to scare you or anything, but if he doesn't come out of the coma we may never find out what really happened.''

''Right now, I don't give a shit what happened. I just want him alive and well.''

''Sure. I was just . . .'' Tracy stopped in mid-sentence and looked out at the shiny surface of the bay. An uneasy silence began to lengthen.

Veronica couldn't shake the negative feeling that David would die, and it bothered her. Most of all she hated the feeling that there was nothing she could do to help him except pray. She stared, absently, at the water to her left and wished for a moment she could be floating on her back without worry.

Finally, Tracy broke the silence. ''This sure is beautiful. This part of Florida. Are you from around here?''

Veronica cast a sidelong glance and smiled. ''Is that called changing the subject?''

''Yeah, I guess so,'' Tracy said sheepishly. ''But I really am interested. Are you a native?''

"In Florida you're a native if you've been here more than a year. I've been here nine years. Born in Roanoke, Virginia."

"Ah, yes," Tracy said. "The Star City of the South."

Veronica turned to look at her. "You been there?"

"Yeah. I worked a PBS shoot there once."

"Well, I wasn't there long. Daddy was accepted into the F.B.I. when I was seven and we moved to Arlington."

"Your father was in the F.B.I? Wow! That must be neat."

"He's retired. Lives on Anna Maria Island, south of here."

"He lives alone? Are your folks divorced?"

"My mother died a few years ago."

"Sorry." Tracy looked out at the condo complexes bordering the road on either side. "The F.B.I.," she said. "That must be really exciting."

"Daddy says it was half boring and half scary as hell." She made the curve northward onto I-275. Traffic was heavy with tourists. "That's what David always says about being a cop. I guess this is the scary-as-hell part. I just hope he comes out of it alive."

Tracy put her hand on Veronica's arm. "He's going to be okay, Veronica. Really."

Veronica sniffed into a thin smile. "I know. And you can call me Vee. Remember?"

"Okay, Vee."

She pulled into the parking lot at Harvey's Fourth Street Grill, just north of Thirtieth Avenue. "We're here."

They got out of the car, and Tracy pointed at the restaurant. "What a cute little place."

Harvey's sat, incongruously, at the end of a strip center featuring, among other things, Joel & Jerry's Deep Discount store and a Larry's Olde-Fashioned Ice Cream Parlour.

To the right of the front door was one of the few remaining testimonials to the early days of St. Petersburg, an authentic green bench. Once, those benches had been all over the downtown area, a virtual symbol of the city. Now, they were collectibles.

Veronica pushed open the heavy door. Inside, all the tables and booths were filled and a dozen people lined the elevated

bar on the left. It was eleven-thirty, and people trying to beat
the lunch crowd had created a pre-lunch crowd. Old-time
posters, enamel-on-steel signs, and potted plants abounded,
and Jimmy Buffett's "Margaritaville" dodged high ceiling
fans from hidden speakers. Above the packed booths hung a
ceiling of striped multicolored parachute cloth.

The young hostess said, "I have two at the bar. Is that
okay?" Veronica and Tracy agreed, and sat on a pair of stools
at the end of the bar near a TV set.

The bartender, a tall Nordic type with bushy blond hair
and sad eyes, took their order for two Coors, gourmet burg-
ers, and fries, then walked away.

Veronica pointed at the flashing neon Coors sign on the
far left wall. It spelled out COORS FOR FLORIDA against a map
of the state by lighting just the F, O, and R of Florida every
few seconds. "I've been trying to figure out a way to steal
that sign for my kitchen since last September."

Tracy laughed. "I don't blame you. It's great. But you
know what? They've got the same sign in California, only
the state outline is different, of course, and the 'for' is from
the middle of California."

"Wonder what they do in Maine?"

"Probably 'Coors *in* Maine,'" Tracy said. They both
laughed and sipped at their beer.

With so little information to go on, their conversation soon
turned from Angela's death to a newly discovered mutual
interest in the movies, and they launched into an in-depth
discussion of the chase scenes in *Bullitt, The French Connection, The Seven-Ups,* and *To Live and Die in L.A.*

"Yeah, that *Live and Die* chase was super," Tracy said.
"I just about freaked when they were driving the wrong way
on that highway. I've been on that road lots of times. It was
really bitchin'. But you know, the movie I worked on last
year had a good chase, too. The picture's called *F/X.* It came
out a couple of months ago. Did ya see it?"

"Not yet."

"Well, there's a chase where this special-effects van is being chased by a cop car. I doubled Martha Gehman," Tracy
said with pride. "She played Andy, the girl who works with

the special-effects guy. That was Brian Brown. What a hunk! And I got to work with some other great people. Brian Dennehy, Mason Adams, Cliff De Young. Jerry Orbach was even—''

"Wait a minute!" Veronica had noticed on the TV above the bar that Channel 13's "Pulse Plus at Noon" had just started and they had flashed a graphic on screen that read PERFECT CASTING. "Can you turn that up?" she asked the bartender.

Anchorwoman Leslie Spencer was reading the national news headlines: "The crew of one of the eighteen air force F-one-elevens that raided Tripoli is still missing. Actor Clint Eastwood was sworn in this morning as mayor of Carmel-by-the-Sea in California. And now back to the top local story of the hour. We take you live to Pass-A-Grille and reporter Mark Keppler.''

The scene switched to an intense young man with a thin moustache, a mike in one hand, and a small notebook in the other. Behind him several onlookers were waving foolishly as bystanders usually did. Behind them was an ugly house with lots of windows and a yellow crime-scene ribbon stretched around it. "Thank you, Leslie," Keppler said. "Movie star Angela Mastry—in town to make the movie *Perfect Casting*—was found dead this morning, here in this abandoned house on Sixth Avenue in Pass-A-Grille.''

"What was she doing there?" Tracy asked.

"Damned if I know," Veronica said.

Keppler continued: "Detective Christopher Cross of the St. Pete Beach Police Department told me that Miss Mastry had been shot twice in the chest and probably died instantly. The body was discovered by a St. Pete Beach police officer called to the scene by reports of shots having been fired just after midnight. Also found at the scene was an unidentified unconscious man. He was transported to Palms of Pasadena, where his condition is listed as fair.''

"Nothing fair about being unconscious," Veronica muttered.

"Police have not released his name, but they say he had not been shot. It is still uncertain at this time what happened here in this weather-beaten old house on Pass-A-Grille last night. But one thing's for sure. Angela Mastry, star of several motion pictures, and in our area to make another one, is dead, the victim of a shooting. I'm Mark Keppler, Channel Thirteen news.''

Veronica was shocked and sorry that Angela was dead, but she also had an uncomfortably selfish sense of relief that Angela was no longer a threat. "We better call Carla and see if she needs any help with the media,'' Veronica said, grabbing both checks and heading for the register. "Look,'' she told Tracy as they left the restaurant, "this morning, in my rush to get to the hospital, I forgot to feed my cats. My house is just a few blocks from here. Do you mind? We can call Carla from there.''

"Fine,'' Tracy said. "I've spent most of the last six months in hotel rooms. I forget what a real home looks like.''

As they entered Veronica's house, the first to check out the new visitor was the gray male of her two long-haired cats.

"Oh, she's beautiful,'' gushed Tracy. "What's her name?''

"*His* name is Rum Tum Tugger. He's a year old.'' She pointed to the bedroom doorway, where her yawning tabby had appeared. "And that's the little lady, Jennyanydots.''

Rum Tum Tugger came up to Tracy and placed his furry head beneath her hand, as if to say, "Okay, pet me.'' As was her custom, Jennyanydots merely stood, shyly, in the corner.

"What unusual names,'' Tracy said as she scratched Rum Tum Tugger under his chin, making them friends for life. "How'd you come up with them?''

"From T.S. Eliot's *Old Possum's Book of Practical Cats*.'' She noticed Tracy's blank look and explained, "It was the basis of the Broadway show *Cats*.''

"Oh!'' Tracy's face lit up. "I saw it in L.A. I loved it.''

Veronica called the production office. Liz said both Jon and Carla were busy with reporters, and asked if Carla could call her back. Veronica agreed and hung up.

She returned to the living room and turned on the stereo, shoving in her favorite cassette of all time, Carole King's *Tapestry*. As King started singing "I Feel the Earth Move,''

Veronica said, "Well, since this is your first time here, why don't I give you the twenty-dollar tour? We'll start with the kitchen, which is not my favorite room."

"Oh, really?" She hurried to keep up with Veronica. "Why?"

"I don't like to cook. I know that makes me less a woman," she said sarcastically, "but that's tough. Daddy's really rather good at it. But mostly I do the easiest stuff I can."

Once in the kitchen, she opened a can of Nine Lives and split it between her two feline friends. As usual, Rum Tum Tugger, the more aggressive of the two, leaped up on the counter next to the can opener to help.

"How does David feel about you not cooking?"

"He's learned to live with it. We eat out a lot." *At restaurants like T. Nelson Downs,* she thought bitterly. *Why did you have to take Angela to our favorite restaurant?*

"This house is so unusual," Tracy said, looking at the three-inch-high mahogany baseboards around the living room.

"It was built in the twenties," Veronica explained. "This is the northeast side of St. Petersburg. Sixty years ago all the wealthy people lived here."

As the cats ate with relish, Veronica led the way into her office. "This used to be a bedroom, but I converted it into an office, where I can write and read and do all sorts of pointless tasks. It's decorated in 'Early Goodwill.' Nothing in here ran me more than fifty bucks."

"You've got a computer." Tracy crossed the room to look more closely at it.

"Yeah, well, *that* was more than fifty, but that ugly little Kaypro is the real love of my life. I got it three years ago. I know the whole world's using an I.B.M. or a clone, but I love this little guy." She patted the metal case.

"I like this room," Tracy said as she touched the antique bar that served as a stand for a Citizen Premier 35 printer. She turned to the six-foot-high bookshelves. "And look at all these books!"

"I have," Veronica said. "I've even *read* most of them. That's my vice, reading." Dozens of mystery novels shared shelf space with books on journalism, radio, and television.

Tracy pointed to the big color picture of a craggy-looking man on the wall. "Who's this guy? Looks tough."

"That's Robert B. Parker, the mystery writer. My favorite." She glanced at the Regulator clock like the one in her dad's house. It was almost one in the afternoon.

Tracy was peering more closely at the paintings of rainy streets in London, Paris, and Amsterdam that were hanging above Veronica's desk.

"They're not real," Veronica explained. "Just prints. I've got a thing for rainy days and city streets." Veronica led the way into the second bedroom. "The master bedroom," she said. "Although, since I'm usually the only one in it, I suppose I could call it the mistress bedroom."

Tracy smiled. "I hear you."

"Yes, it is a queen-sized bed. Daddy thought I needed a bed 'befitting my stature.' " She wrinkled her nose.

"Are you really the only one in it?" Tracy asked as she went to the window and looked out across the brick surface of Coffee Pot Boulevard at the calm water of the bayou.

"Well, David does stay over sometimes."

"Glad to hear it. Are you guys gonna get married?"

"I don't know. Marriage doesn't agree with me."

"Nice view," Tracy said at the window. "Is that what they call Tampa Bay?"

"No. It's Coffee Pot Bayou." Veronica drifted toward the window. "I wanted to live on the waterfront, but I couldn't afford the really good waterfronts, like Tampa Bay or the Gulf."

As they turned to go back down the short hall to the living room, Tracy spotted a framed photo next to a bottle of Nuance on the dresser. "Is that David?"

"Yeah." Seeing his picture made her ache. She couldn't erase the fear that he might not ever wake up from the coma.

"And you don't want to marry him? You must be blind."

"Or careful. I was married once already."

"Oh, that's right, you mentioned that the other—"

The phone pierced the air.

Veronica stepped into the living room and lifted the receiver.

"Carla here. Look, I can't talk now, but Jon's calling a full-blown news conference for tomorrow at nine. I need you and Tracy there to help out."

"Okay. Tracy's here with me."

"She is?"

Veronica detected something odd in Carla's voice. *Probably my imagination,* she thought. "I'll tell her. Do they have any idea who killed Angela?"

"They think her ex-husband did it."

Veronica's throat tightened as she hung up the phone.

She sat and hoped it was not prophetic that Carole King was singing "It's Too Late."

CHAPTER TWELVE

IT WAS A FEW MINUTES PAST NINE. THURSDAY MORNING. Veronica stood along a side wall in the Grand Ballroom of the Don CeSar talking to Sam Zimmerman, a newsman from her station, WAQT. The room was packed with people. The hotel hadn't turned off the Muzak yet, but it was nearly overpowered by the idle conversations going on among the reporters.

Sam, a lanky, bearded man with a perpetual laconic smile, surveyed the crowded room. "Looks like a media convention. Tampa *Trib*'s here. St. Pete *Times*." He pointed to a young woman seated near the front of the room. "Stringer for *USA Today*."

"Who else is here from radio?" Veronica asked. She frowned at a videographer nearby who had lit a cigarette, ignoring the no-smoking signs.

Sam ticked them off his fingers. "You got your PLP, your FLA, your Q-105, and there's Dave McKeever from BRD down in Bradenton."

She recognized television crews from channels 8, 10, 13, and 44—all but one of the local stations. There was also an independent video crew Carla had mentioned. They were shooting for "Entertainment Tonight."

The crowd ran the gamut of style. A few members of the *Perfect Casting* cast and crew were there in shorts, T-shirts, and flip-flops or running shoes. The TV videographers and the newspaper photographers wore jeans, T-shirts, and running shoes. The radio and newspaper reporters were less casual, and the TV reporters were neatly dressed, the men wearing ties.

Jon Vasta, clad in a blue satin Mira Loma Productions jacket, a white dress shirt, and pressed jeans, walked to the podium, brought the gooseneck mike down to his level, and addressed the group. "First, let me say one thing: The death of Angela Mastry last night was appalling, tragic, and—so far, at least—unexplainable. The police are doing their best to find out what happened."

As he was talking, TV lights were switched on and electronic flashes sparkled as photographers caught him in action.

His eyes spanned the room. "I realize that most of you knew Angela only through her work on screen, but some of us here in this room had worked with her on other films. We all loved her and shall sorely miss her."

He gestured in the direction of three chairs placed to the left of the podium. "Allow me to introduce the other two stars of *Perfect Casting*, Paul Haden and Raynor Fitzhugh." Veronica noticed that the two men had left the chair in the center empty like a cheap Hollywood version of the "riderless horse" in John Kennedy's funeral procession.

"We will remember her for the good actress and nice person she was," Vasta continued. "I assure you she would want us to go on and make the very best film we can. We will, of course, dedicate *Perfect Casting* to her memory. Now, any questions?"

Instantly, the room erupted into a grade-school classroom with hands waving and shouted questions bumping into one another.

As Jon fielded the questions, Sam Zimmerman edged closer

to Veronica. "Max says Mastry's ex is your current main squeeze," he whispered, releasing a whiff of cigarette breath. "That true?"

"Yeah. That's true." She looked straight ahead.

"Did she know that?" He scratched his chin through his beard and watched Jon Vasta, in the front of the room.

"I don't think so."

Sam lowered his voice again. "Did you know that they may charge him with the murder? I got the word just before I left the station. My source in the state attorney's office. Seems Detective Cross told them he's got probable cause. He's going to put a guard at the door."

She turned and looked at him. "Why? They think he's going to grab his I.V. bottle and sneak away?"

"Way I hear it, they found her dead at one end of a hall and him with the proverbial 'smoking gun' in his hand out cold at the other end. You hafta admit it looks bad."

"It's crazy, Sam. If David wanted to kill Angela he wouldn't have shot her in a deserted house on Pass-A-Grille."

"Yeah, that's the weird thing. What were they doing there?" Sam staged-whispered. "They found some bullet holes in the wall and managed to retrieve one of the slugs. My source says they're proceeding slowly and carefully 'cause they're sure he did it."

"David wouldn't kill her, Sam. He's a cop, for God's sake. What possible motive could he have?"

"I guess he had a fight with her at some restaurant last night. That's all I know at the moment." Sam leaned closer. "Another thing may be bothering them. His prior."

"What do you mean?"

"He shot and killed a man six, seven years back."

"I remember. I was at WSUN then. But the guy was a drug dealer. David was never charged."

"I know. But cops remember things like that about other cops. Don't worry. I promise I won't use anything about your guy unless I get confirmation. Then I've got to go with it. You understand?"

"Sure. I know." Veronica touched his arm and looked up at Jon Vasta, whose face showed the strain he was under.

Haden and Fitzhugh, who had not yet been singled out for many questions, suppressed visible signs of boredom. Carla Jahns made "wrap it up" motions in Vasta's direction from the back of the room.

Vasta raised his hand and said, "That's all the time I have for questions about Angela Mastry right now." Immediately, the TV lights were switched off, plunging the room into the dimness of recessed lighting. Vasta blinked and pointed to Carla. "Our production manager, Carla Jahns, will be glad to help you with individual interviews with Angela's costars until noon." He gestured again to Haden and Fitzhugh. "But I do have an announcement before you all go."

Reporters who were halfway to the door paused. Videographers beginning to pack their gear looked up.

Vasta played the moment, and then gestured to his left. "I am pleased to announce that Angela's best friend, actress Tracy Morgan, will be taking over her role. I'm sure Angela would have wanted it that way. Tracy will be available for interviews until noon."

Veronica watched as Tracy came from behind a column in an entrance so contrived it reminded Veronica of a Hollywood fund-raiser on television. She wore a blue-and-white sundress with spaghetti straps and a low neck. She smiled and waved at the reporters as electronic flashes strobed and videographers turned their lights back on, adjusted focus, and grumbled. Jon Vasta left the podium to Tracy, who began fielding questions and posing for the photographers. He joined Carla at the rear of the ballroom. As they both left the room, Veronica heard him mutter, "Now, I've got a movie to make."

Veronica watched Tracy posing and smiling at the podium, and wondered why she hadn't said anything yesterday at lunch about her big break. Maybe she didn't know until this morning, Veronica thought, but she couldn't help wondering if the chance to replace a star was a motive for murder.

The heavyset sound man was leaning on his control panel beating time with his fingers to a tune he was humming to himself. The boom man sat nearby with his shirt off and the long boom with a mike attached balanced across his knees. He had his head back, eyes closed, soaking up the rays of the sun, which was directly overhead. In a folding chair, the script girl, perhaps in her late twenties, sat nervously pulling loose strings from her cutoffs. Her eyes were hidden by reflecting sunglasses. There was a trace of white sun-blocking lotion on her nose.

The news conference had delayed the start of that day's shooting, and the crew had the first setup ready before Vasta had even finished. They had been hoping it would be what they called a "one deal" day, meaning there'd be only one setup for the whole day. Now, with the prospect of several setups facing them under the hot Florida sun, the crew members were impatiently waiting for the three stars to finish talking to the reporters.

Vasta was about to shoot the discovery of the second body in the film, a scene that involved only Paul Haden, Raynor Fitzhugh, and a handful of extras. And later, he planned to pick up a twilight poolside conversation scene between Paul Haden's character and the character which, until twenty-four hours ago, had been played by Angela Mastry. It would be Tracy's chance to jump into the film with both feet, Veronica thought, as she sidestepped the cables snaked around the pool and onto the beach and reported to Carla Jahns for her assignment.

It was almost two in the afternoon. As she wiped the sweat off her face, Veronica tried to recall why she ever moved to Florida in the first place. Again she was one of the people assigned to crowd control as the scene was shot in which the character played by Paul Haden literally stumbled across the body on his way to the beach. She was beginning to feel like a distant relative given a job because her daddy the director insisted. She didn't seem to be doing much for the two hundred dollars a week she was getting. One of the few bright spots had been watching Paul Haden walk around in swim trunks for the last two hours.

One camera on a dolly rolled backward on wooden tracks as Haden came down the steps and past the outdoor pool to the sand, where actor Terry Chellis was sitting on a folding chair, waiting for his big scene as the dead body. That was what had taken most of the first hour. The grip crew had to adjust the wooden track after almost every take to get it solid enough for the next shot. The problem was that the last six feet of it extended into the sand, and the boards kept sinking on one side or another under the weight of the big Panavision camera. Another camera, mounted on "sticks," moviespeak for a tripod with wooden legs, was used to film Haden actually finding the body. That scene took only forty-five minutes to get in the can. Forty-five minutes for thirty seconds of screen time.

Surrounding the little pocket of technicians were a half dozen production assistants, including Veronica, trying to hold back a crowd of probably a hundred tourists, hotel guests, fans, and hotel employees eager to see Paul Haden closer than they ever had in their lives. From time to time, as they'd see what a boring process shooting a movie really was, several people in bikinis and Hawaiian-patterned shirts would wander away, only to be replaced in moments by a new batch of gawkers.

When they were ready to resume the scene, the assistant director would use a bullhorn to beg people, "Please be quiet, folks! Do not make any noise until you hear me say 'Cut!' "

Veronica's primary job for the last hour had been to keep the crowd out of the shot. It was supposed to be a practically deserted beach except for several extras gathered around the body. In fact, the beach had been closed to the public for a hundred yards on either side of the rear of the hotel. But as soon as the camera started rolling, there were always a few onlookers who edged over to see better, and Veronica would have to try to move them without speaking.

Doing a relatively mindless job had given Veronica a chance to observe Jon Vasta in action. She discovered a different persona than the gentle Yoda type she had first met.

On the set, Vasta remained a private person, never allowing his face to register his emotions. He was, on the surface, the very image of self-control, his voice crisp and alert.

But Veronica noticed he was sometimes quick to erupt with

no warning, no hostile glance or angry frown to indicate that rage was building up. Once, he shoved a worker he apparently thought was not moving fast enough, then apologized. It was a Jon Vasta she had not yet seen or imagined.

Finally, Vasta had accomplished what he had hoped to, and he went back into the hotel, with several crew members following in his wake.

Veronica walked up to Carla, who stood next to one of the two poolside snack-bar buildings talking to Paul Haden.

"Excuse me," Veronica said. "What's next for me, Carla?"

"Take an hour. Then check back with me."

"Okay." She started away, but Haden placed his hand on her arm and turned back to Carla. "Can we talk about that later? I want to get to know our native girl here."

Carla nodded and strode off toward the hotel.

"Since you've got an hour off," Haden said, "how about spending it with me?" He apparently saw the indecision in Veronica's eyes because he added, "We can talk on the beach. I want to talk to you about Angela."

"Can't we talk here?"

"No." He looked over his shoulder. "I'd rather not."

They worked their way through sandy snowdrifts near the hotel, and started along the beach, where the hungry waves of the Gulf were nibbling at the toasted sand. Along the waterline the sand had been firmly packed by the surf. Because of the storm fences erected to keep out the public during filming, they had a couple of hundred yards of beach all to themselves.

As they walked, Veronica said, "Jon's not quite as much fun on the set, is he?"

"It's his sense of purpose," Haden said. "The Mission. The movie must get made." He reached over and took her hand as if it was the most natural thing in the world. She let him. "It's the ultimate justification for all the good and the bad that go on when you're making a film with Jon Vasta."

"Yeah, but the way he treated some of those people . . ." Veronica's heart was racing. She was talking about Jon Vasta, but she was thinking about Paul Haden. Here she was, a simple girl, not especially beautiful, not an actress, and *the* Paul Haden was walking along the beach with her, holding hands. All they needed was a sunset to turn it into a movie cliché.

"His attitude makes the crew a very subservient bunch of people," Haden said. "They try to do what he wants. They even try to anticipate his next command." Haden stopped and turned to look at her. "Their blind obedience to the Grand Design of shooting a picture and their acceptance of almost anything handed them, even bad manners, is almost masochistic. It's as if they want to be beaten into working." He took her other hand in his. "Jon knows how to manipulate this tendency to his advantage. Fear and insecurity are what get a Jon Vasta movie done."

"Sounds like you've worked with him before." His face was so strong. So handsome. She realized she was staring.

"A few times." He looked at her, smiled, and brought his face closer, very slowly. She couldn't move. His lips touched hers. She didn't try to stop him. He kissed her, slowly and with infinite tenderness, while pulling her body against his. His tanned arms around her back felt strong and wonderful. She had missed that feeling. She had missed that passion. She had missed the excitement of being kissed by someone for the first time. She could scarcely believe that that someone was Paul Haden.

As unexpectedly as he had begun to kiss her, he stopped. He smiled, kissed her cheek, her hand, her fingertips, and, still holding one hand, led her on down the beach. A small crowd of onlookers held back by the hurricane fence several hundred feet away applauded and cheered, and Veronica blushed.

The sky was a cloudless blue that seemed to exist only in Florida. It was a day one would hug if one could get one's arms around it, and Veronica felt like hugging. Gulls swooped in and out, searching on the other side of the fence for scraps from picnics and from small children who probably didn't know what a mob scene feeding them would start. Power boats crisscrossed the blue-green waves, and graceful sailboats breezed along farther out. There was a temporary silence between them that Veronica did not choose to invade.

"We haven't really had a chance to talk," Haden said finally. The fronts of his sandals were shoveling up sand with each step. "But since Tracy tells me you know Angela's ex, I felt I should tell you why Angela was killed." He looked strong and masculine with his hairy chest and his black latex swim trunks.

"What do you mean?" She really wanted to be kissed again, but she forced herself to be serious. "Why was she killed?"

"I think Angela was murdered because of what she knew about Tony Victor's death during the filming of *Slasher Three*."

"That was an accident, wasn't it?" Veronica stopped in her tracks and faced him, shading her eyes with her hand.

"That's what Mira Loma would like the world to believe, but it ain't necessarily so."

"How do you know?"

"I knew Tony. Far better than Angela ever did."

"Were you there when he was killed?"

"No. But I know why he was killed." He pointed at a large mound of sand a few feet away. "Want to sit down? Do you mind?"

"No." She was wearing old shorts. They sat in the sand, and Veronica looked out over the Gulf to the horizon, a simple gray line between blue-green water and bright blue sky. She often regretted taking for granted the tropical paradise she called home. Some people worked all year long up north for just a week of this beautiful sight. She had it anytime she wanted. And now, through some fluke of nature, she was sharing it with Paul Haden, voted *People* magazine's Sexiest Man the previous year.

"Angela and I go back about a year," Haden said, brushing back his sandy blond hair. "She had just wrapped *Slasher Two* when Mira Loma signed me for this film. They tested us together because they had already cast her. She was really beautiful, but there was something tortured about her."

Veronica was amazed to realize she felt a twinge of jealousy. She forced a question. "Did you have anything to do with the *Slasher* films?"

"As a matter of fact, yes. The original *Slasher* was produced for less than two million dollars in 1984, and it grossed a cool twenty-three mil. *Slasher Two* grossed more than thirty million, and it had only cost two-point-two million. Obviously they were making money even though the scripts sucked. So I bought into the third one. I was smart." He said it as a statement of fact, not braggadocio. "I got a piece of the gross."

"I'm sorry," she said, gazing into his hazel eyes. "I don't understand."

He took her hand again and, in spite of herself, Veronica felt warm and excited inside. "The main thing you don't want is to have a piece of the net," he explained. "If you've got a piece of the net, you won't see any money until every charge against the film has been recouped and everyone with a piece of the gross has been paid."

"What do you mean by charges?"

"Charges range from the millions of dollars it costs to shoot the film to the two cents for the little paper clip that holds the script together. And the way studios manage to keep finding expenses, most people with a piece of the net don't ever see a penny."

"You seem to know a lot about the business," she said, thinking that she had found the thing that kept him from being perfect. He could be boring when he talked about the business.

He smiled. "I've done some producing. I even directed once. I'm not just another pretty face."

Veronica looked back toward the hotel and said the exact opposite of what she was feeling. "I've got to be getting back."

Haden stood up, reaching down with both hands to help her up from the sand. He took advantage of that move to kiss her once again and she melted, just as before.

They pulled apart and walked in silence until Haden finally said, "Talking about *Slasher Three*. It was budgeted at four-point-four million dollars, but they had to halt production for six weeks when Tony died. By the time they replaced Tony and reshot his scenes, the film ran over budget by almost two million dollars.''

"Whatever happened to it? I haven't seen it.''

"They're holding it till June.'' He took her hand again as they continued walking back up the beach toward the Don CeSar.

"Why?''

"Because Mira Loma's in court right now.'' He shaded his eyes with his hand. "Tony's family is suing. They heard about the *Twilight Zone* case.''

"That's been going on for years.''

"I know. And I lay you ten to one John Landis will get off. But the Mira Loma people are worried. Like you said, the *Twilight Zone* thing's been going on for years, and they haven't even gone to court yet. But the picture was crippled at the box office. Mira Loma is just a small studio. They can't afford to have a loser with *Slasher Three*. Especially since Angela's dead and there probably won't be any more *Slasher* pictures.''

"You still haven't told me why she was killed.''

"Oh, I'm sorry. I got off on nets and grosses and forgot.''

She checked his face and he looked sincere.

"Tony Victor did a film back in 1975, a bad one called *Dead of Day,* which was never released. But while he was working on that film he was balling . . .'' He gave her a sheepish look. "I'm sorry. He was having an affair with the director's wife. I think that director hired someone to kill him.''

"Ten years later? Get serious.''

"That's because the director was out of the country for most of that time. Avoiding a tax problem. But just three months after he returned to Hollywood, Tony Victor got killed.''

"*Dead of Day*? I've never heard of it.''

"Small wonder. The studio totally mutilated the film. It went though seven rewrites. Then they decided to go back to the original script and they hired a TV director to shoot additional scenes. They cut twenty-seven minutes from the film and added twelve minutes of new material, mostly horrendous violence. It was in general release for one week and then sold to cable.''

''So who was this director?''

Haden glanced out at the water and back at her. ''A guy named Alan Smithee. I don't know him, but I've seen a couple of films he directed. He did *Death of a Gunfighter* starring Richard Widmark in 1967, a Burt Reynolds picture called *Fade-In* a year later, and *Let's Get Harry* just recently. All losers.''

''Why haven't you tried to track down this Smithee guy?''

''Why should I? I didn't much care for Angela, and I hated Tony. Besides . . .'' He stopped. ''It really doesn't matter very much anymore. If Angela was killed because she saw who killed Tony, it's all over now. They got her.''

As they reached the wooden deck where electricians were setting up fill lights for the twilight scene, Veronica turned to Haden and asked, ''Why did you tell me all this if you don't intend to do anything about it?''

''I heard your boyfriend may be in trouble. Some people think he killed Angela. I don't really give a shit who killed her. But I thought you might be interested in why.'' He smiled and walked away.

Veronica retrieved her purse from its hiding place under the counter in the Beachcomber Grill and pulled out a small pad and a pen. She made a note of Alan Smithee and the films Paul Haden had mentioned. *Death of a Gunfighter, Fade-In,* and *Let's Get Harry.* This could be her first good break.

CHAPTER THIRTEEN

VERONICA PUNCHED A LIGHTED BUTTON AND TOOK THE NEXT
call. Friday night. Ten minutes till midnight. Another two
hours and she could go home and worry about David in the
comfort of her own house. He was still in a coma, and she
was sinking in an ever-deepening depression. It was increas-
ingly difficult for her to concentrate on her job.

"This is John from Inverness. I want to give you my opinion about the U.S. bombing raid on Libya."

"That's what we're here for, John. Go ahead." One thing
that continued to worry her was the possibility that whoever
killed Angela Mastry might try to finish off David, too.

"If someone keeps slapping you in the face and you don't
hit them back," John from Inverness said, "then they're going to have you down on your knees. It's about damned time,
as powerful as we are, to say, 'Hey, that's enough.' "

"Okay, John. Anything else?" Problem was, if they
wanted to kill David, why didn't they kill both him and Angela at the same time?

130

"Yeah. There is something else. I'm really happy about the raids. It's about time. It's like getting pushed around by a bully and never doing anything about it. I think we should have done it long ago. People like Qaddafi only understand violence. I know a lot of innocent people will die, but a lot of innocent people are dying from what Qaddafi has been doing."

"Okay, John, thank you." That's what really gnawed at her. David was merely an innocent bystander. If he hadn't tried to help Angela, he wouldn't be lying unconscious in a hospital bed. And maybe she wouldn't be dead.

John from Inverness was still on his soapbox. "I think it was great because they keep pushing us around. If we don't do something about it, who's going to do it? I'm ready to go fight for our country."

"Okay, John. Thanks for your call." She hung up and looked at the clock in the corner. "It's eight minutes till midnight. We can still take a few calls before the news. We're discussing your opinion on the U.S. bombing raid on Libya earlier this week. Let's talk to . . ."—she checked the computer screen—". . . Marjorie in St. Petersburg. You're on the QT."

"Hello?" A hesitant middle-aged woman's voice was followed by Veronica's own voice in the background.

"Marjorie, you need to turn down your radio." There was a seven-second delay that gave Max the chance to delete profanity, and which never ceased to confuse those callers who failed to heed Max's advance warning to turn down their radios. "Okay," Veronica said. "Go ahead."

"I still have mixed emotions. I feel something had to be done, but I'm not sure if it was the right move because we don't know the real truth behind it. I think it was probably justifiable. However, I hate to think of the price we might have to pay because of it."

Veronica was beginning to fear that the price she'd have to pay for David's dinner with Angela would be the death of the man she loved. She shook her head to clear that morbid thought, and tried to concentrate on what her caller was saying.

"In the St. Pete *Times* this morning it said terrorists tried to blow up an Israeli jetliner in London and they killed three kidnapping victims in Lebanon and tossed firebombs into a U.S. marine compound in some other country. See, I'm scared about Qaddafi. He's attacking our allies. How long before he sends terrorists to America? How long before this turns into a war?"

"Okay, Margaret." Veronica looked at the screen again. "I'm sorry. Marjorie. Thanks for your call." She glanced at Max through the glass. "We've got to take a break for CBS News at midnight. Then we'll continue with the last two hours of the 'Slate Show' for a Friday night/Saturday morning. After midnight, we'll be talking by phone with the new mayor of Carmel-by-the-Sea, actor Clint Eastwood, and we'll take your calls, Tampa Bay. Stay with us. I'm Veronica Slate and this is TalkRadio TenTwenty WAQT, serving Tampa, St. Petersburg, and Clearwater."

Over the speaker, CBS News began.

Over the intercom, Max asked, "Hey, babe. You okay?"

"Yeah. Just don't have my mind on Qaddafi tonight."

"I hear you. Eastwood's on the P.L. Ready to talk to him?"

"You bet." She pushed the private-line button. "Hi, Mr. Eastwood. I'm Veronica Slate. Thanks for taking our call. We'll be going on right after the news."

The low, even voice that had turned "Make my day" into a popular catch phrase replied, "No problem. Doing a radio show from my living room suits me just fine. Call me Clint."

"I was going to call you Mr. Mayor."

Eastwood chuckled. "Just don't call me Dirty Harry."

David opened his eyes to a blurred vision in blue and dark brown, like an Impressionist painting, a nice change from the blackness he had experienced for the last few minutes. Or had it been hours? He really couldn't tell. There was a clock on the wall. It read eleven-forty-five P.M. It had been less than an hour since he dropped Angela off at . . . Or, wait a minute. Bits and pieces of the gun battle in the abandoned house on Pass-A-Grille were coming back to him.

He blinked, focused, and saw Veronica, asleep, wrapped

around a magazine in a cheap plastic hospital chair with her feet up on another. She was breathing steadily, softly.

He took a quiet moment to drink in her natural beauty. She was worth coming back from the darkness. Her face was pretty but not glamorous. Her square jaw gave her a look of strength, and he had been drawn to that strength. Her luxurious dark brown hair was beautiful, even though she'd had it cut the first of the year so now it only reached her shoulders. And what great shoulders. He smiled. Veronica had great legs and an especially feminine body, all curves and softness, not like some bony, flat-chested model.

On the wide window ledge behind her chair, three flower arrangements elbowed one another out of the way, and cards were propped up in a neat row as if they were on sale. Beyond the window, a streetlamp and the tops of three palm trees obscured his view of a dark, cloudless sky. The relative silence was penetrated by someone—a woman, it seemed—moaning from a nearby room. The only other sound was Veronica's even breathing.

David started to move and realized it wasn't that easy. He had tubes coming from places he'd just as soon not think about. His movement stirred Veronica and she stared at him for a moment with disbelief in her eyes. She jumped from her chair and came to his side, kissing his free hand.

"You're awake! Oh, my God! Oh, David! You're awake! Oh, my God! I've got to call the nurse!" She fumbled with the call button fastened to his pillow and pushed it several times. "Oh, David, I'm so glad you're awake, and alive." She kissed him, her green eyes bright and damp.

He murmured, "So am I, Vee. So am I."

"Oh, thank God you're alive," she said through her wide smile. "Thank God you're alive."

"What day is it?" His words were imprecise, like someone talking with novocaine in his mouth.

"It's Saturday night." She glanced at the clock. "It's almost Sunday morning." Her smile evened out as she told him, "You've been out like a light for almost four days."

David closed his eyes and then reopened them. "Where's Angela? Is she okay?"

Veronica had known he'd ask that, but she resented the fact that it was one of his first questions. "Why don't you close your eyes, honey? The nurse will be here in a moment." She tucked the sheet in around his chin and patted his cheek.

"What about Angela?"

She bit her lip and concluded that he'd have to know. "She's dead, David."

"Oh, no," he mumbled. "I tried to save her. I really did."

Veronica's response was preempted by the arrival of a nurse.

Convinced by the doctor that there was nothing she could do, Veronica finally went home just after midnight Saturday, fed the cats, slept for eight hours, showered and dressed, and was back in David's room by noontime Sunday armed with the St. Petersburg *Times*.

"What's the matter?" she asked him when he failed to laugh very much as she read aloud from "Hagar the Horrible," "Peanuts," and her favorite, "Captain Vincible." "Are you being poopy?"

"No. I'm just tired."

"C'mon, David, don't try to bullshit me. I've worn your pajama tops too often to be shut out of what you're thinking. What's up? What's bothering you?"

"What do you think is bothering me?" He said it softly, almost sadly.

"Don't play games with me, Parrish." She dropped the funnies, folded her arms, and gave him a mock-serious stare. "I know you're not feeling really great right now, but that won't stop me from beating the tar out of you if I have to."

At that, he smiled tentatively. "No. Anything but that."

"What's wrong?" She unfolded her arms and sat back in the chair, not unconscious of the fact that her blouse pulled taut against her breasts. *Whatever works*, she thought.

"I let them kill her, Vee. I had a chance to save Angela, and I let them kill her."

"You had a chance to save her? Did it occur to you as

quickly as it occurred to me that trying to save her is what got you into that bad marriage in the first place?''

"That was different. I know you can't save an alcoholic. At least I know that now. But this time I was trying to save Angela's life, and I screwed it up. Tomorrow morning a detective's going to visit me. The doctor notified him the minute I came to. I don't know what to tell him."

"Tell him the truth, David." She pulled her chair up closer to the bed. "By the way, what is the truth? I've been waiting for you to feel a little better before I started asking questions. I think you're ready." She reached out and touched his arm. "What happened?"

Slowly, with effort, he told her about the dinner and his fight with Angela at the restaurant, the phony doorman, the van, the high-speed chase out to Pass-A-Grille, the abandoned house, and the shots he'd fired at Angela's kidnapper. When he was done, she looked at him silently for a moment.

"You're really lucky," she said. "You came damned close to being killed.''

"That's the part I don't understand. Why did they just knock me out? Why didn't they kill me?"

"I don't know." Even as she said it she realized that maybe she did know. Perhaps they were planning from the start to set him up for Angela's murder.

"Another thing. Angie told me she had contacted an attorney, guy named Kines, before she left California, and she gave him a complete deposition of everything she knows . . ."—he swallowed—". . . everything she *knew* about the Tony Victor murder." He paused for effect. "Kines was killed a week ago. Probably by someone who wanted to keep her from testifying."

"So presumably they got the deposition?"

"Doesn't matter. She gave me a copy of it."

"Oh, I get it. You think they might come after you once they figure that out?"

"Actually, I was afraid they'd come after both of us, if they know you and I are involved."

"*Involved.* Isn't that a quaint word? What happened to 'in love with each other'? Did that go away?"

"Don't give me a hard time." He frowned. "I'm talking about being involved with Angela and the picture and everything. Mostly, I'm worried about you."

"I'm a big girl. I can take care of myself."

"Why're you talking as if you're in 'Cagney and Lacey'?"

"I'm serious." She stood and walked to the window, her back to him for a moment, looking out at the bright sunshine, the palm trees, and the waterway beyond. "I'm not afraid."

"What Angie found out goes much deeper than just an actor getting killed. It reaches into a couple of dark corners of the industry. It touches some people you wouldn't suspect. It's hard to know who to trust."

Veronica returned to the chair. "What did she tell you?"

He looked down at the foot of the bed. "That Tony Victor was murdered by some bozo with an automatic weapon who snuck onto the set disguised as an extra and disappeared right after. The attorney and his girlfriend were killed by the same sort of weapon. Angie said Tony was dealing drugs."

Veronica remembered her conversation with Paul Haden. He had claimed that Tony had been killed because he had been having an affair with a director's wife. "You think it was a drug deal gone bad?"

"Could be. That would be a good place to start your investigation."

"Wait a minute, Mr. Homicide Detective." She held up her hands. "What's this bullshit about *my* investigation?"

He smiled and gestured to the bandage on his head. "You expect me to get out of my deathbed to look into this?"

"She was your wife, David."

"You like a good mystery."

"Yeah, sure. But if you think I'm going to look into the death of your ex-wife, you're crazy. Must be the bump on your head. Scrambled your brains." She stood again and walked away to the window, but she was adding it up, realizing that she would have to investigate if she wanted to get her man off the hook. She hadn't told him that the police suspected him of the murder because it was only a rumor passed along by Sam Zimmerman. And she hoped it wouldn't happen. But maybe he should be warned. After a few moments, she turned back. "Okay. You're right. I'm curious."

"I was hoping you would be."

Veronica sat again, this time hooking her high heels on the lowest bar of his bed. "So you think I should look into this?"

"Who better? You're working on the movie. You're around all of them. And you've got a dad who used to be in the F.B.I."

"Boy, that's the lamest excuse I've ever heard."

"Best I could do." He managed a thin smile. "I'm wounded, you know."

"Okay. I'll do what I can. But remember, buster, I'm doing it for you, not for Angela's memory."

"Whatever works."

"Where's the copy of the deposition?"

"I had it in my inside jacket pocket when I took her back to the hotel. It's probably still there." He gestured toward the small closet in the room.

She walked to the closet, pulled out his jacket, went through all the pockets, and turned to ask him, "Any more bright ideas, Parrish?"

"It's gone?"

"Uh-huh."

"They must have grabbed it. Shit!"

"Where do you suggest I start *my* investigation?" She gave it a sarcastic twist. "Any ideas?"

"No. Except that there are several people working on *Perfect Casting* who were involved in *Slasher Three*. Angela mentioned the stunt coordinator, Adrian somebody. . . ."

"Adrian Bell."

"Yeah. And the director and production manager and—"

"And the screenwriter, and her stunt double, and half the crew. Think we could narrow this down a little?"

"Look, are you going to take this seriously, or not?" There was a slight edge to his voice. "Angela seemed to distrust the stunt guy. That's where you can start. Nose around a little on the job and see what you hear."

"I don't hear with my nose, Parrish." When he didn't laugh, she leaned forward and touched his cheek. "It was a joke. Lighten up. I'm sorry. I'm just tired and giddy." She ran the tips of her fingers up to his forehead and through the little bit of his curly hair not covered by the bandage. "I am taking this seriously. I'll do what I can. In the meantime, is there anything you can do to protect yourself here?"

He nodded toward the closet again. "Why don't you get my gun. I'll keep it under the pillow."

"You're out of luck, Charlie. The police have it."

"Oh, yeah. Of course. They must have taken it for ballistics tests since I killed the doorman."

She smiled uneasily. "Yeah. That's probably it."

He raised the arm that didn't have a tube attached and said, "C'mere, Vee."

She went back to the side of the bed and kissed him.

He wrapped his one free arm around her neck.

As she pulled away from him, he stared at her. "Now it's you. Now there's something . . . Is there something you're not telling me?"

"What do you mean?" She couldn't meet his gaze, looking instead at the bandage on his head.

"Something's not flying with both wings here. What do you know you're not telling me?"

"Nothing." She stood, walked away, and grabbed her purse from the other chair.

"Don't bullshit me, Slate. How's that go? 'You've worn my pajama tops too often to keep me in the dark.' What aren't you telling me?"

"Jesus! Can't you even make up your own dialogue?" She turned and smiled at him. "Are you going to beat it out of me?"

"No." He sighed. "I'm still a little weak for that."

"Well, if you must know, I'm still pissed that you had dinner with Angela." She glared at him. "Especially because you took her to our favorite restaurant."

"I'm sorry."

"And there's more." She returned to the chair by his bed. "The police think you killed Angela."

"Me? How the hell could . . . I pumped a couple of shots into the doorman and got knocked out. They'll figure that out when they check his body and my gun. I saw him fall. I couldn't have missed. I didn't kill her, Vee."

"You know that. I know that. But they found Angela dead at one end of that hall and you with a gun in your hand at the other end. There was no one else there."

He stared at her.

"That's why I agreed to look into the whole mess," she went on. "Because I don't want you to take the fall for this." She bit her lip and thought, but didn't say, *Unless you did do it.*

David looked steadily at her. "That's one of the things I love most about you, Vee. You care about what's fair. You care about the truth."

"I care about *you*." She touched his hand. "Before you nominate me for sainthood, let me tell you why I'm doing this. I want to find the people who killed Angela before they get a chance to kill you. You mean more to me than truth, justice, and your ex-wife put together. I'm doing it for you." She kissed the tip of her finger and touched it to his cheek. "And I'm doing it for us."

CHAPTER FOURTEEN

VERONICA WAS SITTING AT HER DESK, HALF DRESSED, EATING a bowl of instant oatmeal and trying to punch in her father's number on the phone with the unwanted assistance of Rum Tum Tugger. It was a quarter to ten on Monday morning and she was running late for work at the Don CeSar, but she wanted to do something constructive toward clearing David of Angela's murder.

"Hello?" Her father sounded wide awake.

"Hi, Daddy. How're you feeling?"

"Fine, Ronnie. How's David doing now that he's out of the coma? I saw another story about it on 'Entertainment Tonight.' "

"He's still weak and they're planning a bunch of tests, but at least he's alive." She put down the cereal bowl, grabbed her brush, and started brushing her hair with her one free hand. "Reason I called, I wanted you to hear it from me before it hits the news today. The police up here think David killed Angela."

"The hell you say!"

"I don't know all the details, but it looks like she was killed with his gun."

"I don't believe it."

"Neither do I. I'm trying to find out what really happened so I can get him off the hook."

"That would be best left to a good attorney, Ronnie. I know of a fellow in Tampa who's—"

"No attorneys. At least not yet. I've got to do some digging first. That's the other reason I called. I wondered if you could come up Saturday and go to Pass-A-Grille with me, snooping around a little at the bars and restaurants."

Archie paused a beat. "Well, honey, I'd like to, but I'm afraid Barbara and I have made plans. We're driving over to Orlando Saturday afternoon. We have reservations at the Walt Disney World Contemporary Hotel for the weekend. She has to meet with some out-of-town people on this CircusLand theme-park deal she's doing. She invited me along and . . . well, we've been planning it for . . ."

"That's okay, Daddy. I understand." She wondered if he could hear the lie in her voice. "It's okay. I'll figure out something else."

"I'm really sorry, Ronnie, it's just that—"

"No problem. I really understand. Honestly." She felt like checking her nose to see if it was growing. "Look, I'm late for work. I'll call you later in the week."

"Okay. Take care of yourself. Give my love to David."

She hung up the phone and stared at her reflection in the blank screen of her computer. It was a new feeling sharing her father with another woman. A feeling she didn't much like.

In the lobby of the Don CeSar, they had spent the morning shooting the scene in which the character now played by Tracy Morgan had to bid good-bye to her boyfriend, played by Paul Haden. It was a complicated scene with two setups, some special lighting considerations, and a dozen hired extras and atmosphere people. As usual, Veronica's job was to keep

unwanted people out of camera range and to run errands for
Jon Vasta and Carla Jahns. .

She noticed that Tracy Morgan had apparently not been
able to establish any kind of rapport with her costar. After
each take, Tracy stood by herself off to the side, arms folded
in front of her, her head down. Each time, Adrian Bell would
break through the reverie without speaking, putting his arm
around her shoulders and giving her a hug.

Her costar, Paul Haden, on the other hand, would break
character the moment the lights were killed and start kidding
around with the crew. He appeared able to turn his acting on
and off like a light switch.

They had just finished what everyone hoped would be the
last take of the scene, and everyone was standing still for
room tone, the sound level recorded in each room so that
shots could be matched. After a few minutes, the silence
broke, and Jon Vasta conferred with the camera operator and
the script girl.

Veronica was listening to the gaffer, a young man in a
sleeveless "muscle" T-shirt and cutoffs, who was trying to
explain something to her about the lights.

"Okay," he said. "See, even though Florida is a right-to-
work state, this is a union shoot. So lights like those"—he
gestured at the lights in the lobby—"must be put up by the
electricians, or sometimes we call them lamp operators. I
have to ask for a particular lamp, like those HMI's over there,
and the electrician puts it up and turns it on, whenever I tell
him to."

"What's an HMI?" Veronica asked.

"High-intensity four-thousand- to six-thousand-watt carbon-
arc lamps that run on regular A.C. We bounced them off
those muslin sheets to give it a softer look. We're using HMI's
to reduce the contrast between the actors and the sunlight
coming in the doors and windows of the lobby."

"Is this man boring you?" Paul Haden appeared out of
nowhere and put his arm around Veronica, smiling at the
gaffer.

"No," Veronica said. "I'm learning a lot about lighting."

"Well, how about learning a lot about lunch?" He flashed his CinemaScope smile at her. "Will you join me?"

The gaffer laughed and walked away. Veronica just stammered, "Ah . . . I guess . . . if it's okay with Carla."

Haden kissed her cheek and whispered in her ear. "The fix is in with Carla. You're free for lunch." His hot breath against her ear made her tingle. How could she say no to lunch with the man *US* magazine had called "the hunk of the year"?

The cast and crew went downstairs to the Grand Ballroom, where an elaborate buffet lunch had been set up. Paul Haden told Veronica that, under the terms of their various union contracts, the crew got a half hour for lunch and the company would be charged penalties if they didn't get it on time. So they got it on time, every day. The actors could take more than thirty minutes.

After she had fixed her plate of Swedish meatballs, coleslaw, mashed potatoes, and a dinner roll, and grabbed an iced tea, Veronica sat at a table where Paul Haden had already joined Adrian Bell, the stunt coordinator, and a young man she had seen around the hotel but hadn't met. Tracy was sitting with Raynor Fitzhugh at a table with Jon Vasta.

"Hi. May I sit here?" Veronica asked, winking at Haden.

Bell turned to look at her, and his face altered into a smile. "Hey, babe. Sure. Have a seat."

As she sat, Bell introduced her to the others. "This is Vicki. . . ." He looked back at her. "I'm sorry. What was—"

"Veronica. Veronica Slate."

"Yeah, right. Guys, this is Veronica Slate." He motioned to the young man on the opposite side of the round table. "Meet Todd Keener. He's one of my boys."

Keener, a tall young man who looked to be in his early twenties, half stood and offered his hand, knocking over the single rose in a vase in the center of the table. "Ooops! I'm sorry. Hi."

"Typical stuntman," Paul Haden said, nodding toward Keener, who was busy putting the rose back into the vase and mopping up the spilled water with his napkin. "Veronica and I have already met." He gave her a sexy, conspiratorial smile. "Hello again."

"So how do you like working on a movie?" Adrian Bell asked.

She stuck her straw in her iced tea. "Like everybody says, it's half boredom and half busy as hell."

"Adrian always says stunt work is ninety-nine percent boredom and one percent intense fear," Keener said, looking expectantly at Bell for confirmation.

"Yeah. That's straight," Bell said, stabbing a tomato in his salad. "I was about Todd's age when I got started in it fifteen years ago. Was working for a custom car shop and riding motocross when I had time off. Jon Vasta came to town to make a low-budget biker film. What was the name of that mother?"

"*Choppers from Hell*," Paul Haden said. "Who can forget it? Almost as good as *Plan Nine from Outer Space*."

Veronica laughed at the mention of what most critics called the worst movie ever made. Neither Bell nor Keener reacted. But Haden sneaked his hand down under the table and put it on her bare leg just below where her shorts ended. She swallowed.

"Anyhow, Jon hired me to do a motorcycle gag. That got me hooked. I spent hours practicing instead of going to one of those quick-fix stunt schools. I'd practice day and night, doing high falls, trampoline jumps. I'd run cars and set up cones, driving through them over and over, because when you're doing a gag there's no time to think. It's all reaction."

She was having a great deal of difficulty thinking with Haden's warm hand on her knee, but she didn't want to move it because, frankly, it had been a long time since a man had done that to her in a public place and it felt good. "You like the work?" Veronica asked Bell, trying to appear interested. "You like being a daredevil thrill-seeker?"

"Actually, that's not what it's about. You talk to any professional stuntperson and they're gonna talk about preparation and safety, not cheap thrills."

"At least the money's good," Keener added.

"For some folks, yeah," Bell said. "There's maybe a thousand stuntmen and a couple hundred stuntwomen in Screen Actors Guild. Maybe half of them are working at all, and less than a hundred of them are making the real money."

"What do you call real money?" Paul Haden asked. He squeezed her leg, smiled at her, and removed his hand.

"I pull down a quarter of a million bucks a year, average. See, we all get paid the basic SAG rate of three hundred seventy-nine dollars a day," Bell told Veronica. "Then we get adjustments for each gag we do. We're talking from a hundred to a thousand bucks for driving a car, for example, and from twenty-five hundred to five thou for flipping it over. Like the jet-ski gag we're shooting tomorrow."

"The one you had to postpone from last week," Veronica said. Her mind was racing. She had been excited by the physical contact with Haden, and one voice in her head was yelling at her to cool it, while the other was saying, *Life is short. Enjoy.*

"Yeah. Me and Todd are each getting three thou for that. 'Cause of the danger involved." He grinned at Paul Haden, who was quietly eating his lunch. "We got to take care of the million-dollar baby here" he said without sarcasm. "He's too important to get hurt."

"So a stuntman or even an actor could get injured or killed," Veronica said. "Like Tony Victor on *Slasher Three*." She watched his eyes for a reaction, forcing herself to forget her pulsating libido for the moment.

Bell paused a beat, but covered it by taking a sip of his beer. "Yeah. I've ripped the ligaments in my shoulder and busted my knee. I've had broken ankles, wrists, and toes. It ain't no walk in the park. And I'm getting older. Time for the youngsters like Todd, here, to take over." He nodded at Keener, and something passed between their eyes.

Veronica pushed on. "Were you on the set the day Tony Victor was killed?"

Bell turned slowly to look at her. "Yeah. I was there. It was an accident. One of the extras apparently got a weapon with real ammunition. We still don't know how."

"Is it possible someone not connected with the picture was

there that day? Someone with a loaded gun who wanted Tony dead?"

"Anything's possible," Bell said, balling up his napkin and standing up to punctuate the statement. He leaned so close to Veronica that she could smell his spicy cologne and see the hair his open shirt revealed. "But it's best to leave the past alone. Think about the present. You know what I mean?" His emphasis was obvious. He held his pose a moment longer to make sure she got the idea, then started away.

"I gotta go, too," Keener said, standing up nervously and following his boss. "Nice meeting you."

"Oh, by the way." Bell stopped so suddenly Keener bumped into him like in a scene from a slapstick comedy. "I'm going to need your help when we shoot the jet-ski gag tomorrow."

"Fine," Veronica said.

As the two muscular men walked away, Paul Haden smiled at Veronica. "Great conversationalists, aren't they?"

"Yeah," she said, watching them leave the ballroom. "Why's Adrian so keyed up? I've never heard him talk so much."

"Probably had a pre-lunch snort. He's a noser."

She wasn't really surprised. She'd seen plenty of evidence of cocaine use among the crew members. But she couldn't shake the feeling that Bell was involved with Tony Victor's death. And the more she knew about Victor's death, the better her chances were of discovering who killed Angela. She focused on Haden again. "I've got a question for you, Paul. Would Adrian Bell stand to gain anything from Angela Mastry's death?"

"I don't know. The natural progression for a stuntman is from doing stunts to planning them, which is what he's doing now, to second-unit directing, which Jon has promised him on the next picture they do together. Angela didn't have anything to do with any of that."

"I'm just fishing," Veronica said, as she stood and grabbed her purse.

"However," Haden said, stopping her in her tracks, "Tracy Morgan certainly benefited from Angela's death. And

Tracy is Adrian Bell's chief lady. That could be a connection.''

"Yeah," Veronica said. "That certainly could." She looked at Jon Vasta's table, where Tracy Morgan was laughing, her blond hair shining, her eyes animated. Tracy had evidently gotten what she had always wanted. The question was, at what cost? The death of Angela Mastry?

Paul Haden stood and joined Veronica. He leaned in toward her ear and whispered, "Up in my room I've got some stills they shot the day Tony Victor was killed. Want to see them?''

Veronica laughed. "Stills or etchings?" Even though she sensed he had more than still photographs in his room, Veronica said yes with only a moment's hesitation.

In the elevator on the way to the fourth floor, Haden took Veronica in his arms and kissed her with even more passion than that day on the beach. She melted. It was if he had read her mind. One of her great naughty fantasies had always been to make love in a moving elevator. Kissing Paul Haden was a start.

As they worked their way in the door of his room, slowed by the fact that they were attached at the lips, Veronica glowed with excitement. Paul Haden certainly lived up to his screen image when it came to tenderness. As he eased her onto his bed her mind reeled. Spurts of guilt were sparring with flashes of pleasure. Ultimately, her head won the battle. She pushed him away and said, with as much conviction as she could muster, "No."

Haden sat up, and a slow smile came over his face. His eyes betrayed disbelief and amusement. "Did you say no?"

Veronica swallowed and nodded. "Right. I'm sorry."

"I'm not going to force you." He laughed. "I don't have to." He shook his head. "You said no. That's great."

Veronica sat up. "I'm flattered and all, but it . . .''

The moment was split down the middle by the ringing of the phone. "Sorry, Carla," he said into the phone. "I'll be down in ten minutes.''

He hung up and looked at Veronica, who was trying to get

around him to put her feet on the floor. He stood and walked to the door. "I gotta go, darlin'."

"I know," she murmured. "So do I. I've got a job to do, too." She walked to his side and touched his cheek. "Look, don't be offended. You're very handsome. Any woman would . . ." She stared at her hands. "Well, you know. Trouble is"—she lifted her eyes to meet his—"I'm just too practical for my own good sometimes."

Haden smiled, kissed her gently on the cheek, and said, "It's okay. Just don't tell the *National Enquirer*, okay?"

"What about the stills? Were there any?"

The expression on his face answered her question. They left the room and headed for the elevator, walking side by side but distant. Veronica knew what she had done, or hadn't done, was right for her. But she also knew the experience hadn't been a total waste. It had built her confidence. It had reawakened her awareness of her own femininity. And it had been a nice way to spend a half hour.

CHAPTER FIFTEEN

"HI. I CAN'T STAY LONG. I'VE GOT TO GET HOME, TAKE A shower, stop by Max's video store, and get to work." Veronica kissed David, wondering if he could detect the scent of another man on her body. She sat in the chair beside his bed. "What happened with the police this morning?"

He switched off the TV and put the remote on the table. "You were right. They think I killed Angie."

"That's crazy," she said with less passion than she had intended. She worried whether her cheeks were glowing the way they often did after making out. Her sense of guilt was so intense that she almost wished she had done something to deserve it.

"Maybe it's not crazy," David said.

"What do you mean?"

"According to the investigator I talked to, a guy named Cross, the autopsy shows she was killed by two gunshot wounds, both in the chest, from a thirty-eight-caliber Smith and Wesson. Probably my gun. He's sending it to the F.B.I.

149

lab in Washington. That means he's serious. He's trying to build a tight case." He sighed. "She must have been killed with my gun, Vee."

She had finally turned all her attention to what he was saying. "Then it must have been a freak accident."

"Or a miracle. I fired only two shots. Right at the guy at the end of the hall. I saw him. I know I didn't shoot her."

"Could they have grabbed your gun, reloaded, and shot her?"

"I don't know. Cross wouldn't tell me how many rounds had been fired."

"Did they find the body of the guy you shot?"

"They don't even believe he ever existed."

"Shit!" She stood and paced to the window. "What kind of two-bit—"

"It's not their fault. The St. Pete Beach detectives are very competent. Hell, I'd probably reach the same conclusion if I were investigating the case."

She turned to look at him. "What possible motive could you have to kill Angela?"

He sighed and rested his head on the pillow. "That's one I haven't figured out. They seem to think they've got something, but Cross wouldn't tell me much. We need to find a witness, Vee. We need to find someone who saw the van or heard the shots or saw them take off afterward. It's my only hope of beating this. We've got to prove there were two other guys."

"Okay. It's my turn to get busy. This weekend, I'll do some bar-hopping at Pass-A-Grille. I'm going to talk to Tracy Morgan tomorrow—"

"Who's she?"

"The actress who took over Angela's part. They were old friends. She got the role when Angela was killed."

"It's a motive, but who'd be crazy enough to kill one actress so another could get a part?"

"I don't know. I talked to the stunt coordinator today. He worked on the film set where Tony Victor was killed. He didn't seem eager to discuss it. And I talked a little to Paul Haden." She almost choked at the sin of omission. She had done much more than talk. She felt as if her afternoon romp was engraved all over her face. "I'm going to stop by VideoMax and have a talk with Max on my way to work," she said, a little too quickly.

"So you said. Why?"

"Max is the biggest film freak I know. He can help me find out who the director was who could have killed Tony Victor. A guy named Alan Smithee. If I can find him, I may be able to unravel this." She was eager to go, to get away from the paranoia and guilt in which she was swimming.

David stared at the ceiling for a moment. "Vee, there's something you've got to know."

"Yeah? What?" Had he figured it out? Had Paul Haden called and challenged him to a duel with her as the prize? Was it that obvious that she had been making out in an elevator with a movie star since last they met?

He kept staring at the ceiling, as if putting together the words. "There was a time the night Angie and I went out to dinner when I did want to start all over again with her, just like you said. I have to admit she looked great."

A wave of uneasiness swept over her. "So? What did you decide? Were you going to try again?"

"Does that matter now?"

"It must, or you wouldn't have told me."

He turned to face her. "By the end of the evening, when she was drunk again, as usual, I was angry. With her. With myself for even thinking things had changed. I hated her for what she had put me through years ago and what she was putting me through again. So, in other words, the answer is that I decided it would never work between us. I just thought you should know that I am human. That I did consider it."

"Yeah," she said, her face impassive. "Well, I'm just delighted you saw fit to share that with me."

"I know it erodes your faith in me. But, one thing . . ."

"What?"

His face was tight, his eyes misting over. "I did not kill her." Then, in a smaller voice, he added, "If I did, I didn't mean to do it. I didn't know it."

As if she had been holding her breath for a week, Veronica exhaled and came closer to kiss him on the cheek. "I know you didn't. Somehow, I'll help you prove you didn't. And I forgive you for being seduced by a movie star.'' She laughed nervously, realizing that she was forgiving herself for exactly the same thing. But then, she had begun to rationalize that the important thing to remember was that she hadn't really made love with Paul Haden. Being seduced was forgivable. Lusting in the heart. But making love to him? She couldn't have. She loved David too much.

By seven-thirty Monday night, Veronica had raced home, fed the cats, changed clothes, checked her messages, tossed away half her mail, and started across the Howard Frankland Bridge to Max Wilkinson's video store on Kennedy Boulevard in Tampa.

The dark water of Tampa Bay surrounding the bridge sparkled with reflections from the lights of Tampa, St. Petersburg, and the stars above. She was on the middle one of the three bridges connecting Clearwater and St. Pete to Tampa. To her left about three miles away across Tampa Bay, she saw the moving reds and whites on the Courtney Campbell Causeway. On the right, perhaps five miles distant, was the long ribbon of the Gandy Bridge.

The long bridges of Tampa Bay were a form of therapy for Veronica. Although she was listening to the smooth sounds of WDUV, the area's top beautiful-music station, she was thinking. Thinking how strange it was that she was trying to help David Parrish, a man she hadn't even known a year ago. And thinking how strange it was that she had come within a heartbeat of making love with one of America's number-one box-office attractions, a man she hadn't even known two weeks ago.

There had been a time, immediately after her divorce from Sam Treace, when she had blocked men from her life. There had been a time when she would have rejected any sort of advance from even as handsome and exciting a man as Paul Haden. But her attitude toward men had changed in the last decade.

She had been a teen-ager when she married Sam Treace. Better had turned to worse in less than a year. She'd left him and moved to Houston, and richer had turned immediately to poorer.

It was in Houston, Veronica remembered, that she gained a kind of insular strength and courage born of necessity. Starting as a secretary at KTRH Radio, she began to work her way up to what she had decided she wanted to be, a talk-show host.

Houston in 1975 was a glamorous, glitzy cow town with pretzel-like highways everywhere. But Veronica might as well have been living in a convent, so strong was her resolve. She worked hard at making a living, and ignored the young newly rich oilmen who pursued her. She kept to herself, read a lot, ate TV dinners, and—to feed her soul—acquired an interest in the classical music she heard on KLEF. Sometimes she'd go to the glitzy Galleria mall and watch the ground-floor ice skaters from the third level. Some days she would sit on the roof outside the window of her single room in the shadow of Rice University, listening to the school's marching band practice and missing the only thing she had really liked about her high school days: the band. Where was her French horn now that she needed it?

Veronica realized that David would probably not have liked her in 1975. She had been single-minded, determined, and not much fun. But it worked. In only a year she was a news announcer at KTRH. A year later, the offer came from WSUN in St. Petersburg, Florida. As a news reporter at WSUN in the late seventies, working for a talented news director with the improbable name of Derrick Janisz, Veronica was much too busy to get serious about a man, and much too serious about radio to get busy looking for one.

Veronica often thought the drive across Tampa Bay's long bridges should be tax-deductible, like visits to a psychologist. She seemed to ruminate about her life and her problems every time she drove their long, lonely spans. Sometimes she could even reach solutions to her problems on the bridges.

She glided her blue '83 Honda onto the first exit on the Tampa side of the Howard Frankland Bridge, and headed down Kennedy Boulevard to VideoMax, in a strip center a few blocks east of Channel 13's television studios. As she passed the Krispy Kreme doughnut store just beyond the TV station, the one where she'd met David seven months ago, she thought of him and sighed.

Her father once told her that God has to shake one up sometimes to get one's attention. In 1978, when her mother was killed, she was shaken enough to overcome her selfishness and care for someone else. That someone else was her father.

In the hollow months after Elizabeth Slate's death, Veronica and Archie forged a bond stronger than they'd ever had. That bond gave her the courage to go to college at twenty-five and the confidence to fall in love with Danny Keaton, a handsome young radio announcer who loved her in his own way. Danny was killed the past Thanksgiving, the victim of something bigger than both of them, once again tainting her life with violence.

Now, it was starting all over again. Violence against someone she loved. She liked to think she was too intelligent to perceive a pattern, but often it felt like a plot to take away the people she really cared about. As if loving her could be deadly. Could that be why she resisted any possibility of getting married again? Was it a morbid fear that her husband would die?

There she was again trying to solve a real-life mystery, trying to figure out who killed a woman she barely knew to help a man she'd known for less than a year. She was determined that, this time, she'd fight to keep someone she loved from being taken away from her. She nodded to herself as she pulled into a space in front of VideoMax, as if to confirm her determination. But even as she did, a flash of the forbidden pleasure she'd shared with Paul Haden made her wonder just whom she really loved, and how much.

Veronica always enjoyed visiting VideoMax, because she liked Maxwell Penrose Wilkinson, video dealer by day and her talk-show producer by night.

"Hey, Vee!" Max greeted her the moment she walked in the door. He wore jeans and a red Tampa Bay Bandits T-shirt. Just to his left, a tape of what looked like *Ghostbusters* was playing on a big-screen TV. A huge white marshmallow man wearing a blue sailor hat was attacking a building.

"Hi. Thanks for hanging around. I thought we should talk here, 'cause this is where you keep your reference books."

"That's cool." His smile was dazzling. "Follow me."

Max nodded at the young girl behind the counter, and led the way back to a small office completely papered in movie posters. A small metal desk contained a portable TV, a GE VCR, and wires and black boxes. One entire wall was filled with bookshelves on which books and videotapes shared space. There was room for only two metal chairs among the boxes that littered the floor.

"Sorry it's a mess, but messy office means ordered mind," Max said, smiling and offering her the other chair as he sat at the desk. "So what can I do for you?"

"Well . . ."

"Wait. Wait." He held up his hands and flashed his one-hundred-watt smile. "Before we talk serious, we gotta talk trivia. I've been saving a couple for you. . . ." They had been playing an ongoing movie trivia game since they first met. "What movie from the sixties featured the first major performances of several actors who went on to become stars? The actors were James Coburn, George Kennedy, and Walter Matthau."

"That's easy. One of my ten favorite films of all time. *Charade,* 1963. Cary Grant and Audrey Hepburn starred. Stanley Donen directed. Script by Peter Stone. Music by Henry Mancini."

"Very good." Max gave her a thumbs-up sign. "You get the gold star."

"What? No free tape?"

"What would you do with a tape? You don't have a VCR."

"I know." She faked a sorrowful look. "I'm so ashamed. I feel so cheap. The whole rest of the world has a VCR." She put her hand up as if to stop him. "But don't try to sell me one. I'm still paying for my computer."

"Okay. Just promise you'll buy it from me when you do buy one." He held up one ebony finger. "Just one more.

Then we can get serious. Okay? In the movie *The Graduate,* how many times is Mrs. Robinson's first name mentioned?"

"Jeez! Max, that was almost twenty years ago. Let me guess. Maybe three times?"

"Hey, I gotcha! Gotcha! Gotcha! Gotcha!" With difficulty, he reined in his smile. "Her first name was never mentioned."

"That's a good one. I'll remember that."

"Okay. You paid your dues. What can I do to help you?"

"Like I told you on the phone, they think David killed Angela Mastry."

"That's bullshit."

"I know, but there's some other stuff involved: a murder on a movie set last fall—remember Tony Victor?—adultery, some drug dealing, a dead attorney in L.A."

"Sounds like a great idea for a picture."

"Yeah. Anyhow, what I need is this: I found out that the director of a low-budget film made about ten years ago may have hired someone to kill Tony Victor because he was allegedly screwing the director's wife. This director may even be involved in the death of Angela Mastry, because she knew how they killed Tony Victor. I need to track this guy down."

"So you want to know how to reach him?"

"Yeah. Well, actually, anything would be a help. I thought you could look up a couple of his films and maybe get the name of the studios involved, and I could trace him that way."

"Good idea." He stood and worked his way through the boxes to the bookshelves, where he took down a big reference book. "Give me a couple of his pictures if you know them."

"Okay." She dug into her purse for the notes she'd taken after her first conversation with Paul Haden. "Here we go." She read from her notes. "He directed *Death of a Gunfighter,* starring Richard Widmark, in 1967; a Burt Reynolds picture called *Fade-In* a year later; and *Let's Get Harry* just recently. Paul said they were all losers. But the one he did with Tony Victor was called *Dead of Day.*"

Max sat and started thumbing through the reference book. "So what's the guy's name?"

"Oh, I'm sorry." She checked the paper. "Alan Smithee. Double *e* at the end. Alan is with an *a*."

Max stopped short, looked at Veronica's serious expression, then burst into laughter.

"What?" she said with a trace of resentment. "What's so funny?"

"I'm sorry," Max began, still chuckling. "I'm not . . . I'm not laughing *at* you. I'm laughing *near* you. It's just that . . . it's just that Alan Smithee is a phony name. It's not a real guy." He finally straightened up. "I mean, it's a real guy, but it's actually a *bunch* of real guys."

"I hope you're going to explain this," Veronica said with the air of someone who wasn't in on the joke.

Max finally sobered up and closed the book in his lap. "Okay. It's been a tradition for years that when an actor doesn't want his name attached to a film for one reason or another, he's billed as George Spelvin, or Georgina Spelvin if it's a woman. By the same token, when directors want their names removed from a film, the Directors Guild replaces it with the name Allen Smithee, with two *l*s and an *e* or with one *l* and an *a*."

"Are you serious?"

"Yes. The Guild came up with it in 1967, when Don Siegel replaced the original director of *Death of a Gunfighter*. I should have caught it when you mentioned that film. Richard Widmark had ruined the picture with his ego problems, and neither director wanted his name on the film. The Guild chose Smithee because Smith was too obvious and some real-life members had that name. Another example was *The Challenge*, a TV movie starring Darren McGavin and Broderick Crawford. Oh, yeah, Vee. Lots of name directors have hidden behind the name Alan Smithee. John Frankenheimer did. Michael Ritchie gave up his credit as producer of *Student Bodies* to Alan Smithee. Jud Taylor requested Smithee for *Fade-In* in 1968, and again in 1980 for *City of Fear*. *Let's Get Harry* should have also tipped me off. I just read about that one last week. Stuart Rosenberg asked them to dump it into the Smithee bin after somebody screwed up the film."

"Yeah. Paul Haden told me about that one the other day.

But he didn't seem to know that Alan Smithee was a made-up name.''

Max stood and returned the big book to the shelf. "Looks to me like the only way to track down the right Alan Smithee is to contact the Directors Guild. I'll give you the address and phone number. What did you say the movie was?"

"*Dead of Day.*"

"I can at least look that up and see what year it was released. That might help." He grabbed a different book and started thumbing through the pages. "Here we go. *Dead of Day.* Released 1975. Independent film. Limited distribution. Sold to cable 1979. No cassette." He looked up. "Must be a real dog if it hasn't even gone to tape."

"Or maybe someone didn't want it released for some other reason," Veronica said darkly. "Maybe something happened on that shoot that connects with Tony Victor ending up dead."

"Watch it, Vee. We've got all the conspiracy theories we need. It may have just been a bad film."

"Maybe. But I doubt it."

David was sitting up in his hospital bed trying to answer the questions of the St. Petersburg Beach police detective who had talked to him before.

"As I was saying, Detective Parrish, we're not going to charge you yet, because, frankly, just between us, the moment we charge you we become responsible for your hospital bill."

"God forbid."

"Now, I don't want you feeling like you beat the rap. It's gonna take six to eight weeks for the F.B.I. lab to report on your gun. But I've got a strong feeling—"

"Yeah. I know. That it will be a match."

"And yet you say you didn't shoot her?"

"I don't think so."

"Well. That's a little less sure than what you said last time." He flipped back several pages in his notebook. "Says here, and I quote: 'I didn't kill her.' Now, you say you don't *think* so. So what's the straight story, Detective Parrish?"

"I fired twice at the man I told you about. The one who

had posed as a doorman back at the hotel. I saw him fall before someone clubbed me. That's all I know."

"Is it possible this 'man' you saw was actually your ex-wife? Maybe it was dark in that hallway."

"It wasn't," David snapped. "It was fairly bright from the streetlamp across the street. It was almost as clear as day."

"Well, let me just make this one suggestion: If you make a full confession, the state might work with you a little. I mean, heat of passion, self-defense, some kind of bullshit like that. Maybe you'd get life."

"Are you insane? Aren't you even going to investigate any other possibility? What about the guy driving the van? What the hell have you done to find him?"

"To be honest with you, we don't really believe there was another guy."

"What about the doorman? You said you found the real doorman tied up in a closet. How the hell did that happen?"

"Not related. Didn't even take his uniform. Simple case of burglary. A couple of rooms were broken into that night. We figure the perp tied him up to keep him out of the way." Cross fingered his belt. "It would be a lot easier to believe you if we could find the body of this man you say you shot. Or even the other guy, the one who allegedly hit you. Mighty mysterious that they'd both just vanish. See, at the scene we didn't find anything but some bullet holes and bloodstains. No van. No two guys. Nothing."

"So you come up with the idea that I killed Angela?"

"Seems simple to us. You had a fight with your ex-wife. Coerced her to go to that old house on Pass-A-Grille. Blew her away. Fell and hit your head. Probably not the smartest way to do it, but then murder ain't a smart thing to do."

David closed his eyes. "So are you taking me to jail?"

"Well, not exactly. Your boss over at Tampa P.D. is suspending you till it all gets straight, but—at least for the moment—I'm posting a guard at your door." He smiled. "Just standard procedure, you know."

"Don't tell me. Let me guess. You don't want me to leave town, right?"

"You may think this is funny, Parrish. I don't."

"I hate to ruin good detective work, but have you given any thought to why I'd want to kill my ex-wife? A woman I haven't seen in seven years?"

"For the money, I'd imagine."

"What are you talking about?"

"Now I suppose you're gonna pretend you don't know about the *in*surance." He said it like a Florida cracker, with the stress on the first syllable.

"What insurance?"

"Well, Detective Parrish, your former wife had a quarter-of-a-million-dollar life-insurance policy on herself—taken out just two months ago—and you were the one and only beneficiary. To me, seems like a damned good reason to kill an ex-wife."

CHAPTER SIXTEEN

VERONICA SAT IN THE CASTING INTERVIEW ROOM ON THE third floor of the Don CeSar, the room where she had been interviewed by Jon Vasta just over a week earlier. For the past three hours she had helped Carla Jahns interview local actresses trying for a small part as Paul Haden's date in the big party scene. A part she would gladly have taken herself. She had to skip her usual visit to the hospital and simply call David and say a hurried "I love you" in order to get to the hotel in time.

Now, with Carla gone and everyone at lunch, Veronica was finally able to get to the phone and call the Directors Guild in Los Angeles. It was after nine Tuesday morning there.

A pleasant woman answered after the second ring. "Good morning. Directors Guild. How may I direct your call?"

"I'm trying to find out . . . Well, I'm . . ." Trying to put it together, she realized how strange her request might seem. "There was a movie that I know was directed by a man named Alan Smithee. And I know that Alan Smithee is not a real director's name, and I'm trying to find out who the real director was on this film.''

"I can put you through to Agency, but I don't know if they'll be able to help you.''

"Okay. Well, it's worth a try.''

"Line's busy. Do you wish to hold?''

"Yes." Veronica was eager to find out who the director was who quite possibly had had Tony Victor killed, but the longer the silence on the phone continued the more she worried. She was making the call on Mira Loma's dedicated line, and the long-distance charge would show up somewhere, sometime.

Finally, a ring and another woman's voice. "Agency.''

"Yes. I'm trying to find out the name of the director of a film called *Dead of Day*, released in 1975. And the director—''

The woman interrupted. "*Dead of Day*? Okay, one moment.''

"No. Wait. The director credit on it was Alan Smithee, and I know that Alan Smithee is not a real name. It's one you use for people who don't want to put their name on a film. So I'm trying to find out who the real director was.''

"I don't know if I can tell you that. Hold on, please.''

"Okay." Veronica looked at the closed door, expecting someone to burst in at any moment. She had switched off the lights, and the dust particles floating in the sunlit beams from the windows had taken on an almost sinister appearance. She heard traffic noises from the street three stories below. She half expected to hear someone break down the door and demand to know what she was doing on the phone.

"Hello? In my list here for *Dead of Day* the director is listed as Alan Smithee.''

"I know," Veronica said. "But that's not his real name.''

"What is his real name?''

She felt like George Burns talking to Gracie Allen. "That's what I'm trying to find out.''

"I'm sorry. That's all I have on the list here.''

Veronica slammed the phone down. "Damn!" She glanced at the clock. It was a quarter to one. In fifteen minutes the auditions would resume and Carla would be back. She had to try one other possibility. She dialed VideoMax in Tampa.

"Max, this is Vee. I struck out with the Directors Guild. They say the director's name *is* Alan Smithee."

"They must be protecting his identity. Yeah, that makes sense. Tell you what. I've got a couple friends in the video trade out there. Let me make some calls. I'll let you know what I find out when I see you tonight."

By late afternoon, the casting was done and Veronica had been assigned to the beach, where the second-unit director, Chuck Hollenbeck, was shooting what Adrian Bell called the jet-ski gag, a complicated stunt centering around a mysterious young man who shot a guest and escaped on a jet ski, only to be pursued by Paul Haden on another jet ski.

Naturally, Haden wasn't going to ride it himself. Unlike some of the new breed of tough-guy actors in Hollywood, Haden still protected his beautiful face and his million-dollar presence by turning over the stunt work to the pros. It wasn't narcissism. It was insurance, what with the high cost of losing a star even for a day or two. The company had already lost thousands of dollars when Angela had died. It would be taking no chances.

Todd Keener would be on the first jet ski, with Adrian Bell posing as Paul Haden on the chase jet ski. It was a complicated scene that would take several afternoons to shoot. Aside from the camera on the beach, another was set up on the roof of the Don CeSar, and a third was in a helicopter, which would be flying overhead. Todd Keener and Chuck Hollenbeck were conferring. Adrian Bell was doing a last-minute safety check of the jet skis. According to the list Veronica had checked after lunch, Jon Vasta was in the penthouse shooting a scene with Raynor Fitzhugh. Carla Jahns had left after lunch for a trip to Tampa, seeking props for the film. She had complained to Veronica before she left that *Perfect Casting* wasn't a large enough production to have what set decorators called a "swing gang" to do it for her.

Since she wasn't in the scene, Tracy Morgan was sitting in a lounge chair by the pool in a pink one-piece bathing suit with tiny black dots across the top, eyes closed, soaking up the sun, with the script open on the table next to her.

Veronica went over and sat beside her, wishing she was in a bathing suit instead of the shorts, T-shirt, and Adidas she wore. "Beautiful day, huh?"

Tracy sat up and shaded her eyes with her hand. "Oh, hi, Vee." She reached down beside her and grabbed a pair of sunglasses, putting them on as she closed the script and sat up a bit more in the chair. "Are you working the jet-ski gag?"

"Yeah. If they ever get it rigged." Veronica smiled. "Listen, I never did get to tell you I'm happy for you getting the part and all."

"Thanks. I always told Jon I could handle a lead. He never seemed to think so until now."

"Too bad it had to happen because of a tragedy."

"What?" She frowned. "Oh, yeah. Angela." She took a plastic bottle of No-Ad tanning lotion from a big straw bag with pink ribbons woven through it, and began spreading the white lotion slowly over her slim thighs. "It's really terrible. I didn't know David, of course, but from what Angela had told me, he doesn't seem the type to—"

"He didn't kill her, Tracy." She glanced over her shoulder. No one seemed to be paying any attention. "I know it."

Tracy stopped short and slowly, deliberately screwed the cap back on the lotion, never taking her eyes from Veronica. "You know it? What do you mean?" She returned the plastic bottle to her bag. "Do you know who killed her?"

"No. But I'm trying to find out. I think you can help me."

"Sure." Tracy's eyes darted around at the technicians busy at work on the beach. "You know I'd be glad to help any way I can to find Angela's killers. She was my best friend."

"Great. Here's what I need." Veronica told Tracy of the mysterious director who was probably behind Tony Victor's death. "I tried the Directors Guild and they wouldn't tell me his real name. I thought maybe you'd know someone who worked on *Dead of Day*. Someone who could tell me who the real director was."

"Nineteen seventy-five? That was before I got into the

business. But I'll ask around. See what I can do.'' Tracy sat up and threw her shapely legs over the edge of the chair. "I better get inside before I turn into a lobster." She stood, pulled on the back of her pink bathing suit, and grabbed her straw bag. "If David didn't do it, what motive would anyone else have to kill Angela?"

Veronica stood, casting a large shadow over Tracy. "I guess I'll find that out when I find out who did it."

A few minutes after Tracy left, Chuck Hollenbeck was finally ready to start filming the jet-ski scene. Keeping in two-way radio communication with the camera operators on the roof, on the beach, and in the rented copter whirling overhead, Hollenbeck used the bullhorn in his other hand to say, "Quiet, please."

Veronica, as usual, was supposed to keep onlookers from getting too close. She had pulled off her shoes and socks and stood ankle-deep in soft, white sand, helping to protect the beach's northern perimeter from strolling tourists who managed to miss the hurricane fence and the large DO NOT ENTER sign.

Hollenbeck said, "Stand by. Roll cameras." He glanced at the sound man. "Roll sound."

The sound man started his Nagra recorder and said, "Speed."

Hollenbeck said, "Mark it."

A production assistant snapped his clapstick, the secret to synchronizing picture and sound in the editing room, in front of the main camera on the beach. The cameras on the roof and in the helicopter didn't need to be slated because they were shooting without sound.

When Hollenbeck shouted, "Action!," Todd Keener ran down onto the beach from behind the snack bar and started the jet ski. He glanced nervously back past the camera at the unseen Paul Haden, and pushed the jet ski out into the water.

Just as Todd cleared the beach and started to race across the waves, Adrian Bell, dressed identically to Paul Haden and wearing a small wig that resembled Haden's hair, ran to the other jet ski, started it up in shallow water, jumped on, and gunned it out into the Gulf toward Todd Keener, who was at least a couple of hundred yards farther out. Out of camera range off to the left and right were two unmarked yachts, manned by off-duty Coast Guard men hired to keep that section of the Gulf clear of unauthorized boats until the scene was shot.

Veronica stood, shading her eyes with her hand, her weight on one foot, the other tucked behind it. Keener was out in the Gulf where there were medium-high waves. Bell was a couple of hundred feet behind, leaning low over his jet ski.

From where she was on the beach, Veronica could barely see Todd, but the helicopter was directly over him, shooting aerial footage. A wave tossed his jet ski up a little, and she noticed that Adrian seemed to have slowed down. He was still quite a distance behind the young stuntman.

Suddenly, without warning, just as another wave crested beneath it, Todd's jet ski exploded in a small ball of orange fire.

There was an eerie silence, as a hundred people held their breath. Then all hell broke loose.

The copter circled where the explosion had taken place. The nearest of the Coast Guard-piloted yachts headed toward the spot. Adrian Bell closed in on the area and circled it. Chuck Hollenbeck yelled to keep the cameras running. ''I don't want another *Twilight Zone*,'' she heard him say before he turned off his bullhorn. Veronica watched the frantic scene, wondering if Todd Keener was the victim of an accident or murder. And if it was murder, why would someone kill him?

Tracy stood, looking at herself in the mirror of her room. She had stripped off her swimsuit and was regarding her own naked body on the way to the shower. Tracy enjoyed the sensual pleasure of being small, and soft, and beautiful. She cupped her breasts in her hands and tossed back her loose blond hair. Real blond hair. From her Swedish-American parents, not a bottle.

The sudden chirp of the telephone ruined her mood and made her jump. Tracy grabbed it. ''Yes?''

''Tracy, this is Liz. Just wanted you to know there was an accident with one of the jet skis.''

Tracy nodded. 'Oh, no,'' she said with more emotion in her voice than in her face. "Is Adrian all right?''

"Adrian's fine. Todd is dead.''

"Todd?'' She gasped. "Did you say Todd?''

"Yeah. Jon's suspended shooting for the rest of the day.''

"Jesus! I don't believe it!'' She dropped the phone to its cradle and sunk to the bed, shaking her head. This was getting out of hand. She didn't know who Adrian and Todd were working for, but it was evident that whoever it was had decided to cover all the tracks. Todd was dead. It was only a matter of time until Adrian would be killed. She could be next if someone realized what she knew.

Tracy went to the dresser and pulled a piece of Don CeSar stationery from a drawer. She opened her portable electric Smith-Corona typewriter and turned it on. She had come up with a plan.

"What do you mean she had an insurance policy? Why in the world would she name you as the beneficiary?'' Veronica was pacing by David's bedside, reeling at the latest news in what was beginning to look like either one hell of a frame or a true case of husband shooting wife for the money. What made her even more irritable was that David had waited until she told him everything about the jet-ski accident that had killed Todd Keener that afternoon before he even mentioned the insurance policy.

"It's worse than that,'' David said. "Detective Cross called this morning. They found her will. She left everything to me.''

"David.'' She sat rigidly on the chair by his bed. "If there's something about you and Angela that you're not telling me, I deserve to know. Don't wait until it's too late.'' She folded her arms across her chest. "I love you. But I can get over you.''

"Thanks for that vote of confidence,'' he said. "I hope you're on the jury. I'll probably get the chair.''

"I'm just trying to be practical, David.'' She glanced out the window at the deepening twilight. "We've known each other only six months.''

"Seven months. But who's counting?"

"Okay. Seven months. I'm not saying you weren't justified in killing her. Maybe there was a good reason. But you need to tell me the truth. I can only help if you tell me the truth."

"The truth is I didn't kill her. The truth is I didn't know anything about insurance and a will. That's the truth." He glared at her. "Jesus Christ, Vee! Whose side are you on?"

She stared at him for several moments, then tossed her hair and continued. "Okay. New business," she said, sitting by his bed and opening a folded piece of Don CeSar stationery.

"Aren't you going to answer my question?"

She ignored him. "I got an unsigned note in my box at the production office right before I left."

"I said, aren't you going to answer my question?"

In a tight, even voice, Veronica said, "Don't push it, David. I'm in no mood to talk about taking sides."

"What happened to 'doing it for us'?"

"I am doing it for us. But I'm also looking out for number one. I learned a long time ago that when it comes down to the bottom line, I am all I've really got."

"What the hell's wrong with you? Don't you believe me?"

"I said I don't want to answer that question right now. I don't want to say something I'm going to regret. Let's deal with the murder first. We can deal with our relationship later."

"If there is a later," David said softly.

"Here's what the note says: 'If you want to know how they killed Angela, see *F/X*.' "

"How they killed Angela? Who wrote that?" He grabbed the note from her hand. He saw that it was typed. "Oh." He read it. "F/X? What's that?"

"A movie that came out a few months ago about a special-effects guy. It's probably not out in cassette yet. And I doubt it's running. . . . Wait a minute. Where'd you put today's St. Pete *Times*?"

"On the floor. Over there."

She got up, grabbed the paper, and turned to the entertainment section. "Great!" she said. "It's at the Beach Theatre."

"I thought you said it was a couple months old."

"Yeah. Old enough for second-run houses." She peered at the ad. "Trouble is, it's only on at seven-thirty and nine-thirty. I'll have to wait till Saturday to see it." She looked sadly at him. "Do you realize what this means?"

"What?"

"Someone knows that you didn't kill Angela."

"Jesus Christ, Veronica! I keep telling you I didn't kill her. This insurance and the will—it's all got to be part of an elaborate setup. Someone's trying to frame me. I don't know why. I don't know how. But someone's setting me up."

"It does look that way," she said simply.

His eyes were frantic. "And the worst thing is, if we don't find out who and how they did it, I'm going to jail as soon as I'm out of the hospital. Dammit! I didn't kill her."

"I know." But even as she said it, she wished someone could convince her. There were so many reasons to doubt David. Why would someone go to so much trouble to frame David for Angela's murder?

CHAPTER SEVENTEEN

VERONICA SAT AT HER DESK, STILL IN THE PANTIES AND T-shirt she had slept in. Her headache was spreading to the sides of her head. All these days of trying to juggle two jobs and a couple of visits a day to David were beginning to drain her strength. She'd been making do on five hours' sleep a night. Six was usually her minimum. She waited, impatiently, while the phone in the production office rang. Finally, Liz answered.

"Hi, Liz. This is Veronica Slate. Can I talk to Carla?"

"Sure. Wait a minute."

The previous night Veronica had had a tough time concentrating on her show. Her callers were still interested in Libya, but she had begun to get a few asking about the strange goings-on over on the movie set. Two people—an actress and a stuntman—had died in less than a week. Almost too fantastic to be real life. Especially in St. Pete Beach, Florida.

"Carl Jahns. Can I help you?"

She altered her voice to sound the way she felt. "Hello,

Carla. This is Veronica. Can you possibly do without me today? I'm really feeling lousy.'' She hadn't lied like that since high school. Although her headache was still with her.

"Sure, baby. No sweat. We can work around you today. Hope you feel better.''

Veronica thanked her and hung up, feeling guilty and relieved at the same time.

She immediately punched in her father's number and waited while it rang five times. Then a click, and her father's recorded voice. "Hi. Archie Slate here. Only I'm *not* here. I'm out at the moment. Sorry I missed your call. There's a tone coming up and you can leave a message and your number when you hear it. Thanks.''

After the beep, she said, "Hi, Daddy. It's me. Just hoping I could talk you into coming up to see me before the weekend. Talk to you later.'' *He's probably out with Barbara Robinson,* she thought darkly.

One more try. She dialed Max Wilkinson's number at VideoMax. It took only a moment to talk him into going with her on a tour of Pass-A-Grille, the scene of the crime.

Since she couldn't go to see the movie *F/X* until Saturday night, and Max had been unable to locate anyone among his friends in Los Angeles who knew the identity of the Alan Smithee who'd made *Dead of Day,* poking around the scene of the crime seemed the only logical thing to do. She had wanted to do her snooping with her father by her side, but he was apparently too busy with his new lady friend. *Is there anything strange about being jealous of your father's girlfriend?* she wondered, as she dressed in jeans, Adidas, and a U.S.F. sweat shirt.

An hour later, Veronica and Max were driving along Pass-A-Grille Beach, looking for the mysterious old house David had told her about. They passed a small concrete block building painted blue. A sign identified it as the Hotel Castle.

It was a cloudy-bright day. Not much blue sky but lots of illuminated gray clouds. The sound of the surf mixed with various radios and tape players on the beach and in passing cars that—like Veronica's Honda—had the windows open.

Max wore jeans, a VideoMax T-shirt, and New Balance running shoes. As usual, he was smiling and talking at the same time. "I haven't been down here in probably ten years. It's really changed."

"David said the house was about halfway down Sixth Avenue, but there's no street sign."

"Then it must be this street here." Max pointed to the bare metal pole sticking out of the ground near a stop sign, a fire hydrant, and a telephone pole at the corner of a vacant lot.

She turned right and drove slowly down the street. It was there, on the left, just as David described it. An ugly old house. "You know something strange?" Veronica said. "I'm relieved that it's there. It's like proof that David's telling the truth."

Max turned his head. "You mean you had some doubts?"

"I hate to admit it. But, yeah. I mean, you think you really know someone. Then he goes off and has dinner with his ex-wife. And he's named in her will and on her insurance. The way he talked about her, the few times he did, I thought he'd never want to see her again. I was mistaken. I guess I find that hard to understand."

"What?"

"Why he wanted to see her again." She slowed to a stop in a parking space at the curb on the opposite side of the street, some fifty feet beyond the house. "Let's take a look."

As Max and Veronica walked around the exterior of the house, she tried to note every detail. The ugly, dirty-brown shingles covering the house gave "weather beaten" a bad name. She walked down the sandy alley running alongside the house to check out the rear of the house.

In the back, an old real-estate sign was propped haphazardly against a single grimy window as if tossed there by a blind man. The rear door had been stripped for repainting and forgotten. The whole house was up off the ground a foot on concrete blocks, and there were no steps at the door. However, several dozen round concrete tiles were stacked there. Apparent leftovers from another incomplete project.

Of the two windows on the side of the house nearest the

alley, only one—an attic window—was broken. The front of the house looked almost like another house pasted on the front of an existing structure. It was crowded with vertical jalousie windows on both sides and across the front.

"You know what's odd?" Veronica said. "This place looks like it's condemned, but there's only one broken window."

"Yeah. And it's way up high. And get a load of this." He was in front of the house peering in the windows. "Furniture. But no curtains at the windows. Looks like a garage sale."

She looked in at the furniture that littered the front room. She edged over to the front door, and was surprised to see that the police had apparently finished their work. There were no notices or warnings posted on the door. She tried the handle. It was unlocked.

She looked behind her. Straddling the sidewalk to the door like sentries were two huge palm trees, bare but for brownish green fronds at their tops. A smaller, more attractive palm tree sat to the left of the door in the front yard. Across the street was a seven-story white condominium building split by vertical lines of air-conditioning units and small windows. Her hand was still on the doorknob.

Max realized at once what she wanted to do. "Go ahead. I'll stay out here and watch for cops."

She shot him a grim smile, then opened the door.

Inside, the air was close and musty. The hallway in which she was standing went all the way to the back of the house. A door to the right led to the room with all the furniture. The only other door was at the end of the hall on the left.

She glanced down at the floor, and was almost sickened by the wide brown stain on the thin tattered carpet just beyond the door. She knew it was David's blood. It would have been easy for someone to have hidden in the room and hit him from behind.

She walked slowly down the hall, her shoes nearly silent on the carpet, which was well lit by the hazy sun through all the windows. At the end of the hall, on the wall and floor, were several much larger brown stains. Angela's blood. Veronica shuddered at the bullet holes in the dirty wall.

Then she noticed something and looked closer at the wall. On either side of the bullet holes were different holes, the kind one got when one pulled out a large nail in a hurry. They were almost evenly spaced, two feet to the left of the bullet holes and two feet to the right. There were two more about five feet up in the center of the wall. On either side of one of the bullet holes. Curious. The spacing of the holes reminded her of a cross. A cross of death.

She was about to step into the room at the left when she heard Max's voice out front. She hurried back to the front and saw Max in conversation with a squat little woman wearing a flowered housedress.

As she came out the door, the woman glared at her. "Damn! What y'all doin' in there?" She was so tan her face looked like a leather saddlebag. "Damn! That's private property. I'll call the damned cops on you, lessen you tell me whatcha doin'."

Max gave Veronica a warning look. "I tried to tell this nice lady that we're thinking about renting the house."

"That's right," Veronica said, as she came down the three steps at the front door and linked her arms with him. "Max and I want to rent the house. Who owns it?"

The woman scratched her head through short Brillo-pad hair. "Mr. Dahlhauser, over to The Busted Flush." She eyed Max and added, "But I don' think he's going to rent to your kind."

Max's smile became wooden as Veronica led him back to her car. The squat lady watched until they were in the car, then returned to her house, next to the condo building.

"Sorry about that," Veronica said, rubbing her damp hands on her jeans.

"Consider the source."

The Busted Flush was a few blocks away on Gulf Way. As they crossed the street from the angled parking along the beach, Max said, "I don't get it. Busted Flush?"

"It's a poker term. But probably they named it after the boat that Travis McGee lived on in John D. MacDonald's books."

"Travis McGee?"

She poked him. "Don't you read books?"

"I watch tapes," he shot back. "It's my business."

The Busted Flush was nautical to a fault, with a huge painted mural of a harbor scene on a rear wall and a salad bar in an actual ten-foot rowboat. Ships' lanterns were in the center of each table. Fake brass portholes dotted the walls.

After Veronica and Max conferred with the cashier and waited for a few minutes in the tiny lobby, a compact, muscular man who appeared to be in his fifties strode up to them. "Howdy. I'm Vern Dahlhauser. I own this place. Mary said you asked for me."

Veronica noticed the tattoos that covered both his arms. Dahlhauser wore black slacks and a white dress shirt open halfway down his barrel chest. Covering the dark matted hair were a half dozen heavy-looking gold chains. A grin revealed a few missing teeth and some gold fillings in his leathery face. "Wanna come upstairs to the lounge and I'll buy you a beer?"

They agreed and followed him up the stairs.

What Dahlhauser called "the lounge" was actually one small stuffy room crammed with eight round tables. A bar dominated one side of the room. Windows looking out across the awning to the Gulf filled the other side. At the end opposite the stairs was a giant-screen TV tuned to what appeared to be MTV.

As soon as they sat down and Dahlhauser motioned to the young man behind the bar, Veronica started to perspire. She glanced at the ineffectual room-sized air conditioner in the window. It was dripping water into a coffee can as it strained to cool the tiny room.

"Pass-A-Grille's a nice place," Max said.

"Used to be nicer," Dahlhauser responded. "Before the queers moved in. We used to have some nice decent folks here." He looked out the window. "Used to be nicer."

"How long have you been here?" Veronica asked. She noticed a scar on his cheek stretching from his right ear to his chin.

"All my life, except for a hitch in the navy and a year in a hospital." He leaned in and said conspiratorially, "I used

to be an alcoholic. Had to go to a hospital to dry out." He
sat back as the bartender delivered two Michelobs and a glass
of what looked like club soda or 7-Up. "Haven't taken a
drink in five years," he said proudly. He toasted them with
the glass. "Sprite," he explained. "Here's to you."

"That's great," Max said.

"Well, I admit to missing the whiskey sometimes. It was
my only vice." He flashed a gap-toothed grin at Veronica.
"Except for the ladies."

"Mr. Dahlhauser." Veronica launched into the cover story
she and Max had decided on. "We're here scouting locations
for a movie. I'm Veronica Slate. This is my partner, Max
Wilkinson."

Dahlhauser nodded at Max. "Jamaica?"

"Bahamas."

"Close enough. Figured you was an island boy." He
looked at Veronica. "Well, this is a great place for a movie.
Are you with the bunch that's making the one up at the Don?"

Veronica lied. "No. We're representing another studio
planning to make a TV movie."

"There's some great history to this place. We'd put 'Miami
Vice' to shame. Betcha didn't know Pass-A-Grille used to be
one of the drug-smuggling capitals of the west coast of Florida. More stuff come across this beach than Miami'd ever
see. Not many of them got caught, neither."

"So what stopped the drug trade?" Max asked.

"Did I say it stopped?" He laughed. "There just aren't as
many of them these days and they're more careful. Most of
the drug-runners have switched to flying their stuff into North
Port and other places like that with lots of landing space."

"North Port?" Max asked. "You mean down by Sarasota?"

"Yeah," Veronica said, turning to Max. "North Port's one
of those planned communities where they built the streets
first and waited for people to build houses later. Hundreds of
miles of isolated streets. Make great landing sites."

"I'll tell you something you don't know," Dahlhauser said,
turning his glass in his hands. "This little street out here
where you come in . . . that's the shortest commercial busi-

ness street in the world. It's in the *Guinness Book*. Shortest damned business district in the world. How'd you like that?"

"Amazing," Max said, eyeing Veronica.

She forged ahead. "We've been looking around and we did spot a house we'd like to lease for a few weeks. A neighbor lady told us you own it. It's kinda beat up. Over on Sixth."

"Oh, yeah. The old Christy place. I own it, all right. But I'm looking to either sell it or tear it down."

"We're not interested in buying it, but we would like to lease it for a few weeks," Veronica said. "It would be perfect for one of the scenes in our movie."

"Only one problem with that. I'm already leasing it," Dahlhauser said, "to that other movie company. The folks who are making the movie at the Don."

Veronica had suspected that someone from Mira Loma Productions was involved. This seemed to confirm it. "Have they been filming there?"

"No. That's the funny thing. They leased it a week ago and I ain't seen 'em since. 'Course, the cops was over there. You probably heard about that. They found that actress dead there."

"Yes. I know."

"I'm not too surprised. Always had a hard time keeping bums and vagrants out of there." He shrugged. "Can't be everywhere at one time, y'know." He drained his glass. "Probably run the value of the place up a bit, though."

"Why?" Veronica asked.

"People what believe in ghosts. They'll want to live there and see if the actress comes back to haunt them." He laughed.

Funny, Veronica thought, *seems like Angela's already haunting me.*

CHAPTER EIGHTEEN

ON THE FIFTH DAY SINCE DAVID HAD BECOME CONSCIOUS, just over a week since Angela had been murdered, Veronica was making her usual stop to see him on the way to the Don CeSar.

She told him about seeing the house on Pass-A-Grille and talking to the man who owned it, and then their conversation turned to the death of Todd Keener on Wednesday.

"What I can't figure out," she said, "is why they killed Todd Keener. That was no accident on the jet ski."

"He was the doorman. I'm sure about that," David said.

"The doorman?"

"The kid in the funny doorman's uniform that night. When I saw his face on TV I recognized him. He was the one who took a shot at me in the house. The kid . . . I shot . . ." He frowned at the absurdity of his words. "The kid I *thought* I shot."

"If he was involved in Angela's death, that explains why

they killed him." She stretched out her legs and regarded her blue-white Adidas running shoes.

"Okay," David said. "Let's assume for the moment that it was a rigged accident. Who could have rigged it?"

"Adrian Bell, the stunt coordinator. He worked on the film where Tony Victor was killed, too."

"I see a pattern emerging," David said.

"But why would Adrian Bell want to kill Angela? Or, for that matter, why would he kill Tony Victor, or Angela's attorney?"

"Let's take them one at a time." David sat up a little on his bed, being careful not to move the tube in his hand. "Let's say this mysterious director—"

"Alan Smithee. Only that's not his real name."

"Yeah. This Smithee had Adrian Bell kill Tony Victor because he had been screwing his wife. Except that Angela said Tony was killed because of a drug deal gone bad," David said. "Well, whatever the reason, Tony's killed. Angela sees it. Tells her attorney. The director has Adrian Bell kill Angela and her attorney so they won't talk."

"Good except for one thing," Veronica said. "Adrian Bell was here in St. Pete Beach the night Angela's attorney was killed. And he was allegedly in bed with Tracy Morgan the night Angela was . . ." She sat up. "Wait a minute. Maybe that's it. Maybe Tracy lied for him and he was out there in the house with Keener. Maybe he's the one who hit you on the head. Tracy did get a lead role out of this."

"Not strong enough," David said. "Too great a risk to take just to get a lead in a movie."

"Yeah. You're right. Besides, didn't you say Angela told you she had a clause in her contract about drinking or something?"

"That's right. If she was too drunk or drugged to work, they could fire her and collect some insurance money. In fact, she told me someone tried to set her up the day after she got to town. The day we went to the Ringling Museum. They shot her up and left her." He shrugged. "I figured she just made that up to get me involved."

"Maybe. Maybe not," Veronica said, looking at her

watch. "Well, I think it's time I have another talk with Tracy Morgan." She stood and grabbed her purse. "I want to find out if she's the one who sent the note about *F/X*."

"You gotta go?"

"Afraid so." She leaned over and kissed him, something she had done often enough to notice a difference this time. "What's the matter?"

"What do you mean?"

"You phoned in that kiss."

"Sorry."

"What's the matter?" She teased, "Tell Mommy."

"It's the test today. I'm worried."

"What test?"

"The doctor called it . . ."—he fished for a piece of paper on the bedside table and read it to her—". . . arteriography." His eyes searched her face. "I'm scared shitless about this thing." He gestured toward his groin. "The kid who shaved me down there at the crack of dawn said they're going to shoot dye up through my groin to test my brain."

Veronica laughed in spite of herself. "They're going to use your groin to test your brain? That confirms something I always suspected about men."

"C'mon, Vee. It's not funny."

She pulled her chair back over next to the bed and patted his arm. "I'm sure they'll give you a local. Don't worry."

David did not look relieved. "Yeah, but the night nurse said it's a dangerous test. It can kill you."

"Look, if it'll make you feel better, I'll ask one of the nurses to go along and hold your hand."

He didn't smile. He nodded yes, hopefully.

"David, please try not to worry. It's just a test to make sure you're all right. It'll be over in no time. You'll be back in the room watching TV before you know it. Don't worry."

He closed his eyes for a brief moment, then reached out and took her hand in his. "You know what scares me the most about all of this? How do I know if I'm brain-damaged? I mean, it's like being crazy. If you ask someone if you're crazy, they'll say no. But are they saying it because you really aren't crazy, or because you are crazy and they're afraid of you?"

"Oh, come on, David. You're a little weird sometimes, but you're not crazy."

"And what about normal brain function? I heard the doctor talking about normal brain function. What the hell is normal? I think my brain is working about the same as usual, but I do have trouble putting things together before I talk, and my memory seems to be screwed up."

"Wow! You really are a basket case." Veronica laughed and kissed his hand. "David, your mind is wavy gravy because you're still on heavy-duty pain-killers. You had what they call a trauma. You were in a coma for a couple of days. What do you expect? Instant wellness? It's going to take some time, but you're going to be fine. Besides, you have something very wonderful to live for."

"Like what?"

She stood and lifted her T-shirt up and back down in a flash. "My body." Her smile relaxed into tenderness as she put her hand on his cheek. "I miss you, David."

He took her hand and kissed it. "I miss you, too."

As she gathered her purse and headed to the door, he said, "Will you ask a nurse to go with me to the test?"

She looked at his intense face, serious brown eyes above his bushy moustache, and smiled. "Yes. I'll do it right now." She turned at the door. "When's the test?"

"At ten."

"I'll call you at noon and see how you're doing."

"Okay."

As she walked down the hall, Veronica thought about what her mother used to say. *Men are really little boys in grown-up bodies. That's why they need us.*

Luck was with her when she arrived at the hotel. Tracy's first call was after lunch, and she was sitting in the ground-floor ice cream parlor trying to drink a milk shake while talking to a small group of teen-aged girls, fascinated by a real actress.

"Hi, Vee," she said, with a look of "get me out of here"

all over her face. "Do they need me on the third floor?" She
nodded and arched her eyebrows to give Veronica the hint.

"Oh. Uh . . . yes." Veronica played along. "I'm sorry,
girls, Miss Morgan has to get back to work." Then, to a
grateful Tracy, she added, "You can bring the shake with
you."

Ten minutes later, they were sitting in lounge chairs on the
deck outside the first-floor lobby bar. Veronica wore her
usual uniform of shorts, T-shirt, and Adidas. Tracy was
wearing a pink sundress with white trim and flat white
leather sandals.

"Thanks for the rescue." Tracy stretched and peered over
her sunglasses at Veronica. "How come you're not working?"

"I guess they don't know what to do with me. I checked
in with Carla and she said to take a break. Sometimes I
think I'm excess baggage hired because Jon Vasta has a soft
heart."

"Or a dirty mind." She noted Veronica's surprise. "Oh,
he's a crafty little devil. I'm surprised he hasn't asked you to
do some 'special duty' in his bedroom."

"Never so much as a hint. Guess I should feel rejected."

"Or lucky." She looked over her shoulder. "That reminds
me. The other day in the penthouse when I told you about
Jon's stash in the green suitcase?" She lowered her voice.
"That's just between us, okay? I doubt Jon wants the world
to know."

"No problem. I can keep a secret." Veronica rolled over
on her side on the lounge chair and faced Tracy. "Tracy, I
need to know something. Someone sent me a note suggesting
I watch *F/X* if I want to know how Angela was killed. Was
it you?"

Tracy lay back and her body visibly tensed. After a moment, in an artificial voice, she said, "The other day you
mentioned your ex, but you didn't give me any details." She
removed her sunglasses and cast a significant look at Veronica. "C'mon, tell me about it. I love a good story."

Veronica looked at her. Tentatively, she said, "Who wants to hear about another bad marriage? I'd just as soon forget it."

"C'mon. What was his name?" Tracy rolled her eyes upward.

"Sam. Lieutenant JG Sam Treace, U.S.N." Veronica rolled over on her back and as casually as possible looked up. "It was a classic case of having a beautiful wedding and a lousy marriage." What did Tracy see up there? Was someone listening to them?

"Big church wedding?" asked Tracy.

"No. Big garden wedding. We were married in his parents' garden in Mt. Pocono, Pennsylvania. That's a little resort town north of Philly." Above her she saw the edge of the roof that topped the fifth floor of the hotel, the place where the camera had been for yesterday's jet-ski filming. The bright blue sky above made it difficult to see clearly. "Sam was four years older than me and handsome," she continued. "I was a senior in high school. I saw him in his uniform and that was it."

"Can't resist a man in uniform, huh?" Tracy said out loud. Then she whispered, "There's someone up there."

"Right." Veronica strained to see, but the sun made it difficult. She continued the artificial conversation. "After we were married, he reported for flight training at this little naval base in Kingsville, Texas. About the most boring place I'd ever been. That's where I got hooked on movies."

"So what split you guys up?" Tracy was motionless.

"He hit me. I swore there'd never be a second time."

Veronica didn't know what tipped her off. A glint of sunlight reflected off something above. An out-of-place sound. A sixth sense. But she rolled rapidly off her lounge chair, yelled "Tracy!," and grabbed the small blonde's arm, pulling her off her chair. They scrambled up against the wall. A heartbeat later, something crashed through both lounge chairs and smashed into chunks on the concrete below.

The two women sat against the wall, arms around each other, shaking in fear at the close call as a waiter and a man in a suit came rushing out the doors from the lobby bar. Others were rushing up the concrete stairs from the pool area.

Tracy hugged Veronica and whispered, "Thank you for saving my life. They're trying to kill me, too."

Veronica surveyed the crushed lounge chairs beneath the pile of rubble. "I think they're trying to kill both of us." She turned to Tracy. "Who are they?"

It was too late. Several men were helping them up, asking if they were okay, looking at the pieces of what someone said had been a whole section of the concrete wall surrounding the roof. "Must have just crumbled from old age," ventured the waiter. But Veronica knew it had been shoved. The question was, by whom?

The men were stumbling all over one another to help Veronica and Tracy up. They trailed the two women like puppies as they walked in through the designer-perfect lobby bar, which resembled the drawing room of a mansion in the tropics. Just before the entourage reached the lobby, Veronica stopped, grabbed Tracy's arm, and said, "We've got to visit the little girls' room, guys. Thanks again."

She forced Tracy into the ladies' room. Just inside the door, Veronica caught up to her.

"Look, I don't know what the hell is going on, but someone set up David and I've got to find out who. Did you send me that note?"

Tracy turned from the door to where the stalls and sinks were located. "Get real. Why would I do that?" Veronica saw in her eyes the same shifty-eyed look she'd had out on the balcony. Tracy glanced in the large mirror and pushed her hair off her forehead. Her hand was shaking. "Even if I did know how Angela was killed, why would I try to help you?"

Veronica grabbed her by the arm and turned her violently around. "Listen to me. This is a hell of a lot more important than the lead in a movie. We're talking a man's life here. In this state, he could get the death penalty."

Tracy's face tightened. "So what? I didn't always love Angela, but I certainly wouldn't have her killed just to get a lead in a movie." She tried to pull away from Veronica's grasp. "I'm good enough to get it on my own."

"I'm not saying you killed her. Listen to me. I'm saying you know who did. You've got to tell me. Remember, whoever is behind this tried to kill you just a moment ago."

Tracy tried to pry Veronica's fingers off her arm. "Maybe that *was* just an accident out there."

Veronica tightened her grasp. "For Christ's sake, Tracy! You were the one who saw someone up on the roof. You *know* it wasn't an accident."

Tracy twisted free and spat out, "I think you're letting love blind you, just like you did with your air force pilot."

"Navy."

"Whatever. I think that cop of yours killed Angela on purpose and you just can't face it. After all, he's going to make out like a bandit from all that insurance money. I think you should start using your head instead of your heart." She stormed to the door of the ladies' room. "And I think you should leave me the hell alone."

As the door swung shut behind the little blonde, Veronica sighed. It surprised her to learn that Tracy knew about the insurance money. It troubled her to realize that perhaps there was a slim chance that she was a pawn in a domestic squabble that had ended in an accidental killing. Maybe David had decided he wanted Angela back. Maybe she'd gotten drunk and they'd gotten in a fight. But, even if that was true, why would they have been in the old deserted house on Pass-A-Grille?

Veronica looked at herself in the mirror. There were dark circles under her eyes. Her hair was limp from the humidity. She was tired and confused. Tired of working two jobs and trying to sustain David's spirits. Confused about her feelings for him and her temporary lust for Paul Haden.

She went to the nearby pay phone in the hallway and called David. She happened to glance at the ladies' room door just as Carla Jahns emerged and walked to the special penthouse elevator. Her skin tingled. Could that have been why Tracy had suddenly become nervous and antagonistic? Was Carla involved?

David answered. After making sure he was all right, and learning that the nurse did hold his hand and that she was young and cute, Veronica told David she loved him and said good-bye.

She fished her G.T.E. calling card out of her wallet and dialed her father's number. Standing first on one foot, then the other, imagining her phone bill at the end of the month, but eager to get his advice, Veronica told her father everything that had happened in the last week. He listened patiently, asking an occasional pertinent question. She finally wrapped up her story with a plaintive question. "How can I find out who Alan Smithee really is? I think that may be the key to the whole thing."

"Didn't you say the movie was made back in the seventies?"

"Right. Nineteen seventy-five."

"Seems to me the logical thing to do is talk to someone who's been around a while. Anybody on the crew like that?"

"Not really. They're mostly young, and some of them were hired here. They're local union guys."

"Okay. How about that Mrs. Jahns you told me about?"

"Carla Jahns? I don't know. I'm afraid she might be involved. I'm not sure I trust her right now."

"And didn't you say Raynor Fitzhugh is in this movie?"

"Yes."

"He's a very good actor. As little as I go to movies, I've seen him on a couple of TV movies and that big miniseries, what'd they call it? 'Diamonds and Pearls.' I bet he's been around Hollywood long enough to know something that could help you."

"That's a great idea, Daddy. I bet he would. I'll see if I can talk to him today." She looked at the lobby, busier than it was when she'd picked up the phone a half hour earlier. "I better go, Daddy. Just one more thing. I miss you."

"I miss you, too. Want to come to Disney with us?"

"I'd like to, but I need to see a movie."

"Oh. That one. Okay. Give my love to David."

She said good-bye and went to a wing chair to sit for a moment. Her legs were sore from standing so long.

She smiled as she thought about how much she loved that man. Her father always seemed to know what to do, which way to turn, who to believe. She wondered, *Is that something that's basic nature to men? Or just to fathers?*

CHAPTER NINETEEN

RAYNOR FITZHUGH BRUSHED BACK HIS LONGISH WHITE HAIR and surveyed in the mirror the bearded face his late wife, Eula, had called "full of love and character." He felt merely old and worn. Being alone in his pursuit of a motion-picture acting career for the past twelve years had begun to age what had once been a handsome face.

Fifty-four years ago, Fitzhugh recalled with his usual acute recall of dates, places, and names, he had been a dashing young actor whose suave good looks had led to a role on Broadway in *Art and Mrs. Bottle,* starring Jane Cowl. He'd had a youthful crush on a fellow cast member—a young Kate Hepburn.

That show began a New York theater career that lasted—with a brief break for the war—until the crazy, painted tribal hippies of *Hair* took over Broadway in the late sixties.

He had performed with the best: Lynn Fontanne, Alfred Lunt, and Noël Coward in 1933's *Design for Living*; the sweet, lovely Helen Hayes in 1935's *Victoria Regina*; and even Laurence Olivier and Katherine Cornell in *No Time for Comedy* in 1938.

After the Second World War, Raynor Fitzhugh—although only thirty-five when the war ended—had been dubbed a "character actor," spending most of the next thirty years playing father, uncle, or old friend to bright young actors and actresses like Charlton Heston, Maureen Stapleton, Paul Lynde, and Eva Marie Saint.

Eula, his wife of nearly twenty-seven years and a veteran seamstress in some of Broadway's best costume shops, had died in her sleep in 1974. That was when Raynor Fitzhugh had made his lonely trek to Hollywood, where he had spent the last dozen years making eight movies and waiting patiently for death.

He was seventy-six, although his official bio listed him as seventy-two. He was alone and lonely and no one knew. Female companionship was hard to find when one was old enough to be everyone's grandfather.

A knock on his door jolted him from his reverie.

He had nearly forgotten the earnest young woman who'd asked, during lunch, to come to his room for a discussion of something she considered important. As attractive as the tall brunette was, he wished for a fantasy moment that she was coming to be with him. Ah, well.

Turning from the mirror and walking to the door of his large and, he assumed, expensive hotel suite, Fitzhugh tried to place this young Veronica Slate among the women working on the film. When she had approached his table at lunch, he'd said he remembered her, but he did not. *Guess I'm suffering from old-timer's disease,* he thought with a smile.

He opened the door to the tall, good-looking woman with dark brown hair to her shoulders and a pretty smile. "Veronica! Do come in." Fitzhugh cleared a stack of newspapers from a chair by the window and offered it to her. "Place is a bit of a mess. Been reading the local papers, trying to get a handle on the area." And, he didn't add, to keep from being lonely.

"No problem," said Veronica. As she sat, he was pleased that she wore shorts that revealed her lovely legs. So many young girls today were hiding their assets with dungarees and unattractive oversized shirts. Her French-cut *Perfect Casting* T-shirt revealed curves that he appreciated.

He realized the scent of cherry pipe tobacco hung in the air, and asked, "I hope the aroma of my pipe-smoking doesn't bother you, my dear."

"No. I love the smell of a pipe. It's cigars and cigarettes I can't stand."

"Indeed."

The young woman gazed at his face for a moment, then looked at the four photographs in dark frames that he had brought with him to give his hotel room a feeling of home.

"It was wonderful then," said Fitzhugh, following Veronica's gaze to a large photograph of a scene from the first real musical comedy of the modern era, *Oklahoma!* "The shows were truly entertaining," he said. "No need for showing off bodies and saying bad words to get attention. Good songs, exciting dancing, romance, comedy, and entertainment were the keys. I miss it."

"So do I," Veronica said. She sounded sincere.

"But we're here to discuss the more recent past, aren't we?" said Fitzhugh, as he sat back in his chair and ran his fingers through his snowy hair. "What can I do for you?"

"I'm dating the man the police have accused of killing Angela Mastry."

He smiled. "Are you in the habit of dating accused murderers?"

She frowned. "I've been dating him for some time. Long before he was accused of murder. Anyhow, I'm convinced he didn't do it. But I'm running into trouble finding any proof."

"Are you a private investigator?"

"No. Just curious."

"And in love, no doubt." He could see that in her eyes, luscious green eyes that probably could coax the truth from any man who fell victim to their gaze.

"That, too," she said with a small smile.

"In what way can I help you?"

"I'm not sure you can, but my father seemed to think you'd be most likely to lead me in the right direction."

"Your father? How interesting. Do I know him?"

"No. Of course not. It's just that he's my . . . I guess you could say my mentor, my adviser. He's very intelligent and usually right. He lives near here."

Fitzhugh chuckled. "My. You seem to be in love with two men. One of them your father."

"You could say that."

"That's admirable. So many children turn on their parents these days. It's the cause of so much sadness."

"Do you have children?"

"None. My wife, Eula, and I were too busy with our careers. Now she's gone, and soon I'll be gone, too." He smiled to lighten the mood. "But I'm sure your mother is pleased that you get along so well with your father."

"Mother's dead."

He saw something gray and sad creep into her eyes. "I am sorry. Well, at least you have your father. That helps."

"Yes. It does."

"Well, my dear, I'm sorry I've gotten us off the track. How can I help you?"

"I have information linking the death of Angela Mastry with the death last fall of an actor named Tony Victor."

"Tragic accident, that." He closed his eyes for a moment and nodded his sympathy. "I recall. Accidentally shot."

"But he wasn't. It was murder. And Angela apparently knew that. We think that's why she was killed."

"Can you explain?"

"In 1975, Tony Victor made a movie with a director who had his name removed from the film because it turned out so badly. That director's wife allegedly had an affair with Tony. I think that director had him killed."

"What was the title of the film? Do you know?"

"It was *Dead of Day*."

Fitzhugh leaned back in his chair and closed his eyes. The time had come for him to tell the truth without regard for his own safety. He was just around the bend from death anyhow. "Miss Slate, allow me to tell you the truth about Tony's death."

"Please."

"I met Tony when we made *Dealer's Wire* in 1982." He glanced at her and saw the interest glowing in her lovely green eyes. "You might recall that was the film that brought him national prominence. I had a small role as the manager of the halfway house in which Tony's character lived."

Her eyes lit up. "Yes. I remember. That was before the beard, wasn't it?"

"Why, yes. How kind of you to recall. As the production went on, I got to know Tony really well. In point of fact, we emerged from the production close friends. I suppose he saw me as a father figure. His own father had died in World War II." He reached for his pipe in the nearby ashtray, then asked, "Do you mind if I smoke?"

"A pipe? No. Go ahead."

He fingered some tobacco into his pipe and tamped it first with his forefinger, then with the small aluminum pipe nail. "Since I was even then an elderly man . . ." He chuckled, struck a wooden kitchen match into flame on the side of its box. "And because I had a relatively small role, I was able to spend considerable time sitting around watching." He lit the tobacco and began drawing on it, waiting for it to catch. "That was how I came to notice a man who was frequently on the set. A man whose presence troubled me."

"Why?" asked Veronica.

"He seemed rather out of place. A tall, slim man, as I recall. He was Irish. Shock of red hair. Seemed always to be wearing a three-piece suit no matter what the weather." He frowned at his pipe, which had already gone out. "There was something—I suppose the word is *menacing*, or *malevolent*—frightening about him. When he'd arrive on the set, Tony would always find an excuse to go off in a corner and huddle with him."

"Could he have been Tony's manager or a producer?"

"No. I knew his manager. And the producer of *Dealer's Wire* was nearly as young as Tony and always wore those silly fleece-lined vests over a flannel shirt." He lit another match and finally got the pipe going. "No. This man was an outsider. And after he had left, Tony would return to work. But I could see the paranoia in his eyes. Naturally, I put two and two together and guessed that it had something to do with drugs, not at all uncommon among the younger members of the cast and crew."

"Did you go to the police?"

"No." He shrugged. "I'm not proud of that fact now. At the time, I was merely trying to survive. I needed the income afforded me by my role in the film. I was afraid to jeopardize my job. So I remained silent." His pipe had gone out and he hadn't the energy to restart it, so he laid it in the ashtray. "Even after I discovered that he was a dealer."

"How did you find out?"

"He told me. At the wrap party, he was so drunk that I was elected to drive him home. Once there, he invited me in. He vomited on the way to the bathroom, then began to cry. As I tried to sober him up with hastily prepared instant coffee, he poured out a tangled web of his troubles to me. The gist of which was this." Fitzhugh paused. *Stage training never leaves you,* he thought, as he took what actors called a stage wait.

"Tony told me he had been a teen-ager, clean-cut and not a user of drugs or alcohol, when he worked on his first film, *Dead of Day.* He was subverted and recruited by the director of that film. He was introduced to drugs at that time."

Veronica sat up, obviously interested.

"According to Tony, the director of that film had once been famous. His first major movie had been an unqualified success. Then he'd followed it with a much less successful romantic film. His career was in real trouble. According to Tony, he'd begged for the opportunity to direct *Dead of Day,* and had gotten the chance only because it was an independent film, and a cheaply made one at that. But the problem was he had to raise half the money in order to make the film." He noticed the impatience in her eyes. "I'm nearly done, my dear."

"I'm sorry. I didn't mean to . . ."

He waved away her apology. "Tony said this director needed the money so badly that he made the fatal mistake of selling his soul, so to speak, to a pair of Irish—shall we say— 'businessmen' from Colombia." He noticed her surprise.

"The South American nation, not Columbia Pictures. There are thousands of Irish in Colombia. Wouldn't think so, would you?"

"No," she said.

"At any rate, the two brothers were delighted to launder their money by investing it in his movie-making. Their only requirement, Tony said, was that the director enlist certain select people in the business, such as Tony Victor, to sell the drugs they were importing through Mexico and Florida."

"The director was in debt to big-time drug dealers?"

"He probably still is in debt to big-time drug dealers." Fitzhugh smiled, and stroked his snow-white beard. "Unless he's dead. You see, that's what happened to Tony."

"What is?"

"He confessed to me that night that he had been keeping some of the money he made selling the drugs and he was afraid they'd find out. He begged me not to tell anyone."

"So did you?"

"No. Of course not. As I said, I had no real proof." He leaned back in his chair. "After that, Tony and I drifted apart. He met the young Mastry girl, and soon they had started making *Slasher* in Canada. I really heard very little about him until last fall when he was killed."

"So you know it wasn't an accident?"

"I don't know it for a fact, but I'm convinced he was killed by someone in the employ of those Irish brothers. They probably made it look like an accident to draw attention away from their still-thriving drug business. I imagine when they discovered that Angela Mastry knew what they had done, they hired your young man to kill her."

"No!" She leaped up, her eyes flashing. "David did not kill her! I'm sure he didn't." She added quietly, "Besides, he'd never work for crooks."

Fitzhugh motioned her down. "Relax. It's only a theory. I don't know your young man. Any way you look at it, I suspect the Mastry girl was killed because she knew too much." He frowned. "Unfortunately, both you and I know too much as well."

"Not really, Mister Fitzhugh. You still haven't told me who the director was who caused all this."

"Tony never told me. He was a frightened young man. And I was something of an isolationist, not choosing to get involved in something that was none of my concern."

"So you don't know who Alan Smithee really is?"

"I'm afraid not, my dear. But at least now you know that Tony Victor wasn't killed over some real or imagined affair with the wife of a director. If that was a motive for murder, half the actors in Hollywood would be in their graves."

CHAPTER TWENTY

"THE PROBLEM IS THAT I HAVE NO PROOF THAT JON VASTA is actually Alan Smithee," Veronica said. "Raynor Fitzhugh didn't know. But the clues he gave me about the director having a big hit and then going into a slump with a romantic film fit Vasta like a glove." She paced in David's hospital room. He followed her with his gaze and said nothing.

"I keep thinking the more I know about how they killed Todd Keener and Tony Victor, the more I'll learn about who killed Angela and how they did it." She finally sat in the chair and glared at David. "I think the same man killed them all. I just need to know how he did it."

"What about that movie?" David asked. "The one in the note. Maybe that will—"

"Yeah. Probably. But I don't have a night off until day after tomorrow, and the show's the second film on a double bill. It doesn't start till nine-thirty. I checked."

"Then I guess you'll just have to wait till Saturday night."

"Saturday night." She stretched and yawned. "It seems

like an eternity. . . ." She stopped and a smile brightened her face. "Saturday night. That's it." She grabbed the phone on the table by his bed. "Can I call long distance on this?"

"Dial nine. They bill it to my room."

"Great." She reached in her purse for her little blue address book, looked up the number, and punched it in.

"Who're you calling?"

"Julee Andrews."

"*The Sound of Music*?"

"C'mon, dummy, Julee with a double *e*. She pronounces it 'Jew Lee.' She's the girl who does the Saturday night 'DateLine' on AQT. Don't you remember? She's the one I called last fall when I was in trouble in Tampa. You heard me dropping hints like crazy on her show and you came rolling in with the sheriff."

"Oh, yeah. Hafta thank her sometime. Why you calling her?"

Veronica held up her hand as Julee drawled, "Hullo there."

"Julee, this is Vee. Can you do a big favor?"

"I dunno, sugah. What?"

"Can you work for me tonight? I'll call Sutter and make it all right. It's open calling. Max will take care of you."

"You mean I get to work with that cute little Maxwell? That sure is tempting. But I was gonna go to see mah mama tonight down to Ruskin."

"Please, Julee. I haven't asked you to work for me in months. I'll pay you double."

"Mah goodness, Veronica, y'all do know the way to a girl's heart. If ya promise to clear it with Miz Sutter, I'll do it."

"I promise." Veronica smiled victoriously. "Julee, I love you. You ever need a favor, you got it."

She hung up and smiled at David. "Great. Julee will work for me." She sat back in the chair and said, "I'm going to a movie."

The Beach Theatre was a warm little mom-and-pop theater with pop selling tickets and mom pushing popcorn. It was clean, comfortable, and pleasant. Mostly, it screened second-run motion pictures. The warm family atmosphere and friendly employees helped it compete with the dozens of impersonal multiplex theaters less than ten miles away in all directions.

The Beach Theatre sat on Corey Avenue, a block south of Seventy-fifth Avenue, just across the St. Pete Beach Causeway from Palms of Pasadena, the hospital where David was slowly getting well.

Veronica had changed to her jeans, kissed David good-bye when visiting hours ended, and grabbed dinner at the Ponderosa. It took her less than ten minutes to get to the theater, find a parking space, and reach the box office. She paid for her ticket, bought popcorn and a Dr Pepper, and eased into a seat just over halfway back. Sitting there in the dark with her popcorn and soda took her back to the countless evenings she'd spent in theaters in the sixties and seventies, falling in love with movies.

As she watched *F/X*, an above-average thriller with some good performances, Veronica tried to figure out what trick had a connection with Angela's death. She discounted the scene in which Brian Brown—as a special-effects wizard—created a fake facial appliance for Jerry Orbach and then pretended to shoot him in a crowded restaurant. Angela wouldn't have gone along with that. Besides, she really *was* dead.

Veronica jumped involuntarily at the sudden and violent death of Brian Brown's girlfriend, a pretty, short-haired actress in a clingy slip. She laughed at the chase in which a cop pursued the special-effects van, only to be halted by a dummy in the road. She tried to spot the places where Tracy Morgan had doubled for actress Martha Gehman and—to Tracy's credit—she couldn't.

By the time the movie was nearly over, the only conclusion Veronica had come to was that Brian Dennehy was a vastly underrated actor. His scenes with a young female computer expert were gems. His characterization had that awesome ring of truth.

While she was enjoying the movie, Veronica was frustrated

that she had taken the night off for what was beginning to look like a fruitless search for a clue to Angela's murder.

Finally, near the end of the film, Brian Brown was trying to elude two bad guys in the home of the chief bad guy, played by Mason Adams. Brown used various special-effects tricks to fake them out, but when she saw him set up some sort of folded aluminum frame at the end of the hall, Veronica sat up and paid attention.

In layout, at least, the hall was not unlike the one in the old weather-beaten house on Pass-A-Grille, except that it had doors on both sides at the end of the hall. She watched in amazement as Brown erected the framework and pulled down a sheet of some kind of thin reflective material, probably Mylar. He set it at an angle. Of course! Why hadn't she thought of it?

When the taller bad guy came down the hall, he saw what looked like Brian Brown standing at the end of the hall. He opened fire but, obviously, Brown was just inside the doorway on the left, reflected on the screen. The bullets tore through the Mylar and struck the other bad guy, who had come out the opposite door and found himself behind the screen.

As the bullets hit the second bad guy in the chest and he slumped to the floor, leaving a wide, ragged patch of blood on the wall, Veronica was convinced. That's how they had killed Angela. They must have tied her up against the rear wall. That's why there were holes in the shape of a cross. They simply put the Mylar screen in front of her, and when David shot the doorman he was actually shooting Angela. Then they knocked him out before he could investigate and discover what had really happened.

Brilliant. But why go to all that trouble? Why didn't they just take her out and shoot her in some deserted woods?

More important than that—how could Veronica prove they had done it that way? As she watched the conclusion of the movie, just in case there was another clue, she decided she had to find either that bullet-riddled Mylar screen or the other man who had helped Todd Keener set up David for Angela's murder.

On her way out through the lobby, Veronica checked her watch. It was eleven-twenty-five. Too late to visit David, and the hospital didn't allow phone calls after nine. She'd just have to go home and think it all over. Maybe she'd call Max. . . . No. She'd forgotten that—unlike her—he was where he was supposed to be tonight, at work. Maybe she could call her dad. She was so excited at what she had learned she was bursting to share it with someone she could trust. *He's probably out with Barbara,* he thought, as she pulled out her purse and fished for her G.T.E. calling card. She went to the pay phone in the corner of the lobby.

To her delight, Archie answered after two rings.

"Daddy, I'm getting closer to the truth about Angela's murder." While the manager readied the theater lobby for the last show, a special midnight presentation of *The Rocky Horror Picture Show,* Veronica stood at the pay phone and told her father about her conversation with Raynor Fitzhugh and what she had discovered from watching the movie.

"So you think Jon Vasta is behind all this?"

"It looks that way," she said. "Of course, I have no proof of that. I need to find that Mylar screen."

"Unless they destroyed it."

"Yeah, that's what worries me."

"Is there anything I can do to help?"

That's what she had been hoping for, some help from her father. "As a matter of fact, yes. Can you come up tomorrow? I know you're going to Orlando Saturday, but I'd love to see you tomorrow. You can go to the set with me and meet Raynor Fitzhugh and Tracy Morgan. Maybe we can shake something loose."

"Just like old times, huh?"

"Yeah."

"Okay, Ronnie. But I have to be back by noon Saturday. What time?"

"Be at my place at nine and we can take my car."

"Okay. See you then. Oh, one more thing."

"Yes, Daddy?"

"I love you."

"I love you, too." She hung up, feeling better inside than she had in weeks.

She worked her way through the crowd of *Rocky Horror* fans on the sidewalk, remembering how much fun it had been the fourteen times she had seen it herself. She made a mental promise to treat herself to seeing it again when all this turmoil was over.

By the time she had reached her car, Veronica had decided to take matters into her own hands and look for the Mylar screen. She had been in the room where the gaffer kept the lighting gear locked up. That was where he stored the "gobos," moviespeak for opaque screens used to block unwanted light. It made sense to her that the Mylar screen, which would be used to reflect light, might be there, too. At least it was worth a try.

It was nearly midnight when Veronica pulled into the parking lot in front of the Don CeSar. The floodlit pink building looked even more like a giant birthday cake at night. This close to the Gulf the air was humid and fragrant.

She walked to the side entrance and entered the first floor, one floor below the main lobby. The gaffer's room was just a few feet from the elevator and she paused at the door, checking the elevator lights to make sure no one was on the way down. She checked the lock on the gaffer's door. As she had feared, it was a standard lock, but with a metal shield over the place where enterprising thieves would use a strip of plastic to slip it open. Damn! She had to get the key.

The only person she knew who had a key was the gaffer himself, and she couldn't even remember his name. How could she get in without letting someone else know what she was looking for? She sat heavily in the single hardback chair across the hall from the elevators and tried to think.

Jon Vasta might have access, but he was the very person who shouldn't know what she was doing. Maybe Carla Jahns? No. She'd probably go straight to Vasta. It was really frustrating Veronica to be so near and yet so far. She wanted to find that screen. It would be proof of her theory about Angela's murder. But maybe it wasn't even in the gaffer's room. After all, if it had been used in the commission of a murder, the killers would probably have ditched it. It was probably at the bottom of the Gulf of Mexico or . . . She sat upright as the thought occurred to her. Maybe it was still in the house on Pass-A-Grille. They must have taken off in a hurry after the murder. Maybe they had left it. Standing, Veronica cast one last glance at the locked door and walked rapidly to the end of the carpeted hall and out into the humid night.

Ten minutes later, Veronica sat in her Honda, lights off, trying to build the courage to go into the weather-beaten old house. Despite the security lights on the condo building across the street and the streetlamp, the house looked ominous and mysterious at night. Probably the way it looked to David the night Angela was killed, she thought, except that tonight it wasn't raining.

Finally, as ready as she'd ever be, Veronica got the old army-surplus flashlight from under the front seat of the car, discovered that it still worked, and turned off the dome-light switch so it wouldn't come on as she emerged from the car.

The street was deserted. A house half a block away rocked with music and chatter, the sounds of a party. Lights were on in a few of the condos across the street. There was no traffic. She pushed the button on her watch. Twelve-thirty-three in the morning.

She tried the door to the old house and, once again, it was unlocked. As quietly as possible, she crept through the door-way and illuminated the stained carpet just inside.

She was afraid to risk a search of the front room on the right because it was the one with lots of windows across its entire width and no curtains to keep the light from being seen from the street. Perhaps on her way out.

She tiptoed down the hall, thankful she was wearing her Adidas running shoes. The light from across the street did illuminate the hallway, just as David had said. Veronica realized that, for days now, she had been toying with the possibility that David had been lying to her and that he had killed Angela deliberately. Each thing that was as he claimed it was made her feel more secure and more ashamed of herself for doubting him.

She recalled all those scary movies where the stupid ingenue went into the very house she had been warned against entering and got killed or raped or turned into a vampire. Was she being stupid, too? Probably. But she was burning with the desire to *do* something. To make some progress in solving the mystery.

She reached the end of the hall and played the flashlight beam across the crosslike series of holes on the wall. Yes. It was easily possible they had tied Angela to that wall to await her execution by her own ex-husband.

Veronica turned the beam into the room on the left. The door was open. It was a small room with one window covered with newspapers. A light of some kind behind the house forced its way through the newspapers, illuminating an incredible collection of trash and clothes and knickknacks that were all over the floor and a decrepit couch. She played the flashlight beam across the room. A grimy saltshaker. A stack of old magazines. An overturned ashtray with old cigarette butts scattered around it. A new-looking fire extinguisher. A box of kitchen utensils including an ice pick, something she hadn't seen in years. Several dark trashbags filled with what looked like clothing that had holes eaten in them by rats.

As if telepathy had warned it, something skittered away into the junk as she stepped into the room. She swallowed and wished she was outside, or better yet, home in bed.

She stepped carefully into the center of the room and aimed her light at the only piece of furniture in the room, a decrepit old couch with one leg missing. It sat like a swayback horse with bundles of junk and old newspapers all over it. As she edged slightly to the right, her pulse quickened. She saw what looked like an aluminum rod or a leg sticking out from behind the right side of the old couch. It had a rubber cap on it.

Moving a garbage bag full of newspapers and sending a new group of little friends scurrying, Veronica stepped around the edge of the couch. She grabbed it and pulled it out from behind, tossing it on top of the stuff on the couch.

It was the Mylar screen.

She stuck the flashlight in the waistband of her jeans, while she used both hands to open the screen, hoping against hope that she'd find two bullet holes. Finally, some proof.

She pulled it open by its little ringlike handle and her heart fell. It was a home-movie screen. The old kind one's brother-in-law would put up to show what comedian Richard Lewis called "home movies from hell." It was only about four feet long fully opened, so it couldn't have been used for their purpose. And there were a few tears around the edges, but no holes.

Veronica threw it down in disgust and retrieved the flash-light from her waistband. She was beginning to feel the creeping sense of failure. Nothing seemed to be working. She was learning more every day about how Angela was killed, but she couldn't seem to locate any proof to save her soul.

Weary and frustrated, Veronica picked her way through the debris back to the door and into the hall. She stopped for a moment to examine the holes in the wall again, more convinced than ever that her theory was right, if only it could be proven.

As she turned to go down the hall to the front door she saw the shadowy figure standing in the doorway. She froze with fear. He stood, legs spread apart. From his shadow she could see he was a massive man whose large frame almost blocked all the light from outside. She slowly brought the flashlight beam up his pants, across a wide leather belt, and up a thin tie to his face. It was a pockmarked face with deepset dark eyes.

"What the fuck you doin' here?" he barked. She detected an Italian accent.

She dropped the flashlight beam to his feet. On the way, the beam caught something shiny in his hand. Something metal. As he raised the hand to throw it, she realized it was a knife.

The knife whistled past her face and thudded into the wall behind her. She screamed. The big man started lumbering down the hall toward her. She went in the only available direction, into the room she had just left. His footsteps were nearing as she frantically pulled enough trash out of the way to push shut the door. It had a bolt on it and she slid it into place just as she heard him reach the end of the hall.

Frantically, she crammed the flashlight into the waistband of her belt and piled everything nearby against the door as he pounded on it and tiny rodent or insect feet skittered away.

Veronica knew she had boxed herself into a corner, and she tried to figure an instant solution. He was still pounding on the door. Suddenly, his right fist came through the door and a beefy hand reached around feeling for the bolt.

She looked for a weapon. Anything. On the floor was a hammer. She grabbed it and hit him square on the wrist.

He bellowed but his hand kept feeling for the bolt.

She searched frantically for something else.

His hand found the latch.

Veronica grabbed the rusty ice pick from the box of kitchen utensils.

He slid the bolt open.

She dropped her flashlight, and with both hands and all her strength she stabbed him in the hand. To her amazement, the ice pick went right through his hand and into the door.

He yelled in pain and tried to free his hand.

She picked up the hammer and smacked the heavy wooden handle of the ice pick a couple of times, driving it deeper through his hand into the door.

He cursed and shouted in pain.

She looked at her only possible means of escape, the newspaper-covered window.

He pounded on the door with his other fist.

She looked for something with which to break the window.

He smashed his other hand through the door.

She found the nearly new fire extinguisher.

He yanked the ice pick from his hand with a scream of pain and forced open the door enough that she could see his flabby face contorted in rage.

She grabbed the extinguisher, twisted the valve, and sprayed white smelly foam all over his pockmarked face.

He stumbled into the room and tried to wipe his eyes.

She grabbed the extinguisher by the ring around the top

and, with all her strength, swung it over her shoulders and hit him on the head with it.

He fell to his knees, but was still conscious.

In desperation, she turned to the window and threw the extinguisher against the newspaper. It ripped and crashed through the paper and the glass, letting in a burst of sea air.

Without a backward glance, Veronica grabbed an old coffeepot and smashed away the jagged edge of the glass enough to climb out. She heard the beefy man moaning behind her. Her foot slipped on the old real-estate sign, but she got to her feet, ran around the building down the sandy alley, and climbed into her car, grateful that she had forgotten to lock the door. As she locked it from the inside and started the little Honda, she saw in her rearview mirror the big man emerging from the front door with some foam still on his face and the knife in his hand.

She floored it the half block to Pass-A-Grille Way and took a fast left turn without even looking, racing northward off the peninsula. Glad to be alive but wishing she could stop shaking.

CHAPTER TWENTY-ONE

"WELL, IT SOUNDS LIKE YOU HAD A WHALE OF A NIGHT, Ronnie." Archie Slate waited while Veronica paid the toll on the St. Pete Beach side of the Bayway, then continued. "I just wish you wouldn't go off like that without me or someone along."

"You mean you or another *man,* don't you?" She smiled at her father, who looked crisp and clean in navy blue slacks and a pale blue cotton shirt, and turned into the parking lot of the Don CeSar. "I've never bought the idea that I have to be protected by a man. You know that."

"I know that, yes, but there's a difference between being dependent on a man and being cautious."

"Daddy, I can't just sit around and wait for a man to protect me." She slammed, then locked, her car door. "Something has to be done quickly or David's going to jail for a crime I don't think he committed." She fell in beside her father, and they walked across the street and into the side entrance of the hotel. "I can't wait around for a man to help

207

me. For God's sake, David's in the hospital, Max has a business to run, and you're always out with Barbara. . . ." She stopped, too late.

Archie silently opened the door for her, followed her inside, and broke his silence as they walked up the carpeted hall. "You don't really like Barbara, do you?"

"I don't really know her."

"I understand," Archie said. "A little jealousy is natural. You feel like she's trying to replace your mother. . . ."

Veronica stopped and whirled to face her father so quickly the strap of her blue canvas purse fell to the crook of her elbow. "No one can replace Mom."

Archie raised his hand, palm forward. "Wait a minute, Ronnie. That's what I was about to say." He took her arm, she tugged her purse strap back onto her shoulder, and they resumed walking toward the elevators. "No one can replace Elizabeth and no one should," Archie said. "But I need to have some sort of life. I can't just fish and dream of the past. I have maybe twenty years ahead of me. I don't want to spend them alone."

Veronica pushed the Up button. "I could move back in." She realized that was a ridiculous idea, but she felt protective of her father, and Barbara Robinson didn't seem good enough for him.

He laughed. "Honey, I love you, but that's not practical. You work in Tampa, remember?" The elevator door opened, discharging a small boy in a red bathing suit who ran down the hall without looking at them. They entered the elevator, and she pushed the button for the third floor.

"That's the other side to this," Archie said, his face turning serious. "You need to have a life of your own, too. I know we're all that's left of our family. We'll always have each other. But we also need to have special people of our own. Love is nothing if it isn't shared."

"I'm sorry," she said. "I'll try to get to know her." She glanced at herself in the mirrored wall of the elevator. She wore denim shorts, a pale blue WAQT T-shirt, and Adidas running shoes with little tennis socks. Were her thighs getting fat? Probably. She'd be thirty-one in May. Heading down the home stretch to middle age.

"Ronnie? Are you listening to me?"

"I'm sorry. What did you say?"

"Whether you get to know Barbara or not, one thing's for sure." The elevator stopped, and they stepped out into the carpeted foyer. Archie pulled Veronica over near an antique chair. "One thing's for sure, honey. I'm going to date Barbara for as long as I want to. I hope you'll learn to like her, but I won't stop seeing her just to please you."

"I wouldn't ask you to . . ."

He smiled. "Yes, you would, if you thought I'd pay any attention to you. But you know your old man is a tough cookie."

Finally, Veronica managed a small smile. She patted his cheek and said, "A tough cookie with gooey chocolate inside."

For a half hour, before the first setup, Veronica took her father from one person to another, introducing him and trying to explain, briefly, what each of them did. Jon Vasta invited him to stay and watch them film the first scene. As Archie and Veronica sat in deck chairs around the outdoor pool behind the hotel, he had a few questions.

"Let me see if I've got this straight," Archie said. "A gaffer is the chief electrician, and a best boy is his assistant?"

"Right. But the assistant to the key grip is also called a best boy. A key grip is the man in charge of the other grips, the guys who set up walls and camera tracks and so on."

"Seems to me it would take a year in this business just to learn the terms."

"Probably." She noticed a guy in cutoffs and a muscle T-shirt standing at the Beachcomber Grill, a small tile-roofed snack bar near the pool.

"Wait here, Daddy," she said. "Speaking of gaffers, there he is. I wanna ask him about that screen."

As his daughter strode around the pool and started talking to the gaffer, Archie peered up toward the sun, which was beginning to clear the top of the hotel in its westward arc toward the Gulf of Mexico, in front of him. He closed his eyes for a moment and drank in the warmth. There was just enough of a breeze to make it a nearly perfect day. He sat up and watched Veronica standing on one leg with the other foot gracefully tucked behind her, talking to the gaffer. Her long beautiful legs were something she had inherited from Elizabeth.

He closed his eyes again and considered how well his only child had turned out. She was intelligent, practical, and had a sense of fair play that often caused her to turn fanatic when something threatened those she loved. While it was a good trait, he knew, it was also one that could lead her to danger.

Sure, Archie had been in danger many times in his career with the Bureau, but his daughter . . . His sweet, beautiful child. He couldn't bear the thought of losing her to violence, as he had lost Elizabeth. And why did she become involved in dangerous situations? Love was usually her motivation. He worried that someday she would get in over her head.

Archie shook his head and opened his eyes as a tall, red-haired man in a gray suit brushed past his chair and walked up to the director, Jon Vasta, and the actor he'd met, Paul Haden. It was certainly not a day to be wearing a three-piece suit. The man leaned over and said something to the director. Even from his position some fifteen feet away, Archie could see the anger that flashed on Vasta's face. The red-haired man said something to Paul Haden, and then all three men turned and looked at Veronica, who was at the moment talking to a skinny woman with spiky red hair who had a cigarette dangling from her mouth. Something about the way the two men observed her sent a chill up Archie's back. He started over toward where she was standing. Veronica nodded to the skinny woman and met her father by the corner of the pool.

"Didn't you tell me Raynor Fitzhugh mentioned an Irishman in a three-piece suit in connection with Tony Victor?" He nodded toward the three men, who were still in conversation.

Veronica stiffened. "Jesus, Daddy! Could that be him? He certainly matches the description. And he's talking to Jon."

"Interesting."

Veronica checked her watch. "Listen, Daddy, Raynor Fitzhugh is expected on the set in about twenty minutes. I'm going to see if I can get him down here right now to take a look at this guy, see if he is the Irishman."

"Okay. Go ahead. I'll keep an eye on him."

Veronica pointed to the Beachcomber Grill. "If you want, you can get a drink. I'll be back in a few minutes."

"Okay." He stopped her before she took two steps. "Wait. What did the gaffer say?"

"He said they had two Mylar screens when they got here. Now they've got one." She brushed her hair from her eyes in the unconsciously sexy way she had. "He'd like to know what happened to the other one, too."

Veronica called Fitzhugh's room from the lobby, but there was no answer. She went to his room and knocked on the door. No answer. Back in the lobby, she ran into Liz, who said she didn't know where Fitzhugh was but that Jon Vasta was looking for her.

"Looking for me?" Veronica repeated. "You know why?"

"No," Liz said. "He's in the production office."

The moment Veronica got off the elevator on the third floor she had an uneasy feeling. Something was different. Like when one entered an office where the furniture had been moved since one's last visit.

Jon Vasta was alone in the production office, standing looking out the corner window at the pool area below. He turned when he heard her.

"Shut the door, please." His eyes seemed tired and sad. There was a faint redness to them. He sat at the desk in Liz's chair and gestured to the folding chair opposite. "Have a seat."

Veronica sat, dropped her purse to the floor between her legs, and shook her hair back off her face. "What's up?"

"I wanted to tell you this in person because I like you and I'm grateful for the job you've done here."

Veronica felt that decades-old lump in her chest, the lump she got when called to the principal's office. His choice of words and his tone had not escaped her notice. She sensed she was about to become past tense.

"I'm afraid I'm going to have to let you go." He looked at the coatrack by the door. "It's not really my decision. Carla feels your regular job is getting in the way of your work here." He gazed at the top of the desk and straightened the pad. "We really need someone who's available more often." He glanced at the window, then at the telephone. "And someone who has more actual film-making experience." He finally met her steady gaze. "I'm sorry."

"I don't know what to say." She knew the real reason she was being fired. She was too close to something. Or someone. "I've really enjoyed this job."

Vasta said quickly, "And we've enjoyed working with you. You've done a good job." He blinked and added, "Within certain limitations, of course." He lined up the pens and pencils on Liz's desk. "We'll give you thirty days' severance pay because you've . . ." He brought his sad blue eyes up to meet hers. "Look, Veronica, this is not my fault. There are people I have to answer to. The producers. The people who put up the money to get my films made. They say I must fire you. So I must."

"I thought you said it was Carla." Veronica stood and dragged her purse up to her shoulder. "Has this got something to do with the guy in the three-piece suit out there?"

Vasta's eyes widened and his mouth began to move before he said anything. "He . . . uh . . . no. It was a decision from higher up."

"Do you want me to work the rest of the day?"

Vasta stood, obviously relieved. "No. That's okay. Just get your check from the accountant." He walked around the desk and looked up at her as he offered his hand. "And please feel free to come by and see us once in a while." He presented a leftover smile. "It's been nice working with you."

On her way to the elevator with a check for eight hundred dollars in her purse, Veronica felt rejected and curiously relieved. The movie business was tough, and she had felt like a stepchild anyhow. And she was pleased that she had apparently gotten close enough to worry someone. Carla had not been responsible, that she knew. It had to be the Irishman. She was convinced that Jon Vasta was really Alan Smithee, the man behind the deaths of five people. But the problem still remained: how to prove it.

Archie crept along in the heavy traffic behind the wheel of Veronica's tiny Honda Accord. Three years ago, when she'd bought the car, Veronica had given her father the spare key against the possible day she'd lock her keys in the car. He'd put it on his ring and forgotten about it—until today, when the red-haired man in the three-piece suit had left abruptly with Veronica nowhere in sight. Archie had decided on the spur of the moment that someone ought to follow the man. Since Veronica was unavailable, Archie had decided to take matters in his own hands, borrow her car, and follow him. Just like old times.

For the last twenty minutes he had followed "Red" up the narrow, mostly two-lane beach road past signs that identified such tiny communities as Treasure Island, Redington Beach, Redington Shores, Indian Shores, and Indian Rocks Beach.

Archie couldn't tell one town from another. The roadway was all one long blur of hotels, motels, restaurants, beach-clothing stores, bars, and souvenir shops. Until they reached an area identified as Belleair Beach.

As different as day and night, Belleair Beach boasted quiet yards, trees, fences, and grass. No billboards. No signs. No motels. Obviously the home of people wealthy enough to live the way they wanted. That idea seemed to be confirmed when "Red" turned his gray BMW into the parking lot of the first commercial establishment Archie had seen in Belleair Beach. A bank.

And what a bank. With sculpted hedges, an expanse of unusually green lawn, a graceful sloped roof, and imported stonework around the doors and windows, it looked more like a country estate. Only the small tasteful sign, THE BANK OF BELLEAIR BEACH, gave it away.

"Red" parked and walked in the front door carrying a burgundy briefcase.

Archie tried to get comfortable, which was almost impossible in Veronica's tiny foreign car. He never could figure out how she squeezed her five-foot-ten frame into a little Honda. Or why. She had always insisted she liked small cars. When she'd been married to Sam, she'd driven a little green Ford Cortina. They don't even make them anymore. Then she'd driven a succession of Hondas, ending with this one. He wished she'd get into something bigger and safer.

Archie was so busy thinking about his daughter's automotive preferences he didn't see the curly-haired man leave the bank. What he did see was the burgundy briefcase being thrown in the trunk, and "Red" getting into the car and pulling out onto Gulf Boulevard. He turned right as Archie gave him a few car lengths. Then Archie pulled out to follow him. *Jesus!* Archie thought. *He's going back the way we came.*

It had been years since he had followed someone on Bureau business, but Archie had always been expert at tailing. He was convinced his "mark" hadn't noticed him. For one thing, "Red" had been bobbing his head and slapping the steering wheel much of the way to music that Archie couldn't hear. But the three times he was right behind the BMW, he could hear the bass. Probably had it loud enough to drown out a war. Good thing.

CHAPTER TWENTY-TWO

VERONICA STOOD AT THE POOL, A GULF BREEZE BLOWING her dark brown hair, her eyes frantically searching for some sign of her handsome white-haired father. She'd checked with Carla Jahns, who'd said she hadn't seen him since they'd been introduced earlier. The red-haired stranger was gone. Paul Haden was at the Beachcomber Grill sipping a drink. But Archie Slate was gone. She looked for him, feeling the kind of panic she'd felt as a child when separated from her mother in a grocery store.

Finally, she guessed that her father was somewhere around the hotel following the man in the three-piece suit. Until he turned up, she decided to take advantage of her last day at the Don CeSar to grab the one thing she could use to convince the police that Jon Vasta was a criminal and drug dealer. The green suitcase in his penthouse. His "stash," as Tracy had called it.

Veronica rode to the penthouse level in the special elevator. She knew the door was almost always unlocked, except at night. She walked into the east penthouse, yelling, "Hello! Anybody here?" She didn't want to stumble in on some bimbo enjoying an afternoon delight with a crew member. Silence. Except for gull cries and light traffic noises drifting in from the open sliding-glass doors to the balcony. She checked the balcony. It was much like the one she'd been standing on when she first met Adrian Bell, except that this one looked down on the parking lot and toward the tall buildings of Isla Del Sol, a couple of miles east. She took a deep breath of the fresh spring air, then went back into the penthouse and up the spiral staircase to the bedroom level.

The day she and Tracy had moved the stuff to the east penthouse, the green zippered suitcase had been in the closet.

Today, it wasn't in the closet. Nor on the long wide table beneath one of the windows where another suitcase was sitting open. It wasn't in the bathroom, all gold fixtures and pastel prints. Surely he wouldn't have hidden it beneath the bed. She got down on her knees and dipped her head sideways to look.

"I'll be damned," Veronica said, as she pulled the dusty green suitcase out from under the bed. She put it on the chair behind her and checked the zipper to see if it was locked. It wasn't. Carefully, she zipped it open. The metal zipper sounded like a jackhammer in the relative silence of the room. She opened it and found what she had expected, something she had never seen except in movies. A bunch of plastic bags filled with a white substance. Unless he was smuggling baby powder, it looked as though Jon Vasta did indeed have a drug-dealing sideline.

She tried to decide what to do with it. If she took it, with her luck, she'd be arrested for possession. Besides, how could she prove it came from Jon Vasta's bedroom? She zipped the suitcase shut. She didn't really know the rules of evidence, but she couldn't leave without something to use against Jon Vasta. He had arranged the deaths of several people to cover his drug-dealing sideline and his Irish-Colombian financial backers. She just couldn't let him get away with it.

She finally decided to take it. Even if it couldn't be used as evidence, it could be used as a bargaining chip. Surely,

Vasta would want it back. That might scare him enough that he'd make a mistake. That was what she needed. A mistake.

She listened for any unusual sounds, then went down the spiral staircase. She checked out the living room. No one there. She shut the door, tiptoed into the hall, and decided to walk down the stairs instead of taking the slow-moving elevator.

As she reached the bottom of the first flight of stairs, she realized she might be doing a stupid thing. She was carrying a suitcase full of probably thousands of dollars' worth of an illegal drug, and had only a flimsy way to prove where she got it or to whom it belonged. What the hell was she going to do? If only her father were there, he'd know. . . . *Wait a minute,* she thought. *Where is Daddy?*

Veronica came down the last set of stairs to the ground-floor level of the hotel, and opened the door enough to peek through. There were a few hotel guests walking around, but she didn't see anyone from the crew. She took a deep breath and started out at a fast pace toward the exit about a hundred yards away. She remembered that old theory advanced by one of her high-school classmates. People who act as if they know where they're going are seldom stopped. She prayed it was true.

The green suitcase felt like a neon beacon in her hand. She imagined that it had a loudspeaker in it blaring "coke, coke, coke!" *If you could be this paranoid just carrying the stupid stuff,* she thought, *imagine how crazy you'd get using it.* She was just a few feet from the door, hoping she wouldn't bump into anyone on the way to her car. She planned on hiding the suitcase in the trunk of her Honda, then going back to the hotel for one more try at finding her father.

Through the doors. So far so good. Up to the curb at Pass-A-Grille Way, the only street into and out of the peninsula. Look both ways. It was four lanes with a median here, but became two lanes just south of the hotel. Wait for two cars and a U.P.S. truck. Walk across the street. Even as she crossed the street and entered the parking lot, she felt as if people were hanging out windows of the huge pink hotel behind her, staring and saying, *Look! There goes a woman with a suitcase full of coke.*

Only a few more feet. If she wasn't mistaken, her Honda was parked just beyond that big blue RV. She passed it and reached for her keys in her purse. She looked up and her heart fell to her feet. There was a red Toyota parked there. *Maybe I parked somewhere else,* she thought.

Veronica started a panicky but careful search of the entire parking lot, trying to look casual. What the hell happened to the car? Why would anyone take it? *How* would anyone take it? *Is my mind playing tricks on me?*

The green suitcase was beginning to weigh a hundred pounds of guilt and fear. Veronica was sweating, but not from the sunny day, which was cooled by gentle breezes.

She finally stopped and leaned up against one of the white concrete supports under the entrance ramp, watching without interest the cars going by on Pass-A-Grille Way, trying to figure out what to do.

I can't take a chance going back into the hotel with the suitcase in my hands, she thought, *and I can't hide it here. I can't walk home.* She cast another worried look at the hotel. A woman and two small children were entering the ground-floor ice-cream parlor. A couple of workers in white pants and shirts were washing windows on the outside of the first floor. She looked up at the edifice before her. Curtains were blowing in and out of a window on what looked like the fourth floor, where someone had probably opened a window to enjoy the fresh air. As she watched, a man looked out the window. He looked at her. There was no doubt. She tried to be invisible. He stepped back from the window before she could see who he was.

She heard a steady booming bass beat like a distant marching band as a gray BMW started up from the traffic light a half block away and drove past her heading south toward Pass-A-Grille. A moment later, there was a short, tentative beep from a foreign-car horn. It sounded like a Honda. She looked. It *was* a Honda. A blue 1983 Honda Accord. *Her* Honda. It stopped directly across from her in the far right southbound lane. Her father was behind the wheel. The passenger's door flew open, and Archie called, "Get in, Ronnie! Quickly!"

She crossed to the median, waited for a red Toyota that was passing Archie on the left, ran around the rear of the car, threw the suitcase in the back, and climbed into the seat. "Dammit, Daddy! What in the world were you doing?"

He took off even before she had closed the door.

"I was frantic," she said. "First I couldn't find you. Then I couldn't find my car. And, on top of everything else, I got fired."

"I hope it wasn't something I said," Archie said, smiling.

"I think they were worried that I'm getting too close."

"To what?"

"I wish I knew."

Archie gestured to the backseat, where she'd tossed the green suitcase. "What's in the suitcase?"

"I don't know how they figure street value, but I bet it's at least a couple thousand dollars' worth of cocaine."

"The hell you say!"

"I'll explain later, but I think you've got some explaining to do." She looked out the window as they passed the Pass-A-Grille Yacht Club. "Where are you going?"

"Damned if I know," Archie said. "I'm following *him*." He pointed at the BMW just ahead of the Toyota in front of them. "Have been for almost an hour."

"The Irishman?"

"Yeah." The Toyota turned right at Eighteenth Avenue, just beyond the fire station, putting them directly behind the BMW, about three car lengths back.

She leaned over and kissed his cheek. "Daddy, you are the greatest! Where did he go before?"

As they followed the BMW down Pass-A-Grille Way, Archie told her about the bank in Belleair Beach, the burgundy briefcase, and the trip up and down the beach road.

"What a coincidence that you drove by and I was there."

"Coincidence, hell," Archie said. "This is the only street coming down here, and you were standing right on the curb like a statue. I even watched you from the red light. I couldn't honk because he was right in front of me. I was afraid you'd go back into the hotel.''

"Not with a suitcase full of cocaine.''

A moment later, the gray BMW turned right onto Sixth Avenue.

"Pull up over there, Daddy." She pointed to the curb. "I think he may be stopping.''

Sure enough, he did, pulling into a dirt alley next to a familiar weather-beaten house.

"How did you know he'd stop there?''

"That's the house I told you about.''

"Where Angela was killed?''

"And where I almost got knocked off last night.''

Archie issued a low whistle. "Well, it looks like everything's coming together.''

"Yeah, maybe," she said, slumping in her seat. "Let's wait and watch what happens.''

Adrian Bell was down on his hands and knees frantically searching for the green suitcase he had hidden under Jon's bed. He was beginning to sweat with fear. He ran an excellent chance of being killed if he couldn't find it.

As he searched the closets and the bathroom, Bell was painfully aware that losing the coke or pretending to lose it was what got Tony Victor killed. Victor had been stupid, trying to go into business for himself, so he'd lied to them and said he had lost the stash to undercover cops. They hadn't bought that story. They'd murdered him. Angela had seen them do it. They'd murdered her. Her attorney had known. They'd murdered him. Todd had helped him set up the cop. They'd murdered Todd. If Bell gave them any cause to doubt he could be trusted, he'd be next.

Adrian raced dizzily down the spiral staircase, fear rising in his throat, and rushed to check the kitchen and the living room. He started for the hall closet, only to be stopped in his tracks by the chirp of the phone. After a couple of rings, he sat on the chair and picked it up. "Yeah?''

"Can't find it, can you?''

"No." How the hell did he know?

"That's not good, Adrian. But I know where it is."

A wave of relief turned instantly to dread. "Where?"

"The Slate girl's got it. I saw her get into a car out in front of the hotel just a few minutes ago. And guess what?"

"What?"

"Whoever was driving the car was following Derek on his way back from the bank."

"Do you think Derek knows?"

"Maybe. Maybe not. But you know what you've got to do."

"Get it back?" Sweat poured down his chest.

"Smart man."

"How am I going to find her?"

"Think about it, Adrian. If she was following Derek . . ."

"Oh, yeah. Okay. Count on me. I'll get it."

"Wait. There's more. I want you to get the suitcase *and* the girl. Bring them both back to the penthouse. I'll be waiting there for you."

"Where are you now?"

"In the production office." He chuckled. "I am trying to make a movie, you know."

"What about the shipment coming in this afternoon? You need me for security?"

"No. That's okay. Ruffini will be there. And Derek."

He clenched the phone. "But you said you'd give me more to do if I took care of Angela."

"And I will. Just prove your worth, Adrian. Get the coke and the girl and meet me in the penthouse."

"Okay." He held the phone for a moment and decided to do the prudent thing. He called Tracy and told her what he was about to do and what she should do if they killed him. She sounded frantic and panicky, but he didn't have time to reassure her. He needed someone to reassure *him*.

Archie sat in Veronica's Honda, his back aching from sitting in the little car for almost two hours. He was parked in an angled space on Gulf Way in Pass-A-Grille, facing the white sandy beach with the broad expanse of the Gulf of Mexico beyond it. But he wasn't looking at the water. He was watching the front of a restaurant called The Busted Flush in his rearview mirror.

Archie and Veronica had watched the old house on Sixth for almost twenty minutes before the red-haired man had returned to his car, along with a heavy, muscular man with a bandaged right hand. Veronica had immediately recognized him as the knife-wielding man who had attacked her there the night before. The two men had driven two blocks away to the restaurant called The Busted Flush and disappeared inside.

Veronica and Archie had followed at a safe distance, then pulled into an angled space across from the restaurant.

Veronica stood at a phone booth just a few feet from her car, within view of the restaurant, calling the St. Petersburg Beach police in hopes of reaching Detective Chris Cross.

While he waited, Archie kept his eyes on The Busted Flush. A few cars drove by. The air was filled with the voices of children playing on the beach, gulls crying out to one another, and the waves of the Gulf beating a steady, soothing pulse.

A pretty young girl in a violet bikini ruined her loveliness in Archie's eyes when she stopped, cupped her hands to her pretty face, and lit up a cigarette. *Doesn't she know what an ugly habit that is?* he thought.

As Veronica climbed back in the car, she said, "I couldn't reach Cross, but the guy I talked to promised to give him a message to meet us here."

"Just hope it's in time."

"I also called David. He's okay." She frowned. "He told me to be careful and to listen to you."

Archie smiled. "I know. You think it's a male conspiracy."

She ignored the comment. "Max and I were down here Wednesday. We talked to the owner of the restaurant." She shut the door. "He also owns the house."

"Wonder if he's in on it."

"I don't know. He did seem to know a lot about drug smuggling here years ago. Could be."

"I've got an idea," Archie said, turning to look at his daughter. "The Irish guy doesn't know me. . . ."

"No. I guess not." She rolled the window down.

"That stuffed Italian sausage with a head doesn't know me. . . ."

He could see that she had caught on.

"Oh, no, you don't—" she sputtered.

"The owner of the place doesn't know me. . . ."

"Daddy, c'mon." She grabbed his arm. "You're always telling me to wait for help. Wait for Detective Cross to get here."

He waved her away. "I'm not going to do anything foolish." He patted her cheek. "I'm just going to go in and have a beer and see what I can overhear."

Veronica smiled. "Even in the face of danger you're a poet."

Archie opened his door. "I'll be okay." He slammed the door and started across the street to the entrance of The Busted Flush. Perhaps he wasn't setting a good example for his daughter, but he was tired of waiting for something to happen.

It might even be time to *make* something happen.

CHAPTER TWENTY-THREE

ARCHIE WALKED CASUALLY IN THE DOOR OF THE BUSTED Flush and smiled at the middle-aged lady behind the cashier's counter. "Just here for a drink," he said.

"Upstairs," she told him, pointing to the staircase. He dodged a green chalkboard listing the dinner specials that sat on three spindly legs at the base of the stairs, and climbed to a little twenty-by-twenty room that looked more like a loft than a bar. A Mitsubishi projection-TV was on in the corner tuned to a rerun of "I Love Lucy." A red digital display above the screen said "28." He glanced at his watch. A quarter past one. Past lunchtime. His stomach was growling.

Crammed around a table near the short bar on the side of the tiny room opposite the windows were the Irishman, the sausagelike man with a pockmarked face and a bandaged hand, and a compact, muscular man with tattoos and a barrel chest draped with gold chains. Must be the restaurant owner, Archie thought.

The three men had glanced at him when he appeared at the

top of the stairs, and had immediately gone back to their hushed conversation. There were only two other customers in the cramped bar: a skinny young man in swim trunks, flip-flops, and a white terry-cloth jacket sitting with the girl in the violet bikini he had seen earlier. She was smoking another cigarette.

Archie placed his order for a Coors with the young bartender, and was frustrated to discover that where he had chosen to sit, by the window at the top of the stairs, was a bad place for listening in on the conversation. He was just three feet from a straining room-sized air conditioner that wheezed and buzzed as water dripped into a coffee can.

Veronica was still in the passenger's seat of her Honda, worrying about her father in The Busted Flush, wishing the police would show up, and feeling like a criminal with a suitcase full of cocaine on the rear seat of her car.

Across the low concrete wall separating the street from the beach, youngsters were playing in the sand and the water. Two college-aged boys tossed a Frisbee, aided by a black-and-white dog. A young man and a girl in identical T-shirts were holding hands looking out at the Gulf. It reminded her of that day with Paul Haden. It was a little disturbing that she could be so easily charmed after thinking she was committed to David. But, with the clarity that came only from absence, she was reassessing her relationship with the curly-haired cop.

She expelled a burst of pent-up frustration with a long breath, and longed for a return to normalcy. At this point she'd be grateful just to be doing her radio show, working on her relationship—with David or whomever—and living a calmer life. But first, she had to give Detective Christopher Cross enough to work on so that Jon Vasta and whoever those other two were would go behind bars for a while.

She saw the shadow and smelled the spicy cologne a couple of beats before the gun was thrust in the open window at her face. Adrian Bell leaned down and smiled. "Hi, Veronica. How you doin'? I'm told you've got something. . . ."

He spotted the suitcase in the backseat. "You do. You do have something that doesn't belong to you."

"Look, I don't know what you're planning, but my father is sitting in the restaurant right behind you watching me from that window, and the police are on their way."

He glanced at the restaurant and opened the passenger's door. "Well, then we better get a move on. Why don't you drive? It's your car." He poked her shoulder with the barrel of the gun and she climbed out, walked around, and climbed in behind the wheel.

As she circled the car she looked at the windows above the entrance to The Busted Flush. She saw her father's white hair, but he wasn't looking in her direction.

From the passenger's side, with his gun in her ribs, Adrian Bell said, "To the big pink hotel, please." He laughed.

For several minutes Archie had been pretending to watch "I Love Lucy" while straining to hear the conversation of the three men. The Irishman was writing something on a piece of paper, while the tattooed restaurant owner added figures with a pocket calculator. The sausage in a suit was watching Lucy stomp around in a vat of grapes with her bare feet. The young man and the girl in the violet bikini paid and went down the narrow stairs.

As soon as they were out of sight, the Irishman and the beefy guy stood up. The stuffed sausage grabbed his crotch, adjusting his shorts, while the Irishman said something to the restaurant owner and shook his hand. Then the red-haired man and the beefy man with the bandaged hand headed in Archie's direction. Archie was tensing his muscles, ready for at least an attempt at self-defense, when they both walked right by him and down the stairs behind him without even a glance.

Relieved, Archie glanced at the big TV again. A girl wearing too much makeup was saying, "If you want to be a model or just look like one . . ." He missed the toll-free number because the restaurant owner with ten pounds of gold chains around his neck came between Archie and the TV and pulled up a chair.

"Howdy." He extended his hand and Archie shook it. "I'm Vern Dahlhauser. I own this place."

"Nice to meet you," Archie said. "Name's Archie. I'm just visiting. Seems like a nice place to live."

"Pass-A-Grille? Yeah, I suppose." He raised his bushy eyebrows and revealed a few missing teeth as he smiled. "Mostly, this place is getting filled up with people who are trying to run away from something." He turned serious, as if to warn that something profound was coming up. "When people are running away from the world, they run to the end of an island."

Archie nodded. "I suppose that's true."

"How about you?" Dahlhauser asked. "You running from something or someone?"

"No. Not really."

Dahlhauser's eyes darted above Archie's head for a split-second. He said, "Maybe you should be running."

At that instant, a heavy, muscular arm came around Archie's neck from behind, another arm grabbed him by the belt, and he was lifted right out of his chair by the beefy man, who'd sneaked up behind him unheard because of a lousy air conditioner, a contrived conversation, and a "Lucy" rerun.

By the time Bell and Veronica reached the Don CeSar, it was after two in the afternoon. Adrian Bell stayed slightly behind Veronica as they entered the hotel on the ground level and walked along the carpeted hall past the game room to the special elevator near the ice-cream parlor. He had forced her to carry the suitcase. He held only the gun, concealed by his closeness to her.

Bell pushed the button and they waited. And waited. Veronica toyed with the idea of just running, but she wasn't sure where she could run. She was also not entirely certain he wouldn't just shoot her in the back.

She glanced down the hall, which led through past some elite shops to Le Bistro, the ground-floor nightclub. It was only a few minutes past two, but sandwiches were served there most of the day. As she looked down the hall and Bell impatiently pushed the elevator button, Veronica saw a familiar face turn the corner from Le Bistro. It was Paul Haden. *Thank God!* she thought.

As he passed the small art gallery, Haden recognized her. At the same moment, Bell noticed Haden, and Veronica felt the deadly pressure of his gun in her ribs.

"Hi, darlin'," Haden said, as he approached them. "What are you doing here?" He kissed her lightly on the cheek and glanced at Bell. "And with such a disreputable man." He nodded at Bell.

"We're going . . . uh . . ." she stammered. "We've got to . . . see Jon. I've got to return his . . . suitcase." She arched her eyebrows, hoping he'd catch the hint that she was in trouble.

"Wait a minute," Haden interjected. "I thought I heard this afternoon that Jon fired you, honey. What did you do, steal his suitcase just for spite?"

Nervously, Veronica started to answer, but she was stopped by the elevator doors opening. Bell pulled her into the elevator. She smiled at Haden and said, "Maybe he wants to hire me back." Knowing her chance was passing by, she tried a long shot. "He knows Alan Smithee and Alan spoke up for me."

Something she hoped was recognition flashed in Haden's eyes. He nodded, smiled, and said, "Well, good seeing you. If you get a chance later, drop by Le Bistro. I'll buy you a drink." He nodded at Bell as the doors closed. "And you, too, Adrian."

As the elevator began moving up, Bell said, "Nice try." He put the gun back in his belt.

Veronica closed her eyes, wondering if Paul had gotten her hint. What would he do if he had? She realized she was probably on her own.

At the penthouse level, they got off the elevator and went in the open door of the east penthouse.

Inside, Jon Vasta was sitting on an overstuffed chair. On a straight chair opposite him was the red-haired man Archie had been tailing all afternoon. She wondered where the muscleman was. More important, where was her father?

"Ah. Miss Slate. I'm glad you could come." The red-haired man motioned to the couch. "Have a seat."

She pulled away from Adrian Bell's grasp with a frown and sat on the couch.

To Adrian Bell, the red-haired man said, "You did well. If you'd like a treat, help yourself." He gestured at a couple of lines of cocaine on the glass table in the dining area. Nearby was an entire bag, slit open at the top.

Bell smiled and went to the table and snorted a line.

"Aren't you going to introduce us?" the Irishman said to Jon Vasta, who had gotten up and was standing off to the side, looking uncomfortable.

"Yes," Vasta said, a streak of sweat rolling near his Yoda-like eyes. He gestured at the tall man with curly red hair and freckles sprinkled across his face. "This is Derek Morahan."

Veronica ignored Morahan and asked Vasta, "Why did you invite me to this little meeting? You planning to give yourself up?"

Vasta looked truly surprised. "Give myself up?" He looked at Derek Morahan, who laughed, a bell-like peal more feminine than brittle.

"My goodness, Jon, you were right." He adjusted the muted red tie, which brightened his gray three-piece suit. "This one is a feisty bitch." His Irish brogue didn't fit his words. "Well, Jon, I'd like to thank you for the use of your penthouse. Why don't you go back downstairs and continue with your work? I know you have a picture to make."

Vasta stood, still sporting a confused look on his face. "I don't understand, Derek. What has this girl got to do with—"

Morahan stood and glared at Jon Vasta, who looked even shorter under the gaze. "Really, Jon. You don't want to know about everything that's going on. Do you?"

Vasta nervously started for the door. "No." He looked at Veronica and said, "I'm sorry I had to fire you." Then he left.

"Now, Miss Slate, you have something that belongs to us, and we'd like it back." He walked over to the couch, grabbed the suitcase, and opened it. "Good. Our little green suitcase of Colombian marching powder is safe and sound. How wonderful.'' He turned and flashed an evil smile at her. ''How good for you.''

''It's all falling apart, you know.'' She was bluffing mostly because she didn't know what else to do. ''I've told the police everything I know and they'll be here any minute.''

Morahan laughed. ''Goodness. I've heard *that* before.''

Adrian Bell laughed and rubbed his nose with a forefinger. A trace of white powder stuck in his moustache.

Morahan sat again, crossing his legs and clasping his hands around his knee. ''I am curious, my dear.'' He grinned at Bell. ''Just what is it you know?''

''I know Jon Vasta hired you to kill Tony Victor because Tony was skimming. I know you've been putting up the money for Vasta's films for years and using people like Adrian here to deal your drugs. I know you killed Angela's attorney and then Angela herself because she saw you kill Tony. I know you killed Todd Keener because he helped with Angela.'' She took a breath and flashed a thin, triumphant smile. ''And I know how you killed Angela so it would look like David did it.''

''My goodness,'' Morahan said. ''You have been doing your homework. It's only a shame that you are mostly wrong.''

Veronica started to speak, but was cut short by a sound at the door where the big man with the bandaged hand had just arrived. The olive-skinned giant looked as if his muscular body had been poured into his charcoal suit. He came over, ignoring both Bell and Veronica, and strode directly to Morahan's chair.

''Ah. Mr. Ruffini. How are things at The Busted Flush?''

''He's tied up.'' He sneered at Veronica. ''I'm supposed to kill him after the shipment comes in.''

''What have you done with my father?'' Veronica cried. ''Is he hurt?'' She started to get up off the couch, but Bell forced her down. ''What have you done to him?''

''Stop fucking around,'' said Mr. Ruffini, raising his bandaged hand. ''We got a schedule to keep.''

Derek Morahan muttered something to the chunky man in

what sounded like Italian, then turned back to the group. "Actually, we didn't kill Angela," Morahan said. "She was killed by your boyfriend the policeman."

"I know." Veronica started to rise, but was forced back down on the couch again by Adrian Bell's hand. "But it's all over now. I know how you did it."

"Take her out there," Morahan said, nodding toward the open sliding-glass doors leading to the balcony.

Bell stood Veronica up and walked her out onto the balcony, with Morahan and Ruffini following behind. Morahan was carrying a small black leather case.

"Okay," Bell said. "What now? You gonna throw her off the roof?"

"No. You are," Morahan said. "Here's the scenario we've devised: You and the woman came up to Vasta's penthouse and you did a line. . . ."

Bell glanced nervously at the traces of white powder on the glass table just inside the doors. Veronica could even see his fingerprints in some spilled powder.

"You got in a fight, became violent, and pushed her off the roof," Morahan concluded.

Bell seemed to be digesting it all. "Yeah, but they'll arrest me for her murder."

"No. No. No." He dismissed the thought with a wave of his slim white hand. "You needn't worry. They won't be able to arrest you." The Irishman reached in his briefcase and brought out a hypo. "You'll be dead, the unfortunate victim of an overdose." He nodded to his beefy sidekick. "Hold him."

"What the fuck?" Adrian Bell was startled, and he stepped back as Ruffini lumbered toward him. "What's going on, guys?"

"You also know too much, Mr. Bell," the red-haired boss-man said. "I'm afraid you're of no use anymore."

Bell straightened, pulled the gun from the back of his belt, and pointed it at Ruffini, who stopped only long enough to grin. With amazing agility for a man his size, Ruffini rushed forward, batted the gun from Bell's hand, and slapped either side of Bell's head with his beefy fists. The gun flew to the corner of the balcony about six feet away.

As Bell grabbed his head in pain, Ruffini hit him in the stomach with his left fist, doubling him over, and brought both big fists down hard on the back of Bell's head. The handsome stuntman went down to his knees like a sack of flour.

Veronica edged toward the glass doors with escape on her mind. Ruffini stomped over to the sliding-glass doors and stood, leering defiantly at her. Morahan bent over to administer the liquefied coke into an artery in Bell's neck. Veronica stood still, not knowing what to do.

As Morahan leaned over the stuntman, Bell's fist shot straight up, catching the Irishman under the chin and sending him reeling backward. He fell against the wall and crumpled to the floor. Ruffini turned and saw Bell stand up. For an instant, both men focused on Bell's gun, on the floor just beyond Bell.

Morahan shook his head and tried to get up. Ruffini stared at the gun. Bell edged closer to it. Veronica stood in the corner trying to get closer to the small metal chair there.

Both Bell and Ruffini arrived simultaneously at the gun. Bell grabbed the gun from the ground and aimed it at Ruffini's chest. Ruffini backed up against the waist-high wall of the large balcony. His face was contorted in anger.

Morahan struggled to his feet and started for Bell from the side. Veronica grabbed the aluminum chair and swung it at Morahan's head. It connected, but he was angered, not injured.

Ruffini raised his arms and started toward Bell.

Morahan tossed aside the chair. He grabbed Veronica's arm with one hand and slapped her with the other.

Bell squeezed off a shot point-blank at Ruffini. Ruffini snarled as the bullet started a red gusher in his shoulder. Bell fired again. Ruffini bellowed as his chest started turning red.

Morahan took one look at Ruffini, who was staggering toward Bell like a character from *Night of the Living Dead,* and dropped Veronica's arm. He ran through the sliding-glass doors and out the front door of the penthouse.

Bell was too busy to pursue him. He backed up against the inside wall of the balcony and took one more shot at the still-struggling Ruffini. Veronica closed her eyes in horror when she saw that Bell had shot him square in the face. Ruffini sat down abruptly on the floor of the balcony like a baby failing at his first attempt to walk. His face was bloody, his expression quizzical. Then he fell over on his side, apparently dead.

At that instant, Paul Haden came rushing in through the living room. He yelled, ''What the hell's going on?''

Adrian Bell dropped his gun arm to his side and said, ''Ruffini was going to kill me.'' He looked incredulous. ''After all I've done, Ruffini was going to throw me off the fucking balcony.'' He looked down at the dead Ruffini, giving Veronica a chance to run to the comfort of Paul Haden's arms.

''They've got my father down in Pass-A-Grille and there's a drug shipment coming in, Paul.'' She closed her eyes as he held her tightly against his left shoulder. ''You've got to help me stop them.'' She felt his right arm leave her back, and she opened her eyes to see a gun in his hand.

Adrian Bell chuckled. ''I'll be damned. You mean to tell me she doesn't know . . .''

The sudden explosion almost burst Veronica's eardrums. She turned to see the shocked look on Bell's face. Blood was gushing from a bullet hole in the center of his forehead, just above his eyes. He crumpled to the floor.

''I'm sorry, babe,'' Haden said. ''I had to shoot him. He was going to kill us.'' He stuck the gun under his belt at the back.

''I understand,'' she said, kissing his cheek, hearing sirens.

Haden said, ''Okay. You stay here and tell the police what happened. I'm going after Morahan.''

''No way. My father's in danger. I'm going with you.''

Haden shrugged and said, ''If you're coming with me, let's go. We'll leave this for the police to clean up.''

CHAPTER TWENTY-FOUR

THEY TOOK VERONICA'S CAR BECAUSE HADEN DIDN'T HAVE one. He was driven anywhere he wanted to go. He was being driven again this time. By Veronica. On the way down to The Busted Flush, Veronica told him the whole story, from Jon Vasta's hiding behind the name Alan Smithee through all the deaths that had come from the need to protect a massive drug-smuggling operation.

"You're really a bright girl," Haden said, opening his hazel eyes wide. "To put it all together. Who would have suspected Jon Vasta? I wonder why he did it."

"Jon had some clinkers after *Jeremy Starr*. I figure he had a hard time getting financing and the Irish-Colombians were ready to invest. Especially when they got a bunch of dealers inside the industry as part of the deal."

"Amazing."

Veronica pulled into an angled parking space on Gulf Way, near The Busted Flush. "What are we going to do?" she asked.

"Just follow me." He reached in his jeans pocket and pulled out a pair of sunglasses. "My show-biz disguise," he said, smiling. Haden got out of the car, gun still stuck in the back of his jeans, covered by his blue Izod shirt. Veronica shut her door and followed him. There were dozens of people on the beach behind them, but they seemed too involved in the sunshine and the surf to notice Haden and Veronica.

As they reached the Eighth Avenue entrance to the restaurant, Haden halted her with an outstretched palm. "Wait here," he whispered. He went inside. Veronica waited for a few moments, worrying about her father and praying that this soon would be over, with Jon Vasta and Morahan behind bars. She was thankful for Haden's help. It was good to have someone on her side who could really do something. As quickly as that thought entered her mind, she regretted it. It wasn't David's fault that he was in a hospital bed and unable to help her.

Finally, Haden came to the door, opened it, and said, "They're in the banquet room in the back. Come with me."

Veronica took his hand and walked with him through the nearly empty restaurant. It was that slow time of day between lunch and dinner, and the two handsome young men she saw at a table as Haden led her through a door next to the salad bar were more interested in each other than in their surroundings.

They entered the large rectangular room. Carts filled with metal folding chairs and dozens of folded-up banquet tables were along two side walls. There were four long narrow stained-glass windows in the wall at the far end of the room, where Derek Morahan was sitting on a folding chair behind an ordinary card table counting stacks of bills. The restaurant owner, Vern Dahlhauser, was running the calculator for Morahan, who was softly calling out figures. Her father was in the corner tied to a chair with strips of gray gaffer's tape across his mouth and eyes. He was motionless. His head was bowed. Dahlhauser and Morahan looked up, then continued their task.

"What have you done to my father?" Veronica started for her father, but Haden stopped her.

Dahlhauser said, "It's okay. We just helped him take an afternoon siesta."

She squeezed Haden's arm and whispered, "Aren't you going to do something?"

"Yeah, babe," Haden whispered. "Just hang tight."

As they stepped farther into the room, a feeling of uneasiness began to seep into Veronica's mind.

"It's all over, Morahan," Haden said. "Thanks to Veronica here, we know what you've been doing and we're turning you in to the police." There was something strange about the way he said that, she thought, almost as if he was saying lines from a script.

Morahan finished counting the package of bills in his hand, told the total to Dahlhauser, who punched it in, and slowly stood up. He grinned and raised his arms in the air like a bad guy captured by a marshal in the Old West. "Well, Sheriff, I guess you caught us red-handed." He dropped his arms and broke out laughing, and Dahlhauser joined in.

Haden took Veronica by the arm and walked her into the center of the room with him. He reached behind his back and pulled out the gun. "I don't think you boys should be laughing," he said, as he and Veronica neared the table.

She couldn't understand why no one seemed worried. Were they convinced that Haden was just an actor and not a threat? Why weren't they jumping him or pulling their own guns or something? Like indigestion, the irritating texture of doubt started gnawing at her insides. Something was wrong.

When they reached the table, Haden took the gun, twirled it twice like a cowboy, and stuck it back in his belt. He turned to Veronica and started laughing.

Her cheeks burned with anger. "What's going on?"

The other two joined in, the laughter like salt in a wound.

Haden smiled at her. "Guess."

Suddenly, the truth stood quite still in a corner of her mind. She had been seduced by the oldest trick in the book.

"You're the one," she said, not totally confident.

"Bingo!" Haden said. "You got it right."

"But I thought—"

"I know." He stepped up to her and patted her cheek gently with his hand. "It was wonderful. You thought it was Jon Vasta." He rubbed his hands with glee, and his handsome face didn't look so handsome to Veronica anymore. "You forget, I also had—what did you call them?—'a couple of clinkers' after *Jeremy Starr*. I wanted to direct. But nobody wanted to let me. I was too young." He turned and saluted Morahan. "Nobody but my Irish-Colombian pal here."

"So you killed them all because they found out about you?" She glared at him. "When's the killing going to stop? When everyone who knows anything is dead?"

Haden smiled. "Sounds good to me."

"But why did you set up David?"

"Because of who he is."

"I don't get it."

"He's in Homicide, right?"

"Yeah."

"Well, didn't he used to be in Narcotics?"

"Sure. Back when he was with the St. Pete police."

"Well, if you were going to live through this, you could ask him about Derek Morahan, and, more specifically, ask him about Derek's brother Dennis. The Morahan brothers, couple of Irish-Colombians. They got into the family business."

Morahan came around the table. "We came to Florida in the early seventies and took over the drug ring run by Orlando Navarro here in Pass-A-Grille." He tilted his head to the side. "You never heard about the Morahan–Navarro war?"

She shook her head.

"It was a bloodbath. Cops thought they had a gang war on their hands. We wiped out fifteen of Navarro's men and then grabbed old man Navarro himself and cut off his head."

She forced her revulsion back down to her stomach. "I still don't get the connection with David."

"Well, your man David started hanging around Pass-A-Grille scoping things out. He got the goods on my brother Dennis and arrested him. When he found out we had the fix in to get Denny off, your guy shot and killed him."

"I don't believe that."

"Doesn't matter. I know what he did. And I've been looking for a way to get David Parrish without killing a cop ever
since. You see, when you kill a cop it ruins business. And
we got a great business going. This setup was nearly perfect."

"So it wasn't to cover up what Angela knew about Tony
Victor's death?"

"That was a nice bonus," Haden said. "But it wasn't the
real reason."

"Well, it's all going to end today," Veronica said. "I called
the cops and they'll be here—"

"They was here, already," Dahlhauser said. "I told them
we didn't need any fucking tickets to the policeman's ball."
He erupted into laughter, and the other two joined in.

Veronica was losing hope. She'd really believed Detective
Cross would show up in the nick of time. Now, it was really
up to her.

"You see, Veronica," Haden said, as he reached out again
and patted her cheek, "you were part of the setup from the
start. Why did you think Vasta hired you so easily?"

"He's in on this?"

"No. But, like Adrian Bell and lots of others, Jon had a
habit. I said, 'Hire her or I cut you off.' He did it."

"So what are you going to do now?"

"We're going to send you and your dad on an all-expenses-
paid cruise on the Gulf of Mexico," Haden said. He lifted
her chin with his forefinger. "Sorry about this. I should have
fucked you when I had the chance. I liked you."

Through gritted teeth, Veronica said, "Sorry I can't say
the same about you."

Morahan and Dahlhauser chuckled. Without warning,
Haden slapped her hard on the right cheek, then smiled. "I'm
sorry, what did you say?"

She rubbed her cheek and tried to hold back the tears that
were streaming unbidden from her eyes. "I said—"

This time he didn't wait for her to finish. He slapped her
on the same cheek and she staggered, ending up with her

back to the other two men. He grabbed her by the shoulders. "I would have been the best you'd ever had, babe." He was squeezing her tightly now. "Too bad you'll never know." With that, he kissed her violently. She threw her arms around him to keep from falling and felt his gun, still stuck in his belt.

A plan. She melted into the kiss and gave it back to him. His hands moved off her upper arms to encircle her back as his tongue explored her mouth. She reached the gun and squeezed him with her other arm to cover as she pulled it quickly but gently out of his belt.

When he let go of her, Veronica raced around him toward the door, turning to point the gun with both hands at the three men. They all stood around the table, silently watching her. Finally, Morahan placed the last package of bills in the burgundy briefcase and closed it. "Look, Paul, I don't care what the fuck you do with her. The boat's due in less than twenty minutes. I'm getting out of here."

"No, you're not!" Veronica screamed, trying to keep the shaking of her hands to a minimum.

"Oh, give me a break," Morahan said. "You don't know how to use a gun. You're a fucking disc jockey."

It was the moment of truth—the first time she'd ever had to fire a gun outside the shooting range to which David had taken her. Morahan started around the table with the briefcase in hand. Veronica pulled the trigger. Her hands jumped back nearly to her chin. The explosion was deafening in the cavernous room. But Morahan clutched his shoulder and looked up, absolutely amazed.

For a moment no one moved. Then Morahan kicked the card table, flipping it up. It hit Veronica in the chest, then fell to the floor. Paul Haden grabbed for the gun. Morahan raced out the door into the restaurant. Dahlhauser was right behind him.

Haden grabbed her wrist with one hand and tried to wrest the gun from her hand with the other.

She strained to pull the trigger, but the pressure on her wrist was too great. She backed up, forcing him to follow, and tried to get enough leverage to kick him between the legs.

No luck. The pressure on her wrist was intense. She bit his other hand and he bellowed in pain.

Suddenly, behind Haden, there was a crash as a row of folded metal chairs fell to the terrazzo floor. Haden's head jerked away for a split-second. He let up on her wrist, and she pulled the trigger. She felt the impact of the explosion, and felt the blood splatter her T-shirt a beat before she saw the look of amazement on his face. He let go of her hand and staggered backward, tripping on the overturned card table and holding his side as if trying to keep his insides from falling out. His eyes were wide.

Veronica crumpled to her knees, the gun dragging on the floor in her limp grasp, tears streaming down her face and her breath coming in large, sobbing bursts.

Late-afternoon shadows moved into the room and sat in corners like uninvited guests. When she finally stood up and wiped her eyes on her bare arm, Veronica noticed a couple of cooks and a waiter standing in the doorway, staring. They were looking at the gun, still in her hand. And it hit her like a bolt of lightning that she would be accused of killing Paul Haden. She'd be in the same trouble she was trying to get David out of.

Thinking of David reminded her of her father. She turned to see him lying against a pile of fallen chairs struggling to free himself. She ran to his side and pulled the gaffer's tape off his eyes and mouth.

"Ouch!"

"Sorry, Daddy. Are you okay?"

"A little groggy." He smiled at her as she untied him. "I've gotten out of shape since the Bureau."

She helped him stand up, and eased him into a folding chair. "I'm just glad to see you alive."

Archie nodded toward Paul Haden, on the floor in a pool of blood. "Did you shoot him?"

She nodded. "He was the one."

"I know. I came to just before you got here. I was faking it trying to figure out how to escape."

"Good. Then I don't have to tell it all over again."

At the door, the onlookers gave way to a pair of emergency

medical technicians who went to work on Haden. Just behind them was a young uniformed officer of the St. Petersburg Beach police. "Excuse me, ma'am," he said. "I'll have to ask you and the gentleman to come with me."

Veronica offered him the gun, butt forward. He reached in his pocket for a pencil, stuck it through the trigger guard, and took it from her. "It belongs to Paul Haden," she said.

His eyes widened, and he looked back at the man being lifted onto a stretcher. "*The* Paul Haden?"

"He's the one," Veronica said, putting her arm around her father and heading for the door.

Shortly after Veronica and Archie were escorted from The Busted Flush, Detective Chris Cross joined them in the small St. Pete Beach police station.

"We got Morahan. I had to call in the D.E.A. and the F.B.I. and everybody else, but we caught them offloading the cocaine from an alleged pleasure boat, the *Precious Baby*."

"How did you know where to look?" Veronica asked.

"A lucky break. That girl that's starring in the movie—"

"Tracy Morgan?"

"Yeah. She called us this afternoon, said Paul Haden shot her boyfriend—"

"Adrian Bell," Veronica told her father.

"Said he told her where they were making the drop and to nail the bastard for him. Then he died."

"Like something out of a movie," Archie said.

Veronica asked. "Am I going to jail for shooting Haden?"

"Well, I imagine thousands of fans would be pissed at you if he dies. . . ." He smiled. "But he's not going to die. You got him just below a rib. Flesh wound. E.M.T.'s say he apparently passed out from shock. And from what the character that owns the restaurant is saying, I have ample reason to believe you shot him in self-defense."

Veronica hugged her father. "Thank God," she said.

CHAPTER TWENTY-FIVE

To Veronica, the weekend was a blur of detectives, reporters, cold coffee, sandwiches, and tabloid headlines. They finished talking to her father soon enough that he could still make his trip to Disney World with Barbara Robinson. He asked Veronica if she'd be okay. She lied and said yes because it was apparent Barbara was part of his life, if not hers.

But on Monday morning, April 28, Veronica and Archie sat in chairs, side by side, in David's hospital room, filling him in on the details of what had happened that hadn't been on the TV news over the weekend.

"St. Pete Beach is really on the map now," Archie said. "Although not for reasons the Chamber of Commerce would be pleased to discuss."

"Did you see me on NBC Nightly News Friday night?" Veronica asked. "The Channel Eight people sent the tape to the network."

"Yeah," David said. "You looked great. Tired but great."

"Jon Vasta is going to announce a replacement for Paul Haden tomorrow morning," she explained. "He's going to go ahead and reshoot the picture. Rumors are he's got Michael Douglas."

Archie laughed. "Well, Haden certainly got more than his share of publicity."

"Oh, and Tracy Morgan called me Saturday night," Veronica said. "Can you believe it? She said she may be indicted as a co-conspirator. She apologized for not helping me out earlier."

"And the skinny woman . . ." Archie looked at her for help.

"Carla Jahns."

"Right. Carla Jahns offered Veronica her job back."

"I said no, thanks."

"What about your job at the radio station?" David asked.

"Well, Mrs. Sutter chewed me out for missing two nights, but when I pointed out that all the news reports referred to 'Veronica Slate of WAQT Radio in Tampa,' she cooled off."

"What happened to Paul Haden?"

"Haden survived the gunshot wound," Archie said. "But the combination of a good plea bargain and advice from his manager convinced him to devote some time to telling the D.E.A. investigators everything they ever wanted to know about the Morahan Brothers and their Irish-Colombian drug ring."

"You know what really pisses me off?" Veronica told David. "This whole thing was aimed at getting you. They gave me the job on the movie just to get to you. They created the phony will and insurance policy just to get to you. They even killed Angela just to get you. What kind of people are these?"

"Violent people," David said. "Life means nothing to them."

Archie added, "Someone else's life, that is."

David asked, "What happened to Morahan?"

"They got him at the boat," Veronica said. "I talked with Detective Cross this morning, and he says just the preliminary investigation alone shows that Morahan made cash deposits of more than nineteen million dollars in his account at a Bahamian bank from 1984 to 1986. And Cross says he's been importing drugs since 1974, as near as they can tell. They're very happy to see him.''

''So. Am I off the hook?'' David asked.

Veronica looked at Archie first, then said, ''For murder, yes. You may have to stand trial on some minor charges. It's all really complicated, and I'm sure Detective Cross will call.''

David closed his eyes for a moment. ''Thanks.'' He turned his head and looked at her. ''Thanks for going to bat for me.''

Veronica smiled. She glanced at her father and gave him a signal with her eyes.

Archie stood and made a show of checking his watch. ''I hope you two will excuse me for a moment. I need to run down to the lobby.'' He headed for the door and flashed a small salute at David. ''Want to see if Veronica is on the cover of *Newsweek*.''

Her father gone, Veronica pulled her chair to the edge of the bed, put her head down, and gave David a long, lingering kiss.

''Doctor says I'm getting out day after tomorrow.''

''I know,'' she said, looking at his hand, which she held in hers. ''I'm glad.''

''Looks like I won't be back on the job for a while, what with the court stuff and getting over this fracture and all.''

''Probably not.'' She still had her head down.

''Vee?'' She heard something in his voice. ''Are we over?''

She brought her eyes up to meet his. ''What do you mean?''

''We're over, aren't we? You just don't want to tell me.''

''Don't be silly.'' She squeezed his hand. ''We've had a rough couple of weeks.''

''Do you think we can ever be the same?''

''We don't want to be the same. We want to be better.''

''I'm not very good at this.''

''At what?''

''At being an invalid. At depending on other people. I feel so stupid, being weak and tired and drugged out.''

"You had a bad accident, David. Coming back takes time."

"You know, I've been having a hell of a time seeing straight. Everything is like double images."

"That's the drugs. It'll pass."

"I get tired really quickly, too."

Veronica glanced at him with mock consternation. "Are you going to turn into some sort of hypochondriac? Give me a break already. You are going to live, you know." She poked him gently in the side. "You've got to live so we can love again."

He looked hopefully at her. "You want to love again?"

"I think so," she said in a small voice.

"You want to love me?"

"I think I still do."

"You aren't sure?"

"Right now, I'm not sure of anything."

"What's going to happen when I get out Wednesday?"

"I want you to come stay with me."

"You sure?"

"Yeah. I can take care of you."

"You certainly can."

With that, Veronica went to the door of the room, pushed it shut, and returned to crawl carefully onto the bed alongside David. She put her arm around him, kissed him, and said, "I know. This reminds you of *Love Story*. But this time, no one's going to die."

David smiled and touched her lips with his finger. "I'm really glad to hear that."

ABOUT THE AUTHOR

A former broadcast journalist who was once an assistant to director Robert Altman on a film for 20th Century Fox, Lary Crews divides his time between speaking at writers conferences and writing Veronica Slate mystery novels. He lives with his wife Linda, and their three cats, Jellico, Mistoffelees, and Bustopher Jones, in Sarasota, Florida.

Mr. Crews is interested in comments from his readers. You may address them to: Lary Crews, P.O. Box 3381, Sarasota, FL 34230.

Watch for

OPTION TO DIE

next in the Veronica Slate series
coming soon from Lynx Books!